MORE THAN SHE
Dreamt

SANDY FAYE MAUCK

Rose Arbor Brides Book I

More Than She Dreamt
Rose Arbor Brides—Book 1
Christian Historical Romance

ISBN: 978-0-9968806-0-2 (pbk)
ISBN: 978-0-9968806-1-9 (ebk)
ISBN: 978-0-9968806-2-6 (hbk)

Cover design by:

Lynnette Bonner - Indie Cover Design.com

Cover model and author photo photography by:

A Storybook Moment.com

Scene separator photos by Dreamstime.com and Handcuffs.org

All scripture passages are public domain KJV of the Bible.

Dedication

To my Savior, without you my words would have
no meaning.
Because of you, I give out of a grateful heart.
You are my first love and heavenly prince.
I will ever dream of that new life in the eternal
to spend with you.

To my wonderful romantic-hearted husband
you support me in all I do.
I am so thankful God brought us together.
I love you, my earthly prince.

And to all who hope in a new life beyond
the hard wilderness.

Hope deferred
maketh the heart
sick: but when the
desire cometh, it is
a tree of life

Proverbs 13:12

CHAPTER ONE

Bitter Springs

Arizona Territory — 1905

The ground stared up at her like a wrinkled face, blistered and moaning for water as Katie mindlessly pulled the weeds that cropped up between the cracks. If she didn't keep after them, they would soon rule over the vegetable garden the way her uncle ruled over her—depriving her of life and sustenance.

"Besides," she told the pesky weeds, tossing them aside, "there isn't enough water to share." How did the little intruders have the audacity to grow in this drought?

She wiped her brow with the back of her hand to push back the menacing curls and her bonnet fell back on her weary shoulders. She blew at the obstinate tendrils, but they would not comply. Sighing, she sat back on her knees and squinted at the expansive sky. Not the slightest promise of a thunderhead was in sight. Would the monsoons ever come?

Day after day, she searched in vain for the tiny wispy clouds that would appear out of nowhere and when you blinked would grow into long, fisted arms and expand into a massive thunderstorm. She longed for those drenching downpours, which cooled off the land for days. But today, the sky was a cloudless, dingy blue and the sun relentless.

Bitter Springs. The name choked in her throat. How fitting the name was. But she couldn't be bitter with anyone but herself. Thoughts about leaving home so many years ago had been barraging her lately and today was no exception. Shame rose to attack again as she retraced the vision. She had waved goodbye as her heartsick mother stared hollowly after her, leaning on a pillar of their stately porch. Her father with his head down, slowly shook it and turned to go into the house. It haunted her like a ghost of remorse—an indictment against her. She justified herself so well then or so she thought. Morgan asked her to marry him and he swept her away with promises of a new life and her desire to escape high society made it an easy sweep. But now her beautiful mother was long gone, along with her dear father, and she couldn't bring them back or run to their loving arms for comfort. And with Morgan buried at the bottom of that wretched mine, only Charlotte was left.

Charlotte. What would her sister be doing right now? Most likely she would be dressed in a fancy frock, donning a regal hat adorned with tulle and ribbon, sipping lemonade in a lush garden surrounded by San Francisco's high society. Her sister thrived in that culture, but Katie loathed the proprieties of social rank. She never had any desire to go flouncing about in bustles and corsets, listening to obnoxious women chatter incessantly about nothing the way Charlotte and her mother had done so many years ago. If Charlotte ever did extricate them from their miserable life, would Katie and the children be expected to go back to the life of high society? She sighed deeply. Wasn't there a pleasant sort of life somewhere between slavery and snobbery? She sorely missed some of the comforts of childhood but most of all she longed for her music. Would Charlotte and her friends nag her to plunk out worldly tunes on the piano like they did in her youth? Well, she didn't mind once in a while and some tunes were fun but they never cared for her music. She heard their haughty voices, laughing in her memory....

"Kat, your music is simply archaic and hymns no less. Really, Kat, you are so out of date." But now she could play nothing, not hymns nor classics, nor modern tunes, not to mention the music of her heart that she was not sure she could resurrect. Would her fingers ever touch the fine ivory again? To be without music was a torment. For a second she heard a familiar piece run through her mind and her fingers moved along the ground to play, lost in the memory of a young girl in a white summer dress with layers of pink ruffles, at her polished ebony piano. But the daydream died when she looked down at her nearly threadbare calico and her dusty, parched fingers, and she sighed. She grasped her fallen, faded sunbonnet, and drew it back on her head and tossed the memories out as if they were weedy intruders as well.

Rooted in the depths of her heart was a tiny bud of hope like a sweet rose that defied its ugly surroundings; the promise of a fully opened rose; the hope of a better life. A life like the dreams she had been having lately. She dreamt of her beloved children dressed in charming new clothes, giggling and playing chase in lush green grass with a picnic of delicious food set before them all. Her stomach growled. Well, she was hungry but not starving. She could be thankful for that. For the moment, she could be satisfied with some rain. She shook her head in dismay. If it did rain, then the weeds would pop up and swarm her like an advancing army.

She sighed and looked up into the face of a chicken.

"Mama, the chickens are trying to singed but I can't hear them."

Katie scrunched her eyes trying to figure out what her little fellow was talking about.

His sister came over and rolled her eyes. "I keep telling him they are not trying to sing. I can't hear them either."

Katie shook her head, amused. "Jeremy, it isn't your hearing problem, son. The poor chickens are panting. They are hot. You and Sarah fill extra water pans for them. Sarah, I think I saw a big one in the barn, by the old saddle."

"Are you sure they aren't singing, Mama?" He cocked his little head at her.

"No, dear, they are deathly hot. Go help Sarah get water to cool them off." He trudged back to the coop, chicken in hand, brown curls bouncing on the top of his head.

Singing chickens. Would there be any joy in her life without her beloved little ones?

With the day's weeds conquered and mute singing chickens well-watered, Katie rested on a tree stump. She dusted off her hands and pulled her little Bible from her apron pocket. She turned to Psalm 50 and read silently until she came to verse 23.

"Whoso offereth praise glorifieth me and to him who ordereth his conversation aright will I show the salvation of God."

Father, you gave me this scripture when we came here to Bitter Springs. I've tried so hard to do exactly that. I haven't spoken against this man nor challenged his tirades. I wish you would deliver us soon but nevertheless, not my will, but thine be done.

Katie bowed her head in humility and then looked heavenward. She shielded her eyes from the blinding sun. Out of nowhere, a small cloud appeared in the sky, toward the distant mountains. It looked like a storm developing. She stood up, watching intently, grasping her little Bible to her heart as the bright cloud materialized not into a thunderhead but into a perfect sculpture. She stood barely breathing and it took all her strength to call the children.

"Sarah, Jeremy, come and see. Hurry!" she shouted, never removing her eyes from the heavenly sight. The small cloud in the sky had become a clear depiction of the Lord at Gethsemane kneeling in prayer. The scripture she had just mentioned in her prayer had come to life. When the little ones came running, Katie pointed and they saw it, seconds before it dissipated.

"It was the Lord, wasn't it? In a cloud and now it's gone," Sarah said in her often dismal tone.

"Liked when he prayed in the garden, Sarrie." Little Jeremy stood with his sister, awe in his voice. But chickens squawked and sent the children quickly back to the coop they had left open, but Katie did not budge.

She stared teary-eyed at the now empty sky.

Thank you, Lord. You were so alone at Gethsemane and with no one to pray with you. I feel alone like that. But you were headed into far more suffering than I can even imagine. Thank you for suffering that we might have life. That was your prayer: not my will but yours be done. I will never forget it.

Katie's head snapped around as the familiar sound of a rattling wagon and pounding horse hooves shattered the heavenly respite. She wiped the tears away with her arm and tucked her Bible back into her apron. The chores were not finished and fear broke out all over her. Her uncle would be irate. Yet even if she had done them all, he would find something wrong. The joy that came but seconds before disappeared as quickly as the cloud. She was reluctantly drawn back into the realm of her harsh existence. Quickly, she called back to the children to stay put as he drove toward the barn. She had survived by weighing her words and movements so as not to provoke the angry dragon that raged inside her Uncle Tyler; a dragon, which held not only her and the children captive, but also Tyler himself. Holding her tongue and trying to be a living witness only wrought a tiny semblance of the peace she craved.

The towering mass of a man stomped from the wagon and stood before her, his jaw tightening. He glared at her with a nasty scowl, looked around, and detected that all the chores had not been done.

"Where are the urchins? Lazy little brats—shoulda left the whole bunch of you back at the mine where your fool husband died. When I brung you, all you did was wear my wife out." The malicious words pouring out of his mouth must have stung even his own heart, because he choked on them in the end.

How could he blame us for Aunt Nora, Lord? We tried so to help her. He wore her out, like he is wearing me out.

His eyes were steel, cold impenetrable steel, and she felt his heart was its like. Katie stood flinching at him as he continued to berate her. He said the same things over and over, day after day. Her nerves were frayed, dealing with this callous man, and she was weary in trying to protect the little ones from him. She felt her shoulders slump, knowing the tongue-lashing wasn't over. But thank God it was a verbal assault and not the heaviness of his huge hands that came against her. He had never hit her, but the fear of it hovered over her like a dreadful looming cloud, ever since he started drinking which began the day Aunt Nora was buried. Recently, he started drinking during the day and things took a huge downturn. Anymore he stank of it most of the time. Sometimes she wished he would never come home but mostly she wished she could find a way of escape. But she knew she must pray and hope for his soul as she had promised.

Katie followed him through the side door into the rickety old house, which kept them neither cool from heat nor warm in the cold. She buffered the clapping door with her shoulder to silence it as it closed. It was common for him to stand over her and boom out more insults and orders about the inside of the house but today he trudged into the front room, plopped in his chair and started to cough. She wondered if he could keep up his drinking much longer. He had aged much the last two years. The thought of him being home more was more than she cared to think about, though she wished he'd quit drinking. He leaned back in his chair staring at the ceiling. Her eyes widened as he abruptly doubled over into a coughing fit. He'd been having more of them lately. Whenever she tried to make him herb tea for his coughing fits he ignored it, like every other thing she did to be a comfort to him.

She busied herself with preparing his meal. After eating, he generally went straight to the saloon, and then they could eat in peace. When she was through with his meal, she peeked over at him and noticed he had fallen asleep. A sigh rose in her lungs and caught there, stifled. She did not want to arouse the sleeping giant. He reminded her of Goliath screaming out his taunts to the Hebrews. Was this what they felt like—being mocked by the giant man who harassed them with his huge stature just because he could.

Katie took his plate of food to the table and carefully set another plate over it to keep it warm. Her stomach churned and her heart beat wildly but she made her way like a wraith to the back door. Her hand gripped the knob, turned it and released it slowly, relieved that she had oiled the hinges recently. The children had been near the chicken coop, so she headed there. The cackling assured her she was right. She made her way through the squash and pumpkins and into the pen.

She looked pitifully at her precious little ones. Jeremy's eyes were filled with fear until she spoke.

"It's all right, children, it's just me."

Sarah's frown turned to a dimpled smile. "Mama," she said with a hushed voice, beating her little brother into her mother's arms.

They are so innocent. Please, Father, help us. It seems I went from one wilderness trial to another. Is there ever going to be a way out?

She so wanted to tell them this life was not what she had hoped for them. And to tell them she would take them where no one would frighten them and they would be warm and full and happy. But Katie spoke none of it, afraid to give them false hope. Instead, she cuddled them close and prayed for a miracle.

Their oppressive life had made Sarah somewhat somber and Katie thought it a good thing considering their circumstances. Unlike his big sister, Jeremy was friendly and vocal with a happy little personality that was hard to repress. Who wouldn't laugh about singing chickens? But as precious as he was, he seemed to be a torment to Tyler so Katie kept him far from his reach. They were kind and adorable children and would have won the heart of any simple cold heart but not Uncle Tyler. His heart was locked and it seemed the key was thrown away. Aunt Nora said his father had mistreated him as a child. Whatever the cause, the alcohol made it worse. Truly there were spirits in the bottle. From the young society parties in the city, to the rowdy mining camps and now her uncle's indulgence, Katie assessed it a horrid affliction of mankind.

"Mama, is he gone?" Jeremy looked up into her face with hopeful big brown eyes.

"Not yet. He's taking a nap." She held Sarah close and petted Jeremy's mop of brown curls. "It's all right, dear ones." She comforted them, never fully convinced herself. "But I should go back in now."

This time of day, the children stayed out of sight until they heard Uncle Tyler leave for the saloon. Katie knew he usually didn't nap long and if she didn't get back soon, he might come looking for her. She instructed them to stay out and returned to the house.

She stooped to pick some zucchini and crookneck squash so not to go in empty-handed. But she was too late. She heard him bellow and then the dishes began to crash. She cringed in despair, drew herself up and left the vegetables behind.

Oh, Father, get me through this battle, please.

She did not want to go in, but it was necessary to keep him from coming out to look for the children. She was forever picking up broken dishes after his tirades. Weary of mourning her Aunt Nora's china, as it had dwindled to a few pieces. She stepped into the kitchen, shaking.

"Food's cold. Can't you do nothin' right?" He stood glaring at her, holding a saucer in his hand. The demon in him knew it caused her grief.

"I'll warm it—" She stood at the door, flinching. Then she looked at his hand—the last saucer of Aunt Nora's china. No! He dropped it and it shattered into pieces sending a jolt through her already frayed nerves.

"Finish them chores 'fore I git home or else." Tyler turned away to leave and slammed the door behind him.

She often wondered what or else might actually mean but had determined long ago not to find out. She looked at the shattered china and remembered the day Aunt Nora's body lay crumpled on the floor like a tossed dishrag. The older woman had completely worn out. Uncle Tyler held Aunt Nora and wept for a long time. He cried out to his dead wife and to his mother. That was the only time she ever saw him soften.

The thought of being in heaven with dear Aunt Nora sounded wonderful. But what if she died like Aunt Nora?

What would become of her precious little ones? She shuddered at the thought. No matter how bleak life looked, she mustn't lose hope.

The children peeked through a cracked open back door.

"Wait there. I need to pick up the broken china."

"Why does he break the dishes, Mama?" Sarah asked.

"He is angry deep down. His father was a harsh man, I guess."

"Why doesn't he just forgive him?"

"Ah, a question for the sages of time, Sarah. If he could, he wouldn't be bound by his own judgments against his father. In other words he has become the thing he hated because he couldn't forgive." Katie finished cleaning up the broken china and the children came inside. She bent over and looked into their little faces. "So children, we will continue to forgive him for his anger against us, won't we?"

"Yes, Mama," Sarah said and Jeremy nodded.

Jeremy stared at Uncle Tyler's untouched food on the table. "Can we haved some pie?"

"No honey, the pie is for Uncle Tyler." They had lived on the leftovers and all the best was always for Tyler. He often reminded them what a curse they were to him.

He had no idea how much she longed to relieve him of his curse and leave, but she had next to nothing to go on.

"When Aunt Nora was alive, we had little bits of pie." Sarah spoke to the floor.

Katie winced, then turned to the cupboard and retrieved a wrapped treasure she had hidden. She handed them a big chunk of piecrust she had saved back. The fragrance of cinnamon tickled their noses and brought the happy reactions she hoped it would.

"After supper."

They thanked her like she'd given them a whole pie. Yet it was only a measly scrap of piecrust. They chatted and shared silly stories from the chicken coop as they finished their supper, then the children worked at doing the dishes while Katie finished her chores.

They gathered in the kitchen for their special time of day, when they could be together in peace. But it would have to wait. Despair fell like a pall when they heard the sound of the wagon returning. Katie shoed her little ones off to the bedroom with their buttery cinnamon piecrust and they scurried like mice.

Tyler swung the door so hard Katie just missed being hit. She leaned against the cupboards with her hand to her heart, trying to catch her breath.

"Fools—they are all fools!" Tyler stormed into the living room. He had enough drink to accentuate his normally angry demeanor. This had happened before when he argued with someone at the saloon. She wondered how anyone got along with him.

"Woman, you're a fool, too." He turned and pointed at her but stopped short when he saw that she had her hand on her heart. "Get me the pie." His eyes were glazed and for a moment she wasn't sure he could even see her clearly.

She moved quickly but was so nervous she nearly dropped it. Once delivered, she snuck back to the kitchen to make a plate of food for the children. When she quietly went to the bedroom and put her hand to the knob, she overheard them.

"Sarrie, we need to pray for Mama."

"Yes, Jer'my let's pray."

Katie let go of the door and took a deep breath. How blessed to have these little ones who without coaxing would carry her to the Father in prayer. Waiting until the prayers were said she passed the plate to them and turned back toward the kitchen, hoping he would just go to bed.

After eating his pie, he tired and went to his room. Katie tidied up and joined the children. They were all soon cuddled in bed and she held them close like a mother hen.

"We prayed," Sarah whispered. Jeremy nodded his thick brown locks in agreement.

"Thank you, my dear ones. I'm so blessed." She cuddled them close and kissed their cherub cheeks. Their eyes struggled to stay open so they quickly said their evening prayers and the little heavy lids quietly closed for the night.

Father, I know you have a better life for us. I believe, please help my unbelief.

And Katie fell asleep and dreamt of picnics, colorful flower gardens, laughing children and a gentleman she had seen vaguely in a dream once before.

CHAPTER TWO

Escape

"Howdy, Ma'am." The freckled-faced boy grinned at Katie as she finished fixing the fence post.

"Hello," Katie answered him, smiling, despite her weariness.

"This here letter got put in with ours down to the post and my Ma was thinkin' it might be yours."

Katie looked at the letter and smiled. "Yes, yes thank you." She could have hugged him.

"Yes'm, you're welcome."

"Please tell your mother, thank you."

"Yes'm."

When the boy turned and sauntered away, Katie ran to sit on the stoop to read the letter quickly before anyone could know she had it. Tyler was not there and he could not take it from her but she clung to it just the same. The Lord had been speaking to her about his deliverances in the scriptures lately and her hope was high. She felt sure her uncle had taken her previous letters and kept the money Charlotte had sent to her, giving her only the letters. She opened it hungrily, anticipating the miracle that would take her out of her miserable prison. For so long she imagined train tickets from Charlotte or a letter saying they would come and get them soon. Would this be the day? She saw the money inside and quickly scooped it into her pocket, as if some hand would come and snatch it away. Then she read the words, half starved for any news, any hope of deliverance.

Dear Katie,

I hope this finds you and the children well. We have been so busy with city elections that I have scarcely had a moment to write. One of Father's old friends from New Hampshire is running for mayor here in Oakland and expects me to handle all the luncheon plans and such as that. It is quite an honor. Isn't it a small world that someone from our own neck of the woods would be here in San Francisco and running for mayor? He mined for a season, just like your Morgan, however he struck it rich, as they say. We are hoping he will win.

I will try to write as soon as I can. Granville's family will be coming for the holidays or I would try to find a way to bring you out for a visit. They are highly important people and expect the house run their way, so it will keep me on my toes and they are family, you know. Well, I must be off to the dressmaker.

Your loving sister,
Charlotte

Katie tried to read between the lines as tears blurred the words. She wished the message had been different. It was far from the miracle she hoped to see.

Lord, is she trying to tell me that we will never be welcome?

15

It left her with an estranged feeling in her gut. She felt her hopes crash to the ground. Did Charlotte still see her as a rebellious runaway? Didn't she think she and the children were her family? Perhaps she should write and tell her she would be happy to be a maid—after all she was quite used to slavery. She wrestled with bitterness only to have despair take its place. It did not appear that Charlotte would be the one God would use to deliver them. She sensed the finality in her spirit, and took a deep breath, trying to absorb the blow. God must have another way but how, where, who? She could not imagine any other way.

She and her sister had always been worlds apart but from the words penned by her sister, a new barrier rose between them—Granville's family. Perhaps Granville doesn't want them. But she would read it again later. She needed to get back to her chores before her uncle came home. She often wondered at the two brothers, her father and her uncle, so completely different. But her father went to live with another part of the family at a young age. That must have been the difference. Her uncle was nothing like her father. He was insufferable.

"How did he think taking care of this place was humanly possible for one woman?" she cried out to the air, waving her letter and stamping back to the barn.

Hot tears fell and dried as fast as they came in the scorching heat.

Will I have to die like Aunt Nora? And what would become of the children? She bowed her head, shamefully. *Oh Father, you know I don't really believe that. I am just so tired. I have tried to help this man but I cannot get through to him. Please, you have promised deliverance for us and I promise that even after you deliver us, I will continue to pray for his soul.*

Tyler was later than usual and it had given her time to complete her chores, but she soon found out the reason for his tardiness. He reeked. He must have gone to the saloon first. This set her on edge. She wasn't ready for unexpected changes. A blanket of dread fell over her. He was a mean drunk just like his whole being—mean, hard, and cruel.

She started toward the back door hoping the children had heard him and hid themselves, but not so, for Jeremy came darting through the back door. He stopped dead in his tracks as Tyler glared at him like he was a rat that dared to come into his lair. His little body stood paralyzed by fear at his twisted face.

"Would you like your supper, Uncle Tyler?" Katie set herself between Jeremy and Tyler creating a diversion. He didn't bite. His eyes pinched and he moved toward Jeremy, shoved Katie aside and pursued his prey.

Terrified, Jeremy fell to the floor and started to cry. Sarah looked through the doorway standing behind Jeremy. When she saw Tyler coming at Jeremy, she screamed. In his stupor, he couldn't see nor walk straight and his arms were flailing every which way. When Tyler heard Sarah scream, his eyes blinked wildly. He backed up and stumbled over the kitchen chair, knocking it down. Katie made her way to Jeremy and held him, wrapping her other arm around Sarah who was sobbing. Tyler made his way out of the house with the screen door slapping open and shut behind him. She heard him snap the whip and ride off like a madman, groaning.

Jeremy clung tightly to his mother. She knew he was

not hurt but frightened.

"He's gone now. Are you okay, dear?" Katie rocked him while her mind spun. Jeremy nodded. Katie's jaw set tight. The mama bear in her rose up and she made a decision that her uncle would never scare her precious little ones again. Maybe it had to get this bad before she would leave. She had been afraid to leave partly because he might come after them but also because she was afraid to make another mistake. Right now she didn't have a drop of fear, except that he would come back before they left. It pushed her to hurry. She knew she had fulfilled any obligation to Aunt Nora to take care of Tyler. She had more than worked for her room and board.

She felt free. A peaceful determination came over her as she pulled Jeremy closer. She looked down at Sarah who had stopped crying.

"Sarah, we are leaving," Katie said as she brushed a tear from her daughter's little cheek.

Sarah roused. A smile replaced her forlorn face and she rubbed her eyes.

"Go and get your best clothes together. Put them in your pillowcases. Don't forget your coats."

Jeremy looked up at his mother, his eyes bright. "Can I bringed Flopsy?"

She kissed him. "Yes, of course. But no rocks or anything like that. Go with Sarah. Hurry."

Katie went to the kitchen to grab some food for their journey. She felt like taking the whole rest of the pie or throwing it across the room, but didn't. Let it be a reminder of how well taken care of he had been with her there. She took things that wouldn't spoil easily and that they were able to carry. When she went to retrieve her belongings, she realized she couldn't bring much of anything. Most of what little they had would have to be left behind.

Sarah and Jeremy stood before her with stuffed pillowcases.

"Bring your daddy's books, I'll find a place to store them along the way." The thought of him coming to ruin their getaway bit at her heels.

Give me wisdom, Lord, and keep Tyler away.

Katie thought about trying to find the money he had stolen out of Charlotte's letters but figured he probably gambled or drank it all away. She made sure she had Charlotte's address and all their papers and they all quickly left the house. She refused to look back, never wanting to remember the awful prison that held them captive. It was time to look ahead to the hope of a better life...somewhere. And pray he doesn't come after us.

CHAPTER THREE

The Way Out

When they started out, Jeremy had the slightest skip in his step. It felt good to escape and see the world. But the taste of freedom was not to be savored until they were far away.

"Where'd we going, Mama?" Jeremy's voice had a tinge of whine in it. Her determined steps were a strain on the children.

"West. We're headed west. West is best, I think."

"To Aunt Charlotte's?"

"I don't know, Sarah. She seems to be quite busy with Uncle Granville and his family." The quiver of hope that once lived in Katie had been quenched that very day by Charlotte's letter, leaving in its place a sharp pain in her heart. She mustn't let the bitterness crop up again.

Katie's mind spun with thoughts of past and present. If only she had other family to go to, but she didn't. She didn't know where they were if she did. She had tried to arrange a trip after Sarah's birth to visit her parents but Morgan, like so many others, had been infected with gold fever. Instead, they were drug from mine to mine where nothing but long lonely days and poverty prevailed. She never saw her parents again. When Morgan's desire for gold took hold of him and it became like chasing cotton from the cottonwood trees, taking them here and there and leading nowhere. Then the mine collapsed and Morgan was gone.

Lord, why did Morgan have to get gold fever?

She had questioned Morgan over and over, about his desire for gold. The irony was that he desired everything he had taken her away from—the very same life she had escaped.

Katie rubbed her neck. It was sore from being so tense and turning at every sound. Fear prodded her on but she could see the children were dragging and probably hungry. They stopped to rest for a minute.

"Mama, what will our new place be like?" Sarah asked.

" I don't know, Sarah. We will have to see. God will lead us."

"Will it be hot? Who will take care of the chickens? Where will we get food?" Sarah's worry echoed Katie's own questions. She was trying to think of answers when Jeremy interrupted.

"God will provide," Jeremy said.

Katie sighed, ashamed at her own fears. "Yes, son, he will. Now let's get moving before it gets dark."

Tyler would be left with all the work. But what did he expect after what he did? He had gotten so mean. When he came to get them after Morgan died, he was hard but quiet. He seemed to honor her grief. Little did she know it would be the kindest he would ever be in the years ahead, barely saying but a few sentences mile after mile. Aunt Nora welcomed her with opened arms. The short time she had with her wasn't bad. Tyler was tolerable. Then loss struck again with Nora's weak heart.

As she lay dying, her aunt's voice haunted her. "He's not really so bad, Katie, he's just had a hard life. Maybe you can make a difference. You are such a sweet Christian girl. Perhaps you can bring him to the Savior." Her aunt's last words came back to Katie like an arrow racing toward her heart but she stopped them cold.

"I'm sorry, Aunt Nora. I tried so hard. I just couldn't do it anymore," she spoke under her breath looking up.

Tyler pushed her farther and farther away with his drunken anger. She had endured until now. Her jaw tightened thinking about when he went after her precious Jeremy. Leaving Bitter Springs was the right thing to do. She had a peace now. It was time to go. She had done all she could. The guilt and sorrow made her uncle drink heavier and she and the children were the scapegoats. But now the goats have escaped.

The sun's stripe of gold and orange washed across the tops of the shadowed junipers. She needed to look for shelter for the night. The children were dragging but good troopers. She had pushed them hard to get to town. Katie wanted to stop and count the funds she had. They found a slab of large rocks nestled in the junipers and rested, nibbling on bread and cheese. Cheese was a treat for the children as it had been rationed to them like so many things.

Katie sighed, thinking for the first time in weeks she was glad it was summer and not cold.

"We need to pray, children."

"Okay," the children chorused.

"Mama, why did God let Uncle Tyler scare me?"

"I don't know, son, but perhaps God wanted us to leave and I wasn't hearing his voice. Maybe we stayed longer than God intended. God's ways are not always our ways."

Jeremy seemed satisfied with the explanation but Katie wondered herself.

I suppose if you had told me to go, Lord, I would have said, I have nowhere to go and nothing to go on. I suppose pushing us on was the only way. Thank you for protecting Jeremy.

They huddled together to pray for both direction and safe places to stay. When Katie pulled out her purse to see what they had to go on, it looked pretty meager. She also needed a carpetbag or valise of some sort. They ventured up Main Street far from the saloon and Tyler's shop, and to the general store. Katie looked for a carpetbag and found one, way in the back, which was inexpensive enough for them. Sarah stood fascinated by a beautiful doll dressed in pink chiffon in a dusty box, while Jeremy stared at the big rock candy canister on the counter. Katie quickly reclaimed them and went outside with their purchased carpetbag. They now had something a bit more acceptable for a train trip. She quickly stuffed their belongings into the bag.

Jeremy looked as if something was troubling him. Finally, he put it into words. "Mama, how did they maked candy out of rocks?"

Katie laughed and it felt good for a minute. "They don't, son. It is candy made to look like rocks."

Sarah's freckled nose scrunched. "Why would they do that? Who wants to eat rocks?"

"Some silly notion, I guess. Maybe you will feel differently if you tasted one." She made a mental note to get rock candy someday.

"I'm not going to eat a rock." Sarah's hand on her hip made it clear she wouldn't.

"They aren't really..." Katie started to answer but a sign distracted her. She knew waiting all night at the train depot wouldn't be safe or comfortable. She hesitated at the front of the hotel then decided to obey the sign that beckoned her: WELCOME COME ON IN. She found the cheapest little room but at least it appeared clean and the bed looked like heaven to the tired pilgrims seeking a new life. The children were asleep in no time but Katie lingered, praying until she could not hold her eyes open any longer.

Just after sunrise, Katie woke, her eyes moving from wall to wall sorting out where she was and how she got there. Yesterday seemed as if it were a big bad dream and she needed to gather her thoughts. She kept flashing back to the awful incident that made them flee. She took the thoughts captive and went on to pray for today's direction.

A train whistle blew and she jerked. It caused the children to wake and she climbed out of bed to prepare. She knew the warning ushered in the eastbound train as it rumbled past the little hotel eastward toward the train station. But it stirred her to get ready just the same. She dug in the carpetbag for food. She knew it wouldn't last long but it would hold back their hunger for a little while. She thought of the many times the rationing back at Tyler's was multiplied by the miraculous hand of God. She would not be afraid.

After asking the woman at the hotel if she would keep Morgan's books until she could send for them, they made their way to the train station.

The stolid little man at the counter shook his head. "No, ma'am, fare to Oakland would be much more than that."

Katie turned back to the bench. She would have to think and pray about what to do. There wasn't much time. Several people came through the door and bought their tickets. As she pondered what to do, she remembered Charlotte's newest letter. Oh, the money. Where did I put it? My apron, of course. She reached into her carpetbag and found the apron, pulling out the wad of money Charlotte had sent. Surely this alone will be enough to get to Oakland and closer to Charlotte.

As she held it in her hand, a swift body breezed by and snatched most of it out of her hand. Horrified, Katie gathered the leftovers, which had dropped into her lap and stood to watch as the boy who stole it ran out the station and across the road like a roadrunner. The couple who had just purchased tickets was engrossed in their own little cozy world and the ticket man was bent over doing something. No one even noticed. In desperation, Katie quickly took what was she had and drug the children to the ticket counter. Before she had time to sulk or answer the children's questions about what had happened, she purchased fare for as far as they could go and still have some left for food and lodging.

Just get us out of this horrible town, Lord.

"That'll git you to the White Rock Station, Ma'am."

"Is it a large town?"

"Nice-sized little town—not too big not too small."

Katie nodded, took the tickets, and stuffed them deep in her new carpetbag, safely. As they sat back down and waited for the train, she remembered the verse in the book of Revelation.

To him that overcometh will I give to eat of the hidden manna, and will give him a white stone, and in the stone a new name written, which no man knoweth saving he that receiveth it.

White Rock.

CHAPTER FOUR

The Train Trip

"All a-boarrrd!"

Katie gathered the children close and lugged the carpetbag to the train. The porter took the heavy bag from her, helped them into the car, and they settled in. It felt wonderful to have someone take the burden for a while and to be treated like a lady again. She had forgotten. She thanked him and he nodded, his bright grin welcoming her.

As the train started moving, her shoulders relaxed. They were on their way. Nothing could be worse than Bitter Springs or the mining towns, could it?

She felt the strong desire to burst out in tears of relief but denied it sharply, when she saw the excitement in her little ones. They were wide-eyed and giddy over the train ride. She wanted them to enjoy it. They had been locked in a prison of fear so long, it took little to bring delight to their sweet expressions.

"Mama, Mama what is that?" The children were seeing things they had never seen. They watched every detail out the window from a windmill to a tree. The more land that passed, the more free she felt. She realized this was the first day since Aunt Nora died that she didn't face long hours of hard work. No wonder it felt so good. She was able to rest— really rest.

"S'cuze me, Ma'am, we'll be stoppin' in Seligman at the Harvey House. It's a right nice breakfuss. And they do set a right perty table." The smiling porter offered.

She smiled wanly. "Oh, is it permissible, I mean, may we stay on the train?"

"Why yes'um, sure can."

It would be wonderful to go and dine at a real breakfast. She remembered, as a girl, the lovely starched linens, polished silver, and flowers at the tables but that was on the eastern trains where they served people from meal cars. She wondered what it cost. And just as she thought about it, she heard the porter tell a passenger up front that it cost 75 cents. No, they couldn't do that.

"Breakfast?" Sarah looked up, her eyes hopeful.

"We can't, sweetheart, not now."

A quick flash of disappointment came over Sarah's face but she took it like always and turned to chat about the countryside with Jeremy.

"But there must be some mistake. We don't know anyone," Katie looked up at the kindly porter offering a breakfast invitation.

The porter leaned down and whispered. "It's from the nice lady 'cross the way. She does this all the time and she'd be insulted iffen you don't take it. She's got plentya money. Tips me real good." He winked. "She don't cotton to being known so don't say a word. Go ahead and feed the young'uns."

"But I couldn't."

"Don't let a bit of pride keep the little ones from a real nice breakfuss. It's done been ordered ahead for you all," he whispered.

Katie looked over and saw the stately woman. She was dressed so elegantly, her pink tulle hat tipped low. She was searching for something in her seat. Katie turned back to the porter and sighed, then nodded. She turned to the children and prepped them to use their best manners when they went for breakfast. She glanced back over to the kind lady once more but she was looking out the window. She was elegant and although older, she had a classic beauty and a sweet expression. How kind of her to think of them. Katie handpressed Sarah's skirt, straightened her flimsy hat, tucked Jeremy's shirt in and they were off.

The table settings were just as Katie remembered. White linen tablecloths and shiny silver spread out before them across the room. Each table had a pretty milk glass vase with a lovely pink rose. Her favorite rose. And it had two little buds attached to the larger one. It reminded her of the three of them. It was as if God had lovingly placed it there just for her. The place was astir with young women going to and fro in white-starched aprons and carrying many plates at once. The children watched in admiration. They were seated quickly and served golden French toast triangles and crusted ham with warm buttery biscuits. The smiling waitress brought a rich ham sauce, preserves, and maple syrup.

Jeremy sat, his mouth open, staring at the huge plate of

food placed before him. "Is thised all for me?"

Katie laughed. "Yes, dear, it is all for you. Let's pray and eat it while it is warm. The porter said we only have twenty-five minutes to eat."

After thanking God for their wonderful unexpected blessing, they spoke little, immersed in their treasured fare.

"Can we saved some?" Jeremy was running out of tummy room but she could tell he didn't want it taken away.

"I don't know. We'll see. Eat what you can." She did wish they could gather the leftovers and stuff it in their carpetbag for the unknown days ahead, but she would trust God and enjoy the blessing now. They treasured every bite. It had been such a long time since Katie had been served in such luxury. She had taken it all for granted as a girl. She wondered about becoming a Harvey Girl but she wanted to get as far away from Bitter Springs as possible.

The older couple who sat behind them on the train followed them as they walked back to the train from the Harvey House meal. The woman was rude when talking to their helpful porter as if he were less of God's perfect creation and Katie cringed at the way she treated her husband. The woman's skirts shuffled sharply and her voice was shrill as she opined incessantly.

"Well, I suppose the food was tolerable but I certainly have had better. They really should polish the silver a bit more and the flowers looked wilted but I can't imagine where they found a flower in this dire land."

Little grunts were all Katie heard from the woman's husband.

As they climbed the steps to the train, the woman's voice rose in obvious volume.

"I just don't understand why people don't teach their children how to talk these days. Allowing that child to talk baby talk, why it is just disgraceful. The child will never be able to function in proper society."

Katie ushered Jeremy ahead of herself, farther from the woman's nasty diatribe. She was precisely the type of woman who made Katie want to leave home and marry Morgan. She held her breath, the blood rising. She glanced at Jeremy but he hadn't noticed the line of talk was about him. She let out the breath and relaxed.

Her imposing kind wouldn't understand if Katie tried to explain about Jeremy's hearing impairment. And constantly reprimanding his speech was worse than punishment for him. She'd like to tell her but she wouldn't because the woman would more than likely become a formidable foe or an annoying nag for the rest of the trip. Katie would just pray. The last thing she desired was any more conflict in her life.

Lord, please don't let this woman be going to White Rock.

Putting to rest the contrary woman's words, she settled back into her seat with her little ones who were happily full and refreshed. How unlike the rude woman, the true lady was who had been so generous to them. She wanted to thank the kind lady but if she wanted to remain anonymous, she would have to forego it and honor her request. Perhaps, the lovely philanthropist saw the joy on their faces and that was payment enough. How nice it would be to be on the giving end of things one day.

"I wished we could eat liked this all the time.' Jeremy rubbed his tummy and leaned back against his mother, his eyelids heavy and closing fast.

"Me, too, that would be wonderful," Sarah said.

"I know, children, but this was a special treat—a blessing from God. We must be thankful for whatever we have, little or much, but it certainly was much today, wasn't it?"

"God will provide." Jeremy yawned and his mop head dropped against his mother's sleeve. She snuggled him close.

Father, bless his precious faith.

They were blessed with another invitation for lunch but she declined saying they were still full from breakfast, which was the truth. A simple piece of cheese would be all they needed. For dinner they agreed. The little towns and countryside disappeared slowly into the darkness and the windows to their new world grew black. Katie sat looking in the window at the reflection of herself and her little ones who were both asleep. It would be hard to sleep but she could manage.

"'S'cuze me, Ma'am, but there be two berths free. People got off at the last stop, so won't be needin' 'em. There's just two. If you come with me, I'll show you." The kindly porter's white teeth shone as happy lamps in the dark.

"But, I cannot afford—"

"No worry 'bout that, Ma'am, s' already paid for, all the way to Los Angeleez."

"We'll be getting off at White Rock."

"You is plentya covered then," he whispered loudly. "Now c'mon, let's get the young'uns settled in for the night.

Embarrassed but elated Katie nudged Sarah, picked up Jeremy, and they followed the porter back to the berths. She settled the children in, took the top berth, and thanked God and blessed everyone who had contributed to their well-being. The rest of the night was pure sound sleep except to peek at the children now and then until the strings of dawn wove through windows of the train.

"All meals?" Katie looked up from her seat at the cheerful porter, her mouth open.

"Yes, ma'am. She had paid for all of them. So God has blessed you folks real good."

"Oh my, I can't accept all that."

"Well, Ma'am, been done already. All taken care of. I done told her you'd be not wanting to accept it but she said it was already done ahead."

"But...how can I ever thank her? Thank her for me, please."

"Will do, Ma'am. Now don't you be feeling bad. She gets pleasure from givin' an helpin'."

Jeremy shook his sister's arm. "Did you hearded, Sarrie? Did you hearded that?"

"Of course, Jer'my. I am right here." Sarah cocked her head.

"But Sarrie, I tolded you. God will provide."

"I know. You always say it."

"Well, it's trued."

"Mr. Porter, sir, what is your name?" Sarah asked.

"Why it's Sampson, missy." He gave her a slight tip of his hat.

"Can we called him Mr. Sambson?" Jeremy whispered.

"If it is all right with Mr. Sampson." Katie smiled sweetly at the cheery man who had brought so many blessings.

He winked. "Well, that suits me just fine, folks. I is

pleased to meet you all."

"Porter, Porter," the annoying woman called from the seat behind.

"S'cuze me folks. I be right back."

"My husband is cold. Do you have a blanket? If you wouldn't fraternize with the passengers so much perhaps we could get some attention."

"Yes, Ma'am. I be right back with a blanket for you, sir."

"Renalda, I am not cold—" her husband started.

"Nonsense. Of course you are. You always get cold when we travel."

Katie listened to their conversation, not because she wanted to but because she couldn't avoid it. The woman's voice grated her like the train wheels on the rails braking to a stop.

Sampson came back with the blanket and it sounded like she wrapped her husband in it. It was summer and hot. The poor man!

Ignoring the obnoxious woman's comments, Sampson came back to visit them.

"I am Sarah, this is Jer'my and my mama."

"Yes, Missy Sarah. You is a precious lot."

"Thank you, Sampson. I am Katie."

"Yes, Ma'am, Missez Katie. Pleased to meet you all."

"God will provide," Jeremy said.

"Indeed. Indeed, little fella." The porter winked at Jeremy and cackled all the way down the aisle.

"Son, you were right. You believed and God has been so good to us."

"Yup. Is it timed to go eat yet?"

"No, not yet." Katie sat her Bible on her lap and read to

the children.

After more meals along the way, Sarah decided it would be more fun just to live on the train for good, stopping every so often at a Harvey House.

"Do we have to get off? I like it here."

"Now, Sarah, we can't live on a train."

"I don't want to live on a train," Jeremy said. "I want to live on a big green hill with a big tree to climbed."

"It would be nice, wouldn't it?" Katie tried to imagine such a place and plopped a nice big house on top of Jeremy's green hill. Could she even hope for such a place?

"Time for the dinner menu, folks. We be stoppin' soon. It be the chicken catch-a-dorie, umm umm, it's a good 'un." The kindly porter seemed to enjoy telling the children about the next meals and watch the expressions it produced.

"Chicken catch a what?" Sarah looked at her mother, her freckled nose wrinkled.

Someone called for the porter and Katie overheard him saying as he left, "No wonder you bless'em so much, Lord. They is the dearest folks I ever did see."

Katie smiled at the porter's remarks, then turned to Sarah. "Chicken cacciatore, I believe he was saying. It is a special sauce that makes the chicken tasty."

As they sat finishing dinner, a choking feeling welled in Katie's throat. She tried desperately to keep the worry at bay but thoughts of where they would live, where she might find work, and what White Rock would be like made her head spin. Whatever it was, they would be stuck there. She swallowed hard.

Jeremy broke her thoughts. "Mama, what is this?"

"It is pie, silly," Sarah answered instead.

"I was asking Mama."

"It's called lemon cream pie. Inside is a delicious custard filling. I haven't had any since I was a girl."

Jeremy sat staring at the pie, deep in thought.

"What is it, son?"

He shook his head and frowned. "Well, Mama I just don't knowed about this pie. I don't think mustard insided it would be very good."

"Mustard? No, it is custard, dear. Custard is sweet. It is made with milk and eggs not mustard."

"But its yellow like mustard."

"Egg yolks are yellow, too, dear."

Finally convinced, he ventured a bite and his eyes twinkled happily.

Katie and Sarah were about to explode into laughter so they stuffed their mouths with pie to avoid it.

Mealtimes had been a great time of exploration for Sarah and Jeremy and a joy to teach for Katie. But mustard—well, that was one for the memory book.

When they climbed the steps, Sampson was there to assist them. Jeremy reached for the kindly porter. "Mr. Sambson, I love catchamatory."

Sarah rolled her eyes. "Oh Jer'my, you love everything."

The porter laughed his hearty belly laugh and winked at Sarah. "That's good, Missy Sarah. It is good to enjoy it all. You chillen' do make my day a pleasure."

In the morning, their scenery had turned to ugly desert so they spent extra time on Bible stories and reading lessons. Katie knew they had to cross the Mohave Desert but the desert's lifeless land concerned her. What would White Rock be like? Then the landscape turned from barren flats to treed hills and farms, huge water towers, and fields of produce. The fields made Katie think back to the garden at Bitter Springs she so tenderly coaxed in the deathly heat. She saw nothing but green, healthy, growing land. She breathed easier. She had hope for White Rock.

Jeremy pressed his nose on the window. "I liked this land. It's greened all over. Maybe we'd could be farmers."

"I am glad we are not in Arizona Territory or the Mojave Desert anymore. Will White Rock be green like this?" Sarah looked hopeful.

Katie looked off into the green fields and golden hills in the distance. "Maybe. I don't know. I hope so."

From the seat behind them, the incessant chatter stopped and the obnoxious woman whispered loudly, as if it were a whisper at all.

"I don't understand these young women traveling across the country unchaperoned. It just isn't proper."

Katie let out a little chortle.

Father, if only she knew—you are a perfect chaperone.

Outside the train window, they started seeing more people. Some stopped to watch the passing train. Often, the children would excitedly wave back to Sarah and Jeremy.

The doting porter made sure the children had little snacks in between meals and would point out special things of interest to them.

"Mr. Sampson, sir, could you tell us what grows up and down the hills out there? It makes such nice patterns."

"Yes, Missy Sarah, them is the vineyards where they grows grapes."

"They grow so perfectly in rows, like little roads. It's so lovely." Katie admired all of it. She hoped she would feel the same about White Rock.

"Yes'um. They grows pert near everthin' in Californy. Soon you be seein' the orange groves."

"I hope White Rock is green. I am going to prayed White Rock is green," Jeremy said.

"Yes, it's green, uh huh." The porter nodded. "It's a right pretty spot. Never took to walking the streets but looked mighty nice to me. Be a good home for you all, I am thinkin'. I know a very nice man who lives there. His name is Mr. Daniel. Maybe you will meet him. He loves the Lord, too." He winked at Katie and hastened down the aisle whistling a tune.

"Mama, your face is red," Sarah said.

Katie covered her cheeks and hoped the women behind didn't hear what the porter said.

As they came closer to the town of White Rock, everything seemed green indeed. There were beautiful spreading oaks with winding arms to welcome them. More oaks fanned out into the distance and made beautiful dots of green on the golden summer hills.

"Wow, I can climbed all those trees. We can maked a tree house, Sarrie."

Sarah tugged at her mother's arm, pointing out the window. "Just like Mr. Sampson said, it *is* green."

Father, thank you for the beautiful land. Now we need a place to live and I need a job.

Katie's heart beat faster as the train wheels slowed with their whining song. This journey was coming to a close and their new life awaited.

CHAPTER FIVE

White Rock

As the train approached their destination, Katie gathered things together. She craned her neck to look out the window to see what the town looked like but huge spreading trees stood as a formidable wall. Even her newfound freedom couldn't quench the fear of the unknown that loomed before her.

The train slowed and gave them a glimpse of the area but the station soon blocked their view. Fear pulsed through her, but she stood firm against it. She could go no further and she was not going back. That was that.

Katie walked by the rude woman and her husband, relieved they were not getting up to leave. The woman grasped Katie's skirt. "You know young woman, you must teach your children how to speak properly. It really is a—"

From the other side of the aisle, the elegant lady pushed between Katie and the obnoxious woman and asked the woman to please not block the way. The woman's mouth fell open and she quickly let go of Katie's skirt. Katie walked on ahead and the elegant lady touched Katie on the back.

"My dear, you have a lovely family and the most well-behaved children I have ever observed on the railroad. You have raised them well." She left Katie with a sweet smile and went farther back on the train as Katie called a soft thank you to her.

"WHI-ITE RO-OCK," the man yelled and Katie climbed down the steps. The kindly porter handed Katie her carpetbag and assisted the children down the steps. She tried to tip him but he just winked, "Already been taken' care of, Ma'am." He tipped his cap.

She winced and realized the kind lady had helped her yet again.

"Oh, my. Will you thank her for me, please, Sampson. And thank you so much for all your help. You were our guardian angel."

He chuckled. "Yes'm, will do. Thank you, Ma'am. God go with you folks."

"God bless you and thank you." She smiled back at the jolly porter and received the blessing into her heart as a precious promise.

Sarah turned back sadly to wave to their big-hearted porter friend as they walked on. "I wish he could come with us. He is such a nice man."

"I liked Mr. Sambson. He knowed God would provide."

"He certainly is a thoughtful man." Katie looked back over her shoulder and noticed he was already busy helping others.

They took in every little sight as they had on the train. To the little ones, an adventure awaited but to Katie a strange mix of faith and trepidation stirred within her. Watchful and cautious and in awe, they explored their new home.

They rounded the train station and a tree-lined street led them into a new world. Katie pulled the children off to the side as a horse and buggy trotted by. Then a wagon came from behind, which made them all stiffen until they saw it carried a wagonload of children. Chattering and giggling, the family waved at the trio, as if they were old friends. The street hosted cozy little rock cottages and gardens blooming in their glory, hemmed in by white picket fences, short white rock walls, and green hedges.

"Look, Mama, pansies, the same as the ones on Aunt Nora's needlework." Sarah was in a visual heaven.

"There are soed many flowers and trees."

"Yes, children, I've never seen some of these kinds." Katie felt a trickle of hope seeing the beauty surrounding them.

"It is a storybook town." Sarah looked around in wonder. "And it is not hot here."

In every direction Katie saw immaculately kept yards and gardens. The ground was not cracked. She didn't see anything dead or drooping and not a scratchy old tumbleweed in sight. As they walked further, there were colorful, Victorian homes with towering cupolas and ornate detailed decor over their porches. Elegant buggies stood waiting in front with horses whose coats were as shiny as the bells around their necks.

Jeremy caught sight of the horses and tugged on his sister's sleeve. "Look, Sarrie."

"Yes, Jer'my, and look at the lady with the big hat in the carriage. She is so pretty."

"Mama, you need a dress and hat like hers."

"Ah, it is lovely, isn't it? When I was young I had beautiful clothes and hats and a carriage with horses."

"You did? I wish we could live that way." Sarah was awestruck.

All the lovely homes and gardens took Katie back to her childhood. She had lived quite comfortably in a huge mansion with servants and carriages and had many beautiful dresses. But she needed to focus her attention on finding a place to live and a place to work. The day was getting on. She must not waste another second on lemony tulle hats and parasols and beautiful homes she couldn't dream of living in now.

"Mama, are we'd at Aunt Charlotte's?"

"No, son, your aunt lives quite far away from here."

"Does Aunt Charlotte know we left Bitter Springs?" asked Sarah.

"No, not yet. No sense in her worrying about us until we are settled."

Katie tried not to show her own worries as she diligently sought a boarding place. How could she afford anything for very long?

Lord, we do so need your help

Not long after her prayer, she heard a carriage behind them. For a second she felt the fear rise but she quickly dispelled the thought, as Tyler would never come by carriage. She hated jumping at every noise.

The carriage stopped next to them and a tall, well-dressed man walked toward them.

He tipped his hat and reached out to give Katie an envelope.

"Excuse me, Ma'am. I believe you left this on the train."

"Oh, no it can't be mine—" she started but he jumped right back into the carriage, tipped his hat, saying he needed to hurry back to the train and was down the street and around the corner.

She turned it over in her hand. No writing. She was stunned.

"Mama, that man was a friend of the nice lady from the train."

"You saw him on the train?"

"Yes, he talked to her a few times. I remember he had the same shiny hair and a dark mustache and his coat had fancy buttons on the sleeve. She gave him a note one time."

"It appears the benefactress is our guardian angel even off the train," Katie said as she pulled money out of the envelope—plenty for a place to stay. "God has surely come through for us. Lord, forgive my lack of faith." It was as if the money, which had been stolen was now restored and with interest.

"Was he an angel?" Jeremy looked up with big wide eyes and his mouth open.

"I don't think so, son, but he is a messenger and that is what angel means. He was a blessing sent to us."

They walked on in awe of God's blessings.

"God will provide."

The females looked at Jeremy, then smiled at each other.

"Maybe we should check the hotel," Katie said when they reached the corner.

"Hotel's closed for fixen', Missy," a voice crackled out of nowhere.

Startled, the trio turned to see an older woman, standing amid her amazing flower garden. The woman's grey hair plopped upon her head like a big cow pie, making Katie want to giggle as she carried her weeds and her trowel to the fence.

"Excuse me, do you know of—" Katie started.

"Uh, let me think. There's Gwennie, folks call her Grandma Gwen and Adelaide and Widah Perkins."

Katie started, "Where can I—"

"Grandma Gwen's is rietch over there. Perky little cottage." She pointed to a dollhouse-like cottage across the street and back a few houses from where they had come.

"Oh, a pretty cottage," Sarah whispered to Jeremy. But Jeremy was scowling.

"Thank you. We will try Grandma Gwen, then," Katie said. When they made introductions they found out the odd but helpful character was Miss Ruby, an extraordinary gardener.

They walked back up the street to the dollhouse cottage. It had a Dutch door with hand-painted tulips. Gladiolas and Sweet William grew all along the little white picket fence. They opened the little gate and walked the white rock trail to the door.

Jeremy started pulling against his sister's hand and dragging his heels.

"What is it, Jer'my?" Sarah tried to pull him to the door but he wouldn't budge.

"Is it Hamsel and Gretel's house where the witched is?"

Katie laughed. "No, son. I am sure she is a very nice lady."

"You are so silly." Sarah giggled and drug her little brother to the door.

"Hush, children. We must be on our best behavior, if we

are to find a place to board."

She knocked and waited and knocked again but it was no use; no one was there. So they made their way back to Miss Ruby, their friendly source of information.

"Ah, she is allus going to visit shut-ins. Could be where she is. Taked care of me back to when I was feeling poorly. Brung me chicken and dumplings and...." Ruby stopped to scratch an itch on her already dirty cheek and made a few new additions.

"Miss Ruby, could you tell us the names of the others again, please?" Katie asked.

Sure. Widah Perkinz. She'd not be me first choice, but ya never know. Third house on Maple." She pointed with her trowel. "Next block down—biggest spread on the block. Highfalutin place, can't miss it. Iffen she can't help, then go to the mercantile. Adelaide, she runs it. Kinda crotchety but I can't think of no one else."

"Thank you again, Miss Ruby, you have been so helpful."

Ruby smiled, revealing a missing tooth or two as the hopeful trio moved on to Maple St. When she found the Perkins house, Katie's hope lilted like a dying flower. Perfect rosebushes lined the lush green lawn and circled the driveway. Hedges of metered proportion brought them to the imposing front door.

"It's so big." Sarah gawked surveying the estate." Even the roses are big,"

"Sarrie, do you thinked a king lives here?"

"I don't think so, Jer'my."

"Now children, you must be completely quiet and sit still if I am interviewed by Mrs. Perkins."

Katie knocked on the door of the huge blue and white Victorian and took a big breath. She handpressed her wrinkled skirt and tucked in her obstinate curl but neither complied.

She waited in front of the huge double doors, looking around at the perfectly manicured estate. Katie noticed Sarah trying to count the windows. Slowly, one side of the door opened and a maid dressed in white and black with a perfectly starched apron and ruffled cap answered the door. Katie explained her situation fully expecting to be turned away as waifs. But the maid returned quickly and asked them to have a seat in the impeccably decorated parlor. There were beautiful rich imported carpets and elegant cushioned high backed chairs and lovely colorful glass lamps, sitting against patterned green and gold wallpaper. Though elegant and much like her childhood home, there seemed a lack of the warmth she longed for.

As they waited, Katie looked over to a mirror on the wall. She did not fit in this place. Had it not been for the children, she would have bolted right out the marbled hallway and back out to the street.

"Hello, I am Mrs. Perkins." A stately but kind-faced woman in a lace-trimmed, cream-colored dress walked into the room. She had touches of grey on the sides of her hair swept high in perfection.

"I understand you are looking for residence."

"Yes, yes we are. My name is Katherine Jensen. We have only just arrived and we need a place to stay and I am looking for work." Katie spoke nervously but kept her bearing.

"And your husband?"

"I am a widow."

"Oh, I see. Did you have to leave your home? Pardon me," she stopped herself and put her fingers to her mouth as if to stop the flow of words. "That is none of my business. I should think a young man doesn't expect to leave his family so soon, does he?" She was speaking more to herself than Katie. Katie fidgeted with the edge of her sleeve and wished she would just get it over with and send them on their way.

"Are your children well-behaved?"

"Yes, quite so, Mrs. Perkins." Katie almost laughed at their frozen little faces.

"Well, I don't usually take on children," she said sizing them up with little twitches in her cheeks, as she thought.

"Where did you say you worked?" She seemed a bit absentminded.

"I haven't found work, as of yet, as we have only just arrived."

"Well, hmm, what do you do?"

"I can do quite a lot of things. I am well-educated and I am also strong for hard work as well." It came out of her mouth involuntarily. Hard labor was not what she hoped to do.

"You don't happen to write well, do you?"

"Why, yes, I could show you."

"Do you know how to set a proper table?"

"Yes, my father was mayor in the East and my mother hosted many elegant receptions."

The woman's silver blue eyes lit up. "Splendid. Is your father still mayor?"

"No, Mrs. Perkins. They have both passed on from this world."

"Oh, I am sorry. Well, I thought I saw well-bred bearing in you. I need a social secretary. One who will help with all of my ladies meetings and teas. It is wearing me out. I'm at my wits end. I am just not as young as I used to be." She looked up in thought. "Hmm, I guess it's true about all of us, isn't it?" She gave a quick chuckle and then cleared her throat to go on. "I must check about the living quarters. I don't quite see how we'll manage the children. It is a matter of logistics, as the Colonel used to say. Let me think on it and if you find another place to board, fine. But I will employ you. We will certainly give it a try. Can you start on the twelfth?"

Relieved she hadn't bolted, Katie accepted graciously.

"I am sure you need to get the children in school. That should give you plenty of time."

Katie started to open her mouth but the stately woman walked out of the room and the maid appeared to show them out.

Outside, Katie took a big breath. "Thank you, Father."

"Mama, school?" Sarah said.

"Well, Sarah, I don't think Mrs. Perkins remembers that children are not in school this time of year. It was best I didn't correct her. Now let's look for the last possibility for a place to stay. Perhaps it will be easier if I tell them I will be working for Mrs. Perkins." Katie was overjoyed to have a good job and in a pleasant place and it wasn't fixing fence posts, pulling weeds or mucking stalls. She had a new spring in her step.

"God provided," Jeremy said.

"Yes, Jeremy, he surely did, didn't he." Katie smiled proudly at him and tussled his curls.

"I like it here in White Rock. It is so pretty and green and...and...happy." Sarah did a little twirl and her braids spun.

"Me, too. I liked it real much."

"Very much," corrected Katie nonchalantly.

"Now, what did Miss Ruby say her name was? Ada...Adel...Adelaide, that's it."

"Yes, Miss Ruby said she runs the mercantile."

"How smart you are, my little girl." Katie smiled at Sarah's lovely little dimples and brushed her cheek with her hand.

They walked toward the center of town, enjoying every beautiful house and the surrounding creation.

"Mama, look." Sarah pointed to a beautiful rose arbor all in bloom with perfect pink blossoms.

It took Katie's breath away. "It is heavenly, Sarah. It would be wonderful to have a rose arbor someday.'

Soon they found the mercantile shop and walked in. An irate voice caused Katie to flinch. At the fabric counter stood two middle-aged women.

"Well, Adelaide, this is just not right. I paid good money for these goods and look at the pulls in the middle. I can't make a skirt out of this, now can I?"

"I don't see anything wrong with it," she spewed back in a flippant tone, making Katie cringe. Katie walked inconspicuously closer to have a look at the goods in question. The lady was right. The goods were not usable at all. She quickly grabbed the children and walked out of the store.

"What's wrong?" Sarah asked.

"I don't think we want to stay there."

"Was it because she sounded angry?"

"Yes, and she was not being honest with her customer."

Father, you must have a place for us all planned out, don't you?

CHAPTER SIX

A Blessed Cottage

Katie and the children walked past the livery stable and near the little post office window. They stopped to rest on a short white rock wall.

"Nothing from Danny today," the postmistress told the older woman, as she sorted the mail. Katie watched as the sweet-faced older woman frowned at the news. She turned and walked toward Katie and the children.

"Good afternoon," greeted the little woman, her silvery-white hair shimmered in the sun. A warm smile took over where there had been disappointment but a moment ago.

"Good afternoon," Katie said, nudging the children.

"Good afternoon, Ma'am," they chorused.

"What a lovely family. My name is Gwen Richards. You are new to town, aren't you?"

"Yes, we are. My name is Katherine Jensen, my children, Sarah and Jeremy."

"How nice to meet you all. Where have you come from?"

"From Bitter Springs in the Arizona Territory." Whoops, she wasn't going to say it but it's out now.

"My, such a long way. Are you visiting?"

"No, Ma'am, we hope to live here." Katie wondered and took the chance to ask, "Might you be the Grandma Gwen, who takes in boarders on Center Street?"

"Why, yes, most folks do call me Grandma Gwen. Why do you ask? Are you in need of a place to stay?"

"Yes, Mrs. Richards. I have secured a job with Mrs. Perkins on Maple Street but she wasn't sure she could accommodate the children."

"I see. Is there only the three of you?"

"Yes, I am a widow."

"Ah, so young." Gwen's countenance dropped. "I lost my Samuel several years ago. I know it is a hard thing. Come, let's go see what we can arrange." Gwen ushered them back toward the storybook cottage. They chatted about flowers and businesses and it seemed so wonderful, yet Katie still looked over her shoulder now and then. Would she turn around to hear the sound of a wagon and horses hooves and be taken back?

"I see ya found 'er," Ruby cackled over the fence, wiping her dirt-laden hand on her apron and waving.

"Yes, thank you so much, Miss Ruby," Katie said.

"Hello, Ruby. Nice of you to help these folks."

As Grandma Gwen ushered them through her tulip-painted Dutch door, Jeremy gawked. He tugged on Katie's sleeve.

"Mama, the door is cut in halfed."

Gwen tried to suppress a laugh but couldn't.

"He keeps us smiling, Mrs. Richards."

"You are all charming."

The cottage had a beautiful white rock fireplace, and on

the mantle pictures of happy people framed in lovely ornate frames. Paintings dotted the cottage walls. The painting over the fireplace caught Katie's eye. It had lush gardens in bloom with a charming little gazebo and sunlight shining from above on the green hills meandering back to the horizon. It reminded her of one of her dreams.

Gwen came and stood next to her. "It is lovely, isn't it?

"It is breathtaking. Did you paint it?"

Gwen chuckled. "Me? Oh no, Audrey, my great niece. She spent many months with us when her parents went to England on holidays. Some years she would go with them and other years she stayed with us. She painted everything beautiful around us. Audrey is quite the artist. She's a sweet girl, a bit capricious but a most accomplished artist.'

"She certainly is."

"Do you paint?"

"I did a little as a girl but my first love was music, if I can still play. I have not seen a piano in years." The longing seemed to drag out in her words.

"Maybe you will be blessed with the opportunity, living here. My husband played beautifully. His piano is in the Overlook House east of the town on the hill. You can't see it from here. It is where the family lived but now only my grandson Daniel and I are left. Samuel is with the Lord and my son and his family went east, but I will share more later." She patted Katie's arm. "Let's get you settled first, you look weary."

Katie and the children were taken with the friendly cottage. There were sweet teacups and saucers with matching dainty English teapots, delicately painted with tiny little roses which sat in an exquisite hand-carved hutch.

A cuckoo clock came to life and cuckooed for them and the children were captivated. Wide-eyed and mouths ajar they stood waiting intently for him to come out again.

Another painting caught Katie's admiring eye, a spring green meadow dotted with happy little yellow and orange flowers. The sun shone in a particular spot as if set apart as a holy place.

"What a perfect place."

"We called it Prayer Meadow, the place where my Samuel proposed to me and the place where I told him he was going to be a father. We spent many wonderful times together in prayer there, in our younger years."

"How precious," Katie whispered, feeling sorrow for Gwen's loss and grateful to hear how important prayer was to her.

"Yes, it is and I will cherish it always but I can't go there anymore. These old bones won't make it up and down and we sold the horses and the carriage after my grandson went to college."

"Do you think you could go with my help? I would help you."

The tears pooled in Gwen's eyes at her suggestion. "What a lovely thought." Gwen reached for her and gave her a quick hug. "The children would love it, too. Now let's go see what rooms would suit you."

"A simple room would do for us, a small one." Fear struck anew as the price had not been mentioned.

Coaxing the children away from the cuckoo, they followed Gwen down the hallway. The little cottage proved to be deceptive, not nearly as small as she thought. Gwen showed them the first room and Katie was in awe.

It looked as if it were comfort itself and the bed with its colorful quilt and lavender wallpaper called to every beauty-starved bone in her body. Each room was charming with ruffled curtains and lovely quilted spreads and big fat fluffy pillows beckoning the weary to come and rest.

The first room with the wedding ring quilt that had taken Katie's breath away was the very one Gwen suggested to Katie, since there was an adjoining room for the children. The children's room was a bright, cheery peach color with light yellow curtains. They each had their own bed and were little cherubs in heaven, surveying their abode.

"Sarrie, the pillow is so soft," Jeremy said, as he rubbed it over and over like a pet kitten.

Gwen smiled at the children and put her hand on her heart. "You will be such a joy to a lonely old woman. I am so glad you are here." And she reached down and gathered the little ones in her arms like the grandmother they never had.

"But I am not sure I have enough for two rooms, Mrs. Richards."

"Pishposh, we'll just wait until you have worked and figure it out. Perhaps you could just do errands or help a bit around here to earn your board. And please call me Gwen. It is so wonderful to have company. My Daniel has been gone for much too long. He is my pride and joy, my grandson. Oh, I am rattling on and you all look famished. Let's go get some supper. We'll just make something quick so you won't have to wait long."

Gwen and Katie worked busily in the kitchen together preparing sandwiches made of tender fresh bread and thick ham pieces cut from a full baked mustard crusted ham, which Gwen said she had baked yesterday to take to shut-ins. They set one wonderful treat after another before the children. There were shiny black olives, apple butter, and savory smelling bread and butter pickles.

"This is even better than the Harvey Houses," Sarah said, her eyes bright with delight.

"It surely is. I am sure Grandma Gwen is a wonderful cook."

"We had chicken catcha-matorie onced, Grandma Gwen." Jeremy beamed, proud to have said such a big word.

Grandma Gwen could hardly hold back the giggle but she bit her bottom lip and managed. "You did? Well, I don't believe I have ever ventured to make such a dish but Daniel sure loves my chicken and dumplings."

"I think I would love chickened and dumpings."

Chickened and dumpings and the look on Jeremy's little expectant face got the better of her and she couldn't suppress the giggle anymore.

"It is all right, Mrs. Richards—Gwen. We spend half our lives amused by his unusual vocabulary. He doesn't mind. I think sometimes he actually enjoys making us laugh, though he doesn't quite know how he accomplishes it."

"I am so relieved. I didn't want to upset anyone. Shall we say grace?"

Jeremy started praying before one more word could be spoken. "Thank you, Father, for your nice blessings. For Grandma Gwen and her nice housed and her appled butter and sammiches and thank you for this not being Hamsel and Gretel's house. Amen."

Katie glanced at Grandma Gwen, whose brows were raised a bit, hoping for an explanation. Sarah came to her rescue.

"Before we knew you, when we first came to your cottage, Jer'my thought your cottage was the witch's house in Hansel and Gretel."

"I think because we kept talking about the town being like a storybook place," Katie added.

Grandma Gwen gave a cute little chuckle. 'What a wonderful prayer, Jeremy. I take it you all know the Savior?"

"Yes, I don't know how we would have survived without him."

The children nodded in affirmation.

"I tolded them over and over God will provide." Jeremy flailed his arms like a frustrated preacher trying to get his message across.

"He did, Grandma Gwen, and every single time God did something wonderful for us," Sarah said.

The trio told Gwen about their amazing journey to White Rock, as they enjoyed their first meal together.

"I would hardly believe such stories if I had not had so many miracles in my own life. God has surely held you all close to his heart," Gwen said.

"One blessing after another came once we left Bitter Springs. But I was not so assured before we left. At the train station, I remembered the money I had put in my apron and as I pulled it out, a boy ran by and snatched it out of my hand. I was so distraught, I hurried to purchase a ticket for as far as I could go and still have some left over for food and lodging. It happened to be White Rock and it reminded me of the scripture—"

"In the beginning of the book of Revelation," Grandma Gwen finished.

"Yes, and here we are."

"You realize even the thief was part of God's provision, don't you?"

Katie was stunned. "No, how?"

"You could go no further. You were forced to stop here. Sounds like God's providence to me."

"I haven't had much time to look at the whole picture, but you're right."

"Well, I am so glad you are all here. You and your wonderful little ones."

"So are we," Sarah said.

Grandma Gwen looked over at Sarah with a sly smile. "Did you know Sarah means princess?"

"Wow, you're a princess, Sarrie." Jeremy's eyes grew wide as he parroted the news to his sister.

"Then Jer'my, you are a prince, since you are my brother." Sarah smiled back at her little brother.

"Grandma Gwen, I'm a prince. What about you?"

"My name actually means blessing, Jeremy,"

"Oh, what a perfect name. You are surely a blessing to us," Katie said.

"Grandma Gwen, but what is Mama?"

"I think your Mama...is quite easily an angel sent to me." Gwen winked at him.

"Yes, she's our angel, too." Jeremy smiled, nodding.

"Children, you must ask our new friend what she would want to be called by you. We wouldn't want to be disrespectful."

"I think the children have chosen my right name. Grandma Gwen it is. Now, I have a little bit of apple crisp left for us. Tomorrow I will make something more special."

"Please, Gwen, we are fine. Don't do anything special for

us. We are so thankful and we are not used to eating much, although we were well fed a great deal at the Harvey Houses."

Gwen stood, hand at her chin, sizing them all up. "Yes, I see you all need a bit of fattening up."

Katie was beginning to see this precious lonely grandma was not to be thwarted. She was intent on spoiling them.

After their delicious meal, as she served their dessert, Jeremy looked at his mother.

"Does Grandma Gwen knowed about Uncle Tyler?"

"Shhh." Sarah hushed Jeremy.

"It's all right, children. I will explain everything to Grandma Gwen."

Katie got the children bathed and ready for bed. Sarah sighed contentedly as she snuggled into her bed, but Jeremy was popping his little mopped head all over his extra soft pillow. She pulled Flopsy, the stuffed bunny and Sarah's little Lambie out of the overstuffed carpetbag, prayed for them, and kissed them goodnight. "I'll be right there in the next room." She pointed to the open door leading into her lavender and lilac room. She wanted to join in and crawl happily into her own bed but she knew she must explain at least some of their situation to Gwen.

"Mama," Jeremy said sleepily.

"Yes."

"God will provide." And he was out like a lamp. She brushed his little cheek with her fingers.

Oh, Father how you speak through the little ones.

"Mama, Jer'my always says God will provide and he is always right."

"Yes, he is. We have a wonderful God who cares about

our every need and he sees even the sparrow fall to the ground. Every part of his creation is precious to him. You know how much I love you and Jeremy? Well, God loves you even more."

"Why did he make us stay so long at Uncle Tyler's house?"

Katie took a deep breath. "God wanted us to be a witness to him. It didn't seem as if we did much but we must continue to pray for him."

"Okay, but sometimes it is hard."

"It is. But he is a hurting, lonely old man, and even if God is angry with the way he treated us, God still loves him and we must love him enough to pray for his soul." Katie was preaching more to herself than to Sarah. She needed to remember. She had to admit it was a great deal easier to pray for him now—not being under his tyranny.

"Good night. I like Grandma Gwen."

"She is sweet, isn't she? Goodnight, little princess."

When Katie came back out to the living area, she sank into a comfy chair, which was so comfortable she thought she might not make it to bed.

"We can talk tomorrow when you are all rested. You go on to bed."

But Katie insisted on telling her a bit about her situation and fears of Uncle Tyler coming after them so she shared a condensed version and then stifled a yawn.

"Just let him try—he'll have to deal with this whole town, I'll see to that." The feisty woman spoke as though the issue was all settled and in her mind, it was.

"Gwen, you are so kind. You are both a blessing and an angel."

Gwen promptly ushered Katie to her room and gave her a wonderful grandmotherly hug, which Katie savored and before long she was snuggling into the most delicious sandwich of comfort she had been in since leaving her childhood home, covered with a lilac wedding ring quilt. Everything smelled so pure and clean. Sweetness permeated the whole room—one which only peace can bring.

Father, this isn't a dream is it?

CHAPTER SEVEN

Comfort & Chaos

Gwen peeked in to see if the little family was stirring. The delicate features of Katherine's face were bathed in sunrays. She had prayed for the little family and was pleased to see her newfound charges were so comfortable and at peace. Katherine was such a beautiful young woman and so gracious. And those children—adorable was what they were—absolutely adorable, but they all needed a bit of fattening up and she smiled as she went back to prepare the full breakfast she had planned for them.

She worked happily making a feast fit for a king, or was that a princess and prince and, oh yes, an angel. She laughed to herself. She would spoil them the way she often spoiled Daniel when he came home for a visit. She missed him. Why hasn't he written? He was so faithful to send his letters. Well, she would not worry. He was in God's hands and she covered him and the Men's Street Mission with her faithful prayers. Now she would have this delightful little family to pray for as well as spoil. She wondered what happened to Katherine's husband and if Daniel would find her attractive. How could he not? The lovely young woman was a little golden-haired treasure. But she must let God do his work and not interfere. Still, she imagined what a perfect couple they might make.

Katie opened her eyes and collected her thoughts, trying to put all the puzzle pieces together. The events of the last few days ran through her mind like a buzzing bee, going from one scene to another and back again. She was drunk with the smell of the sweet lavender. Her eyes traveled around by way of the lilac-flowered wallpaper to the spray of lavender in a vase on the bureau. She stretched and sat up, tracing her fingers over the pattern of the rings, which entwined each other on the wedding ring quilt.

It wasn't a dream. I am really here. Thank you, Father.

She heard clatter from the kitchen and was horrified she had slept so late. Jumping out of bed, she peeked at the children, sleeping soundly. She looked at the oval dressing mirror on the bureau and was taken aback at the vision in the mirror. Her girlishness was surely gone and she looked different—a bit gaunt but she was sure Grandma Gwen would be plotting a change to that soon.

She washed her face, dressed quickly, pulled her fairy tresses up, and thanked God for all his mercy. Her mind flashed back to the lady on the train and her right-hand man, who brought the envelope, the meals, Sampson, Mrs. Perkins and her new job, and wonderful Gwen and her lovely cottage.

Father, please let it last.

"Good morning, Katherine. How did you sleep?" Gwen greeted Katie as she came into the kitchen.

"Better than I can remember and please call me Katie."

"Katie it is. I am so glad you are rested. The children still asleep?" Katie nodded.

"They must be comfy, too. Everyone always says the cottage is peaceful. It is the Lord's presence I am sure." Gwen set out a lovely rose teacup and poured tea.

"Yes, it is. It is heavenly." Katie gave a contented sigh and sipped her tea.

"Now, let's fix you a plate. When the little ones smell it, they will perk up quickly."

Gwen pulled the warm homemade bread closer and sliced it lickety-split.

"This smells wonderful," Katie said. Then as Gwen predicted, the vapors must have danced down the hallway into the little sleepy noses of the children for they were stirring.

Gwen let out a short cackle and motioned toward the hall. "I guess it did the trick."

"Good morning, Grandma Gwen," Sarah said rubbing her eyes with Jeremy in tow.

"Freshed bread?" Jeremy's eyes widened at the sight and smell.

Grandma Gwen reached over, tossed his curly thick locks, and answered, "It sure is, little fellow, and butter and strawberry jam is on the table."

"Yum . . . do we get to haved some?"

Gwen's head tilted as she tried to understand what he

meant. "Why, I made it just for you."

"We were used to rationing," Katie said and Gwen nodded.

It had been several days since her little family had come to stay and they were already working together like a family. Katie took all the harder lifting and bending chores, leaving Gwen the less strenuous jobs of cooking and mending. The work was so much less than what either of them had been used to doing. What a joy to do things for Gwen and be appreciated. But Katie was concerned that their staying at the cottage might be too much for the dear woman and her Daniel would come home and shoo them all out.

The children were well fed, dressed, and giggling in the side yard like little birds freed from a cage. Gwen and Katie stood near the window watching. The children were so happy at the cottage, it reminded her of the dreams she had back in Bitter Springs.

"Katie, I hope you will be content to stay right here with me."

"I don't know, Gwen. It's wonderful being here, but I am afraid we will burden you too much." The truth be told, she never wanted to leave the charming cottage nor the precious adopted grandmother who stood with her.

"Nonsense. You are a joy, not a burden. I just hoped you would like our little town and stay."

"Oh, I do. I have never been so happy. I would hate to leave."

The two women settled back into their chairs. Katie peeled potatoes and Gwen snapped beans. They enjoyed great fellowship, which they had both lacked so long.

"Well, I haven't enjoyed myself this much in years. I do hope you will stay." Gwen peered up from her bowl, hopefully.

"We love being here. Of course, our original plan was to try to get closer to Charlotte's in San Francisco."

"Charlotte?"

"My sister. But I don't believe she really wants us to come. Her letter said as much. She was so busy with society there and her husband's high society family would be coming for the holidays. It sounded as if they were quite particular and she could not invite us to come. I suppose we would be an embarrassment to her." Her head lowered. "She probably thinks me a poverty-stricken hick." A nervous laugh escaped. "Perhaps that is what I have become."

"Anyone with half their sight could see you are a well-bred young lady."

"Mrs. Perkins said the same thing. Perhaps I am not too far gone. I suppose it was rather brazen to leave on my own, though."

"It must have been a hard decision. You are a brave girl."

But Katie didn't feel in the least bit brave and she finally broke down.

"It was so horrible, Gwen. The last day was so—" The tears flowed, pouring out like a waterfall and she was unable to stop the heaving sobs. She finally managed to tell Gwen about the days before they left.

"You poor girl, what a difficult situation." Gwen had come over to the couch and held her. It seemed Katie had not really cried in years and now the dam burst. She had suppressed the pain for the children's sake for so long, becoming numb from the years of oppression and loneliness.

Finally, after a good hard bout, Katie took a deep breath and apologized.

Gwen hugged her tightly. "Oh, sweet child, I am so glad God brought you here. You will be safe and happy here, all of you."

"But I cannot impose—"

"Well, you certainly can't leave. I will be miserable. It has been so lonely without Daniel."

"But we don't want to wear you...out." As the words came out of her mouth, her mind went back to the face of her accusing uncle when he said they had worn Aunt Nora out.

"Nonsense. You have been helping me constantly. Doing things I have a hard time doing. You have no idea how much joy your little family has brought to me. It is a pleasure to have you here and fix meals and do things together."

It was no use. Katie couldn't leave—not that she wanted to. She had already embraced Grandma Gwen and the town of White Rock. What could God add to this to make it any more wonderful? Gwen made it clear to her—she was thankful for their company.

They happily chattered as they went to the kitchen, made themselves tea, and set out little biscuit crackers and juice for the children. When she called them, they came in telling of all their glorious adventures.

"I hearded a frog," Jeremy said in high pitch.

"And the flowers are so pretty. The ones we saw the day we came here have all bloomed, now in all different colors.

You have to come see." Sarah, the quiet one, was just as ecstatic over her finds, pulling on her mother's arm, dragging her mother outside.

"She must be talking about the snapdragons," Gwen said, following them. "I have been waiting for them to bloom. I planted them late."

"Dragons?" Jeremy's eyes doubled in size.

"Just flowers, Jer'my, just flowers," Sarah said. But he didn't look convinced.

"They will bloom here for months."

"How wonderful," Katie said. Her heart ached for the beauty of this town to last.

"All the flowers are dead back home," Sarah said as if she had just given them a funeral. Then her sandy brown braids flipped around and she faced her mother. "Is this our new home? Can we live here forever? We don't ever have to go back do we?"

Katie was speechless. She felt the same way.

"You can stay as long as you like. This is God's provision and if he provided this for you, you have no reason to worry about tomorrow. But don't worry, Sarah, you are not going back to Arizona Territory if I have anything to do with it. Right now this is your home." And when Grandma Gwen spoke in that tone, they were assured—it was settled.

Sarah's smile grew wide, fully reassured. "Mama, is this the way you lived when you were a little girl?"

"No, my home was more like Mrs. Perkins' house."

"Mrs. Perkins' house was big and fancy but I like it here better."

"Yes, dear, my childhood was not quite as warm and cozy as this but I was loved just the same."

"Is your sister older than you, Katie?" Gwen asked.

"Yes, she is two years older. She was the society girl. She loved all the teas and parties and shops. I loved the country and the beauty of God's creation. She would drag me through the city on endless shopping excursions and I would whine. Now, I wish I could enjoy some of the blessings again. I don't care for city life but I don't want to live in desolate mining towns or places like Bitter Springs, either."

"Oh my, no. Well, perhaps White Rock will hold new life for you. I would love to have you all close to me, of course. And you must meet my Daniel."

Daniel. Where had she heard that name?

When they were finished with their tea and biscuits, Grandma Gwen said, "Who wants to go to the post office with me?"

"I do," Sarah said.

"Me too, please," Jeremy scooted off his chair.

"You look so comfy, Katie. Why don't you just stay here and rest for a while?"

Katie started to protest but she really did want some time to pray.

After they left she tidied the kitchen and then meandered in the garden, taking in all its color and fragrance, praying.

Suddenly, a loud knock at the door made her jump. She felt apprehensive. She peeked around the corner of the trellis of the side yard to see if she could find out who it might be. The huge frame was familiar—the grisly face— Markum!

All the rest and peace she had soaked in was drained in

seconds as she fought to know what to do. Her breathing escalated as she pressed herself into the outside wall of the house. She must leave. She ran toward the back gate and down the back path to town, hoping to catch Gwen and the children before they made their way back.

She caught them coming out of the Post Office.

Gwen grasped her arm. "What is it, child?"

"It is a man who works with Tyler. He knocked at the door. I didn't answer it. I was in the garden and saw him. He mustn't know we are here, but the whole town will tell him. Gwen, he is an awful man."

Gwen was thinking fast. Katie was truly frightened. The man must be terrible. She reached in her pocket. "Here, take this key. Do you see the house there on the hill, the light green one? Yes, that is the one. It is a little bit of a climb but go and stay there. Don't worry, no one is living there. Go on in and make yourself at home. I will take care of things here. I'll find a way to send for you when it's safe. God is with you. Don't forget."

As Gwen scooted them all toward the hill, she prayed for direction and proceeded to carry out her plan.

She went into the restaurant and pulled Millie aside, who was known to be a bit of a talebearer, second only to Miss Ruby, who usually blurted things out in innocence not malignantly.

"Millie, listen, we have sort of a calamity here. You know the lovely young lady and her two little ones who came into town awhile back and are staying with me? Yes, those are the ones. Well, there's a bad fellow looking for them and we have to thwart him. Can you spread the word around? Tell everyone not to answer his questions. And for land sakes, find Ruby or we're done for. She wasn't home when I passed her house earlier."

Millie sent out two of her workers out to spread the word—one in one direction and one in the other, while Gwen scurried up the street hoping to size up the fellow who was snooping around her yard and to give Ruby a warning, had she returned home. But Ruby was nowhere to be seen and Gwen braced for the stranger, quite out of breath.

Father, give me strength and wisdom.

Surprised to see him still at the cottage, in the most cheerful voice she could conjure up, Gwen greeted the stranger.

"Can I help you, sir?"

"Yup, I'm lookin' fer a woman—yellar hair and two young'uns. Seen 'em?" His voice was coarse and raspy, his face unshaven and his hair and clothing unkempt.

"Oh, my, did you lose them?" Gwen evaded his question, playing up her elderly innocence.

"Uh, yeah, their uncle's looking for 'em." He pointed to her sign. "You bunk fer the night here?"

Gwen hesitated. "Yes, sometimes but I am expecting my grandson so I am not taking any boarders right now." When she said it, it rang strangely true to her and she thought it odd. Just as she finished speaking the words, arms came wrapping around her from behind in a big bear hug. She jumped nervously. Then she heard the familiar voice.

"I'm sorry, Grandma, I didn't mean to startle you."

"Daniel. Oh, my boy." She turned and gave him a greatly relieved hug.

Danny watched the stranger back away as the reunion started.

"Hmm . . . the bum said the yellar-haired lady got off here. I'll ask around anyhow. Git some grub," he grumbled to himself but Danny could hear. He turned his attention to his grandma.

"How did you know I was coming?" Daniel asked.

"I didn't," she whispered. "Come inside and I'll explain."

"Are you alright?"

"Tea and a biscuit," she mumbled as they walked in to the cottage. "We'll talk over tea and a biscuit."

"Okay, Grandma, what's up? That was a rather shady looking fellow. Something is amiss here." He noticed the extra dishes on the table and some of his childhood games on the rug. "Do you have boarders?"

"Yes, Daniel, a precious young mother and her two lovable children. The man who was outside was looking for them. It's a rather long story but right now we must protect them."

Daniel knew his grandmother had impeccable discernment but she was sure out of sorts. "Sounds serious. Are you sure she's on the up and up?"

"Yes, yes, she is a darling girl and loves our Lord."

"So tell me the story."

"As soon I get some tea made. Tea is what I need."

"Are you feeling ill?"

"No, I'm fine. A little tired is all. I scooted all over town quite quickly for an old woman."

"You come and sit down. I will get your tea." She rested while he made her tea.

Gwen took a deep breath and a sip of tea and bite of tea biscuit, then shared a quick rendition of Katie's story and what had just come about.

"Poor little family. They must have had a rough go of it."

"I'm afraid so. Oh, I almost forgot, she and the children are at the Overlook House. I gave them the key. The poor little family is probably scared stiff."

"That was a good idea. Does anyone know?"

"No. I have passed the word around town to brush him off."

"Good thinking, Grandma. It will all be fine. Let's pray and then I will scout around and see if I can get rid of him."

"Do be careful. He is not a nice man. And of all people, we couldn't find Ruby, to tell her to keep quiet. If he runs into her, it is all spilled."

They prayed for protection and wisdom and to find Miss Ruby before the stranger did.

"The Lord will help me. What did you always teach me?"

"Yes, I know," said Gwen sheepishly." If we worry we are not trusting God."

"Yes, Ma'am." He pecked her cheek and hurried out the door.

This was certainly a strange homecoming.

Daniel followed the stranger around town, watching as he made his way to the small restaurant. Daniel walked in and sat at a table near him and overheard him ask the young waitress about a yellar-headed woman with two young'uns. Daniel prayed.

"No, no one like that around here and we would know. We know everything that goes on in this town."

Daniel watched, amused at her performance, when of all people, Ruby walked in. She eyed Daniel and her face lit up.

"Dan'el, when did you get back to town?" Daniel's heart sank. Of all people, the one person who could spill the beans better than anyone else now seated herself beside him. He took a deep breath.

Lord, help me with this one.

"Ruby, how are you? Have you planted anything new in your garden? I just love your prize pansies...yes, the dark purple ones." On and on he babbled, completely monopolizing the conversation about her garden until she forgot all else and was immersed in her garden world. The friendly ploy was working. He smiled as she chattered on and on about every flower and weed in her yard while her hair plopped around on top of her head like a happy flapjack.

Out of the corner of his eye, he watched the uncouth stranger wolf down his meal, wipe his mouth on his sleeve, drink his third cup of coffee like water, and start out the door. Daniel motioned to the young waitress and asked her if she would fill Ruby in on the situation and walked out keeping his eye on the stranger. He noted his direction and quickly ran around back.

"Danny Boy—so good to see you," the sheriff said, jumping up from his desk.

"You too, Tom."

The two friends shook hands and Tom started telling about new things around town until Danny cut him short to explain the situation with Katie and the stranger.

"Where did he come from?"

"Arizona Territory from what I remember. Must have got off the train. He's looking for the boarders at Grandma's house. She has them hidden but let me explain..." The sheriff listened to a summarized version of the already brief version Danny received from his grandma.

"Let's go see about this stranger." Tom grabbed his hat and followed Danny out.

Danny pointed him out and stayed in the background. Tom walked up to the stranger after seeing him coming out of the mercantile.

"Can I be of service?" the sheriff asked, his tall and muscular countenance looking impressively intimidating.

"Ah, yeah, I'm looking fer a yellar-haired woman and her kids that came out this a way. Her uncle's lookin' for her."

"Why's he looking for her?"

"Worried about her." The stranger wrung his hands.

"Is she lost or something?" Tom prodded.

"No. Just left without saying goodbye."

"Is she under age?"

"No."

"Then nothing to be done. Sounds like she left of her own accord. Maybe she'll come back on her own."

"Maybe." The stranger's eyes were set on the ground through most of the conversation his fingers itchy. He turned on his heel and grumbled to the air as he headed back down Center Street toward the train station. The sheriff and Danny watched as he left.

"Slimy sort. Grandma said he scared her boarder."

"Yup. Not someone I would trust. You haven't met the new boarder?" Tom grinned at him, reminding him of a littler Tom who would do that when he knew something Danny didn't.

"No, why?" He said askance.

"Nice surprise in store for you." The sheriff had a teasing twinkle in his eyes and his face was flushed. Danny tried to ignore him.

"Do you think he'll leave now?" Danny turned back to watch the stranger.

"Hope so. I'll send Jacob to see if he gets on the train, just to make sure."

"Good idea. Will you keep me posted?"

"You bet. Goin' home?"

"Yes, Grandma sent the family to the Overlook House. Thank you, Tom." They shook hands again and Danny hurried back to the cottage, following behind the stranger, hoping the vulgar man would not go back to the cottage and fluster his grandmother.

What did Tom mean by a nice surprise?

CHAPTER EIGHT

Dandy

"Daniel, you must go tell Katie all that has transpired. She must be beside herself. She is rather fearful, coming out of that awful situation. I hope you won't scare her."

"Thank you for the vote of confidence." He loved to tease his beloved grandma.

"You silly boy. Seeing you will be quite a nice change from the filthy evil man who was looking for her. She just doesn't know you are coming."

"I will walk up the creek way so she can see me coming."

"Good idea. Now, wait a minute, she'll need a few provisions until we know for sure he is gone." She scurried around like a chipmunk gathering things for him to take. "This won't be too heavy, will it?"

"You don't take me for a milksop, do you?"

"Oh, off with you. And if you are invited to eat, I am sending plenty for all of you. I think they should stay the night, don't you?"

"Yes, might be best since it may be awhile until we hear back from Tom. I will show them where everything is and be back before dark."

With provisions in tow, Danny hiked the long hill to the Overlook House. It had been a long time. Too long. He stopped to rest for a minute and looked up at the old homestead. The beautiful house was large, but not pretentious; elegant, but not ostentatious. Its large white trimmed bay windows reached out to welcome him home.

When he got closer, the wraparound porch looked as if it was hungry for happy family times—or at least he was. When the bay window came into view, he wondered about the little family staying there for their protection. He saw movement for a second.

Lord, please don't let them be afraid.

"Mama, a man comed up the hill," Jeremy warned, scooting off the window seat where he pretended to be a prince of the big castle.

Katie froze. A sick feeling engulfed her. How did he find them? Where could they hide?

Sarah peered out the window. "Mama, he isn't a mean looking man."

Katie inched toward the window.

Jeremy climbed back onto the window seat. "He has stuffed in his arms."

Katie thought maybe Gwen was sending provisions by way of an errand boy. But when she looked, she did not see an errand boy but a handsome man nearer her age, well-dressed and cheerful looking. He looked at the window and waved to them. She jumped away from the window.

When he came around and knocked on the door. Katie hesitated, unsure. Could it be a trick? When she didn't answer right away, he put in his key and peeked in the door. "Hello, is anybody home? I brought provisions from Grandma, uh...Gwen."

Danny stood looking at Katie for an overly long moment.

Oh, my, she is lovely. Not at all what I expected. Aha, Tom's surprise.

He choked, trying to get out his introduction. "Hello, everyone, I am Daniel, Gwen's grandson. I came home unexpectedly and found you were all in quite a predicament."

Katie let out the breath she had been holding. "Oh, Daniel, I am so glad to meet you. I am Katie but then I guess you know that. I am so sorry to have caused all this awful mess. Please, forgive me. This should have been a pleasant homecoming for you and I have spoiled it."

My, how unselfish she sounds. "Not at all. I am so glad we could help."

He sat down his bags of provisions and told her all that had happened in town.

"I can't tell you how relieved I am. Everyone is so kind." Katie's eyes were watery and Daniel noticed it right away, as he didn't seem to be able to stop looking at her.

"Jeremy, Sarah, come out children. It is Grandma Gwen's grandson, Daniel." Katie called to them as she quickly dried the pooling tears.

"Call me Danny, please. That's what my grandma calls me when she isn't upset or serious." They peered around the corner wall and came to their mother's side.

He reached out to shake their little hands.

"Hello, Mr. Dandy. Did you scared away the bad man?" Jeremy asked.

Danny laughed. "I believe we have. What a delight you must be to Grandma."

"I miss Grandma Gwen, can we goed to see her now?"

"Not yet little fellow, but soon. We thought it best for you to stay the night, at least until we find out more. And you must be Sarah," he said.

"Yes. It means princess. Grandma Gwen told me."

"Well, Princess Sarah, I am your devoted servant." He bowed and she giggled, covering her mouth.

"I feel so bad. I have caused so much trouble for everyone." Katie bowed her head.

"No, no, not at all. I think this town needed a little livening up."

"I should think there would be better ways to liven up a town."

"Listen, don't think another thought about it. I think you are now fully initiated into White Rock as the new family. Everyone here works together pretty well. Only a few black sheep."

"I didn't see any blacked sheep?" Jeremy thought out loud.

"You surely bring the house down, Jeremy."

"Sarrie, I didn't bringed a house down." Jeremy looked confused but Sarah knew enough to join the laughter.

"There is not a thing to worry about, chap." Danny

reached down and picked Jeremy up. "Let's find some food for you, shall we? Grandma was worried about you but I preached her own sermon right back at her about worry."

"Such as, take no thought for what you shall eat or wear. It has become a familiar scripture to us," Katie said, unloading the provisions.

"Yes, a good one. We used it often at the Men's Mission. Sometimes it is harder to live out than to say."

"I am afraid that is often the case with scriptures."

"Oooo...roasted beast. We had it at Harvey's House. But I never did see Harvey. Too many people visited his house all the timed."

Danny laughed. "You went to Harvey's House? In all my meals, I never met Harvey myself, come to think of it."

"Daniel, I hope you will stay and eat with us. If I know your grandmother, she gave up the whole meal to us."

"I would love to stay for dinner, thank you." He felt to stay and just look at Katie might be even better than Grandma's roast, which smelled heavenly.

Katie found all she needed with help from Danny and set a lovely table before them all.

Danny watched like a boy at the candy counter, as Katie served them. He tried to compare her to every young woman he had ever known and they came up short—extremely short. She was beautiful and kind all in the same perfect package. No wonder Grandma was so taken with her. But he was still a little gun-shy of females. Yet, there was something different about this one.

Danny was asked to say the grace and he thanked God for safety, new friends, and blessed his grandma for making them such a delicious meal of God's provision.

They chatted and talked about Grandma Gwen and what a blessing she had been to them. Katie mentioned her new job and Sarah shared their train story about the wonderful lady who had been so kind along the way.

"Mrs. Templeton," Danny said.

"You know her?" Katie stared at him, with her mouth open, and the children looked at each other excitedly.

"She rides the train a great deal. She is rather well-to-do and a great philanthropist. She has given gifts to the Men's Street Mission from time to time."

"What's a flap and rust?" Jeremy asked.

"Oh, little chap, you are a prize. You would have kept everyone at the mission house from ever getting in the doldrums."

Jeremy's little eyebrows scrunched and whispered to his sister, "What are dull drums, chap and flap and rust?"

Sarah shrugged.

"I am not sure I can finish eating," Danny said, trying to catch his breath.

"He is our charmer," Katie said and she did her best to explain to Jeremy what a philanthropist was.

"Hmm, then Grandma Gwen is a flap and rust because she taked us in her house and gaved us coconutted cake."

Coconutted cake? Danny was beside himself with laughter. "I love Grandma's coconutted cake, too, little chap."

Katie snuck back to the kitchen and brought back plates of the much-desired coconut cake in question.

"It has been my favorite since I was a little chap like you, Jeremy."

"Me, too." Jeremy nodded.

"Everything is his favorite." Sarah rolled her eyes and shook her head.

After eating a few bites, Katie and Danny excused themselves and let the children finish their cake while they went into the kitchen to clean up.

"I can do this part. It is the least I can do."

"I can help, I am quite accustomed to it. It was part of the Mission House job much of the time. Besides, who can eat with little Jeremy around?"

"Yes, it can be a dilemma at times." Her laugh was gentle and sweet.

"Here, I'll dry." He reached for the plate. She smiled shyly not coquettish like other women but innocently.

"I was so afraid to use this beautiful china; it is so delicate and lovely." She traced the pink roses with her finger.

Yes, lovely and delicate. No wonder she loves it. It was like her.

"It is a pattern I would have chosen for myself. I don't think I have ever seen one more exquisite."

She praised the china. It meant a great deal to him, after his old flame's distasteful criticism. He watched as she gingerly washed the dish as if it were highly prized.

"I don't think the owner would mind terribly that we used them." He grinned a mite but she didn't see it.

Her surprise caught him off-guard. "Oh, do you know the owner?" Her brilliant eyes locked with his.

"As close as anyone." Now he was teasing and the querying cock of her head made him wonder is she suspected something.

"Are you sure it is all right for us to be here?"

"Why don't you ask him yourself?"

"What?" She nearly dropped the plate, looking around. He helped her hang on to it and their hands touched.

Danny was ashamed. "I am sorry, Katie, I didn't mean to worry you. I confess; I am the owner."

"You?"

"Yes, it was my parents' home and they left it to me. Mother left the china and many other nice things for my future wife as a gift."

Katie blinked and looked down. He had embarrassed her. But she rallied with a good-natured, although reticent smile. "All the more reason to take care of it. It is a treasured heirloom."

"Please forgive me for playing the game with you. I'm afraid I have been surrounded by men so long and many of them characters at that."

"Of course." Her smile widened and it made him feel even worse.

What a cad. What must she think of me now?

Desiring to change the subject quickly, he offered to show her around. He put his arm out to escort her and they strolled the lovely old house, as he told stories of his childhood home.

When they came into the library, Katie's face lit up and her mouth fell open. "How glorious."

Clearly she was enamored. She walked toward the floor-to-ceiling bookcase, looked up, and nearly tripped on one of the Persian rugs. "Oh, the books. And what a beautiful desk."

"My special spot. I want to try my hand at writing sitting there one day."

She turned to look at him and then she saw the paintings. He smiled as he watched her enjoying the things he loved, things pertaining to his beloved family.

"You hadn't ventured in here since you came up, then?"

"No. I felt I was imposing as it was. It must be exquisite with the fireplace lit and reading your Bible by the fire."

Katie was visibly taken with his home and it exhilarated him. His smile grew as he watched her. She happily gazed at everything around her like a child in a fairytale. In the middle of her survey, she stopped abruptly and her hand went to her heart. She gasped, looking right past him like she'd seen an old friend. "A piano." She walked over and touched the edge of the beautiful mahogany grand piano like it was made of gold.

"Do you play?"

"When I was a girl at home." She was in a daze now. He wondered what was going through her mind.

"Please play. It is not good for a piano to sit, you know."

It was as if the piano was drawing her, luring her. She moved slowly, seeming almost afraid but continued to the stool. She swished her skirts out of the way to sit. Her fingers stretched to the keys and played a few notes, then chords, then they began to traipse the entire keyboard in every scale. *Music*—it was too simple a word to call it that. One cannot describe what it did to Daniel's soul. Her fingertips melded with the ivory keys and brought the resounding life to the piano's strings. It was as if she had played every day of her life and with the finest orchestras.

Danny backed away so as not to disturb her as she came to life like a butterfly with new wings of flight. He drank it all in to his mission-weary soul as symphony and harmony danced around the room in perfect unison.

Katie, so beautiful, so sweet and now gifted as well.

A couple of her golden curls fell across her cheek and he was enchanted. Then she played several hymns, some of his favorites and when she sang, his heart was flooded with wonderful memories. Her voice was rich and clear.

He relaxed back into the old Bentwood rocking chair his grandfather had loved, remembering when he used to sit in it and watch as his grandfather played the piano. It was glorious to hear the piano come to life again after all its dormant years since his grandfather had left this world. He turned to see Katie's profile and he found himself a willing captive. She would look heavenward at times and her lashes were wet and her green eyes sparkled. It was as if she wasn't on earth at all. There were moments he wanted to reach for her and touch her delicate cheek. She had such a gentle, gracious spirit, fitting so perfectly in his beloved homestead. Was she real? Was he dreaming her up? Would he wake up back at the mission with the good-hearted but scruffy lot of men?

Jeremy and Sarah wandered in looking like two little cherubs into an unknown world. Their eyes were full of wonderment.

"Is this a piano?" Sarah's eyes grew big as she softly touched the keys.

Jeremy ran over to his mother and it brought her out of heavenly places. "Don't stopped, Mama."

Had they never seen a piano nor heard their mother play? Daniel wondered. They were such innocent and sweet little ones. Life surely must have been hard for them.

"Maybe later, children. I certainly got carried away."

She was radiant as she turned to Danny, "Thank you for letting me play." She looked at him as if he had given her the piano. Something about her made him wish he *could* give it to her. She had come alive after she played. She was even more beautiful than he had already determined with this sort of holy light in her countenance.

"Thank you for playing. It was magnificent." He was entirely enchanted. He never felt this way before. She seemed pure femininity. Something about her made him feel ten feet tall and, yet, weak at the knees.

This is not good. Help me, Lord—I don't want to be deceived again.

He drew his eyes away from her, forcibly. "This was my favorite room. Father would read us Bible stories and my sister and I would sit by the fire. Mother would sit over there by the lamp and do her needlework and listen. When Grandma and Grandpa lived with us, it was music and song. Grandpa Samuel played the piano. He had a gift for music as you do, Katie—" His eyes fell back on her again and his words slowed. "And I dare say the old piano has not been played in such glory since he last touched its keys. I know he would have been honored to have you play it. He was quite the tenor, too. Grandma loved to sing, too, and she and my father would harmonize. My sister sang a sweet soprano, like you."

Katie's eyes brightened and she blushed slightly.

"Mother said God left her out of the musical gifts so she could enjoy it the most. She said she could never have finished all her needlework without it. The needlework above the piano is hers."

Katie turned to look, taking it all in. "It is exquisite work, a painting in needlepoint. Your childhood must have been heavenly. I'm afraid mine was rather stoic, but I was loved and spoiled in many ways. We had many servants and my mother was thoroughly involved in society. My sister, Charlotte followed in her footsteps. It came naturally for her. I studied with a master and he was insufferable but I cannot deny I learned a great deal from him. When alone, the piano was my escape from social functions, along with the big maple tree and a book, when no one missed me."

"I think I would have done the same in your circumstances. This home was a happy place for me." Danny looked around the room and walked over to the garden window, his hands behind his back. Katie followed. "I used to run out in the hills and sing as loud as I could pretending to be my Grandpa Samuel."

"Then you inherited his voice?" She looked at him with such interest it touched his heart. How could a man think at all with this lovely creature so near?

She is waiting for an answer. Wake up, man.

"Uh...they used to tell me I did but I never sang like he did. He was amazing." He pointed to the portrait on the wall near the massive desk.

Katie walked closer, admiring it. "He has a kind face. I wish I could have known him. I see the resemblance," she said comparing Danny to the portrait.

"I'm glad. He was a wonderful man. My grandparents came over by ship from Bristol, England. My grandparents were just little children when they came over but their families were quite close and Grandpa and Grandma were childhood friends. I think that's why it is so hard for her at times. She misses him so much."

"All those years together. It must have been awful for her to lose him. She talks of him often. So that is where the slight accent comes from."

"Yes, and Grandma says I am worse than either of them. They worked so hard at losing their accent to fit in when they came. I loved it and wanted to speak the way my great grandparents spoke."

"I noticed. It...is charming," she said and looked away.

"Thank you." He found her much more charming.

He turned to the grand bookcase. "A great deal of these belonged to Grandpa. He was an educated man in many areas and you will find most of his books had to do with theology. When they came to live with us, he brought the piano and the books and many other delightful things."

"No wonder your grandmother misses being here." Katie perused the shelves. "I could spend half my life in this room, playing the piano and reading. Of course, the other half would be in the garden and out on the hills."

He walked over to her as she took a book off the shelf. She smiled at him and their eyes met again. He wondered if she was she feeling it, too? She was. She was blushing again. Was he blushing, as well?

She looked at the book in her hand, avoiding eye contact. "This one looks particularly interesting."

"Read all you care to and when you come back to the cottage, bring what you want to read with you."

"Jeremy, look, I have never seen so many books." Katie and Danny turned to see Sarah as her eyes followed the shelves all the way to the ceiling.

"Well, they won't be as easy to count as Mrs. Perkins' windows." She explained to Danny about their first day at the Perkins mansion.

Danny lifted Sarah onto the desk so she could see even better. "Now let me think where the children's books were placed. They should be here somewhere."

"Children's books?" Sarah said.

"Yes, little princess, lots of them. If I could remember where they are."

Katie's eyes scanned the shelves. "What about there on the fourth shelf, close to the window?"

"Ha. Grandma always said that a man couldn't find the nose on his face." He reached up and brought down several. He took Sarah from the desk and carried the books over to the coiled rug by the fireplace. The children hurried over and sat looking through the books, laughing and showing pictures to each other.

"Did they have to leave their books behind?" Danny asked.

"They only had a couple. I always wanted more for them." She looked down, ashamed.

"I'm sure you did."

The children squealed and giggled. "Look, you've given them a treasure to enjoy. Thank you, I will see to it we put them on the desk before we leave. I am not sure I could reach the shelf."

"Hmm, the ladder. I was supposed to fix it some time ago. Anyway, please be sure the children bring all the books they want with them to the cottage." He looked around the room and at the children, then turned to Katie. "What a pleasant homecoming this has been."

"It must be hard to be away from this lovely place so long."

Taken with her words, he looked over the room with its high ceilings and family portraits. "Yes, it has been. I hope to come back someday to live here again."

"Mr. Dandy, is this your room?" Jeremy asked, looking up from the picture book he found.

"The whole house is Danny's, Jer'my," Sarah answered, instead.

"But this is my favorite room, Jeremy. However, I received my first spanking, right here."

"You are big, Mr. Dandy. Why did you getted spanked?"

"Oh no, here we go again. Call me Danny, little chap. Leave off the Mr."

Katie intervened. "Jeremy, Danny was a little boy like you when he got his spanking." Clearly the cogs were moving in Jeremy's head.

"Did you eat too muched cake?"

Danny massaged his jaws. He hadn't smiled or laughed this much for years. "No, little chap, I believe I was being a little contrary with my mother, if I remember. My father spanked me right over there by the desk."

"Oh, I gotted spanked, too." Jeremy's eyes opened big, remembering.

"Surely not. A chap as good as you?"

"That is what makes him so good," Sarah mumbled, immersed in her book.

"Who made you so wise, little princess?"

"God and my mama," Sarah said proudly, looking up.

"I think you two are the most prized possessions your charming mother could have."

Danny lingered, fighting the inevitable. He didn't want the day to end. It seemed they all belonged together here in the house. It felt like old times but all new—new and completely wonderful. But the sun was waning and he couldn't stay. And he didn't want his grandma to worry.

"I had better be on my way before I can't see to get back. The sunset is beautiful from up here. Be sure to watch it. Thank you for sharing your supper with me. I will come tomorrow, as soon as I know the coast is clear. Be sure to use the beds and take the covers off all these chairs. Please enjoy my home, treat it as your own." They walked him to the door. Then he turned to look at Katie, her emerald eyes starry, but she looked disappointed. She really seemed sorry to see him go. Was he imagining it?

He thought how nice it would be to come home to this charming woman and her adorable children every day. She loved his house, the library, his family, and even the china. But especially she appeared to love the Lord as much as he and Grandma. Was she someone God brought to him, or was he just showing him he would have a beautiful and kind wife and family someday? Could there be anyone as beautiful in spirit as well as appearance as Katie? Was she really as she seemed?

He sighed. "Goodnight. God will keep you safe. I will let you know when to come back to the cottage."

"Thank you and thank your dear grandmother, please."

They watched him descend the hill and he waved at them.

Jeremy pulled at his mother's sleeve. "Look at the sky,

Mama."

But Katie was not watching the sunset. She could not stop thinking about Danny. She had never met a man like him. He was kind and gentle, yet strong and manly. Most of the gentlemen she had known were obsessed with themselves and their money. And he could never compare to the coarse gold diggers who would have drunk the gold as fast as they had found it. He didn't seem an ambitious businessman like her father. Of course he was nothing like her uncle. He wasn't anything like Morgan, either. Danny was so attentive, caring, and unselfish. She sighed. Well, maybe she just hadn't seen the real him yet. But to have a grandmother like Gwen and his glorious heritage, perhaps he is as he seems. And he was rather handsome. When he looked into her eyes, she wanted to melt. But she was a poor widow. He was just being kind. She mustn't be foolish.

"I love sunsets." Sarah sat at the window seat. "Can we live here? We could bring Grandma Gwen here. Wasn't the china pretty with all the pink roses? Will you read one of the books and start a fire, and will you please play the piano?"

"Sarah, whoa. Slow down. I can't answer everything at once. But let's start with the fire. It is far too warm for a fire but let's go back into the library and pretend we have a real fire and read a book and say our prayers and maybe I will play a song or two again."

"Hooray." Sarah jumped from the window seat and grabbed her mother's hand.

"I liked Dandy," Jeremy said.

"Dan-nee, Jer'my, it is Dan-nee," Sarah coached.

He scowled with hands on his hips. "That's what I sayed, Sarrie."

Sarah shrugged and they walked back into the library.

"It has been a long day, children, and we must see about making up a place to sleep first, before it's too dark. I am not sure how these lamps work here. But Danny said you can bring the books to the cottage."

"Really? Jer'my, did you hear that?"

"Yes, Sarrie. Dandy is niced."

As tired as she was, Katie still could have sat and played for hours but she knew they needed to rest. It wasn't until they were all tucked in for the night that she realized Danny had taken all the fear out of the day. He was so charming and handsome. His big brown eyes made her lightheaded. But it was a good lightheadedness. She couldn't wait to see him again. She chastised herself for feeling so silly but she couldn't seem to help it.

She remembered the way he looked at her when she caught him staring several times. It made her feel feminine and attractive and a surge of desire came over her more than once.

She told herself not to feel so flattered. It was only because she just hadn't been around an honorable man in so long. Did he really mean it when he said he hated to leave?

CHAPTER NINE

Back to the Ship

Danny whistled a tune as he walked through the back door of his grandmother's cottage. "All is well, Grandma. They are all comfy in the big house."

"Ah, now I am relieved. Thank you. Now I suppose you are hungry," she said with a twinkle in her eye.

"Well, we all ate a delicious meal that some beloved person made." He winked. "But I let them have most of the cake. I had one small piece but I sure wanted more. I was too busy showing Katie the house."

His grandma's eyebrows rose. Was he that obvious?

She went to the kitchen and came back with a big piece of coconut cake and sat it in front of him.

"I didn't miss out on the coconutted cake after all." He kissed her on the forehead and dug in.

"Oh, that cute little mop-headed fella, isn't he adorable?"

"He could make a body worse for laughing."

"Yes, I haven't had this much fun in years. Now, tell me what are you doing back in town? I wasn't expecting you for a long time, but you hadn't written."

"They sent in the new missionaries one more time for a visit before they take over. I will have to go back soon and get ready to leave. Then I will say goodbye and show the new folks the ropes before I come home for good. I didn't mean to worry you. I wanted to surprise you."

"Well, I must say, God sent you at the right time."

"He knows what he's doing, as always. He didn't warn me there would be a whole family to aid when I came home but it was a pleasant surprise." He smiled thinking of his time with Katie and the children.

"I was going to make you chicken and dumplings but I thought you might stay and eat with Katie and the children."

"I would have eaten all over again if you had. I am a growing boy, you know."

"Bosh. You are no longer a boy and you'll be growing out instead of up one of these days. How was Katie?"

"I think I startled her at first but then we had a grand time. When she played the piano, it sounded like Grandpa. It was glorious. The children, poor lambs, had never seen a piano, let alone see their own mother play one."

"I am not surprised, Danny Boy. The poor family has been through a great deal. She has not told the whole story yet, but I do know it has been rough for one so young and lovely."

Oh, yes—she is lovely. He had never seen anyone so sweet and lovely.

"The children have had a wonderful time here. They are precious."

"Are they ever. Jeremy had us laughing so hard we could barely eat. I may have to write a book about that little chap someday."

"He is like you when you were small, a real charmer and he says the cutest things. However, you spoke quite well at his age. Jeremy has a hearing ailment. They don't correct him all the time because it frustrates him," Gwen whispered, even though no one else was there to hear.

He sobered. "I didn't know. I hope I did not laugh too much."

"It's all right, really. He appears to enjoy the laughter. I imagine one day it might not be so, though."

"When she played the piano, the children were amazed. It was heavenly." He remembered dreamily, wishing he were back in the house watching her sweet face.

"Yes, you said that." She cocked her head, a sweet smirk on her lips.

"Did I?" He chuckled. "I guess I did."

"It is good someone plays the piano. It has been too long," she said a little sadly.

He was sure his grandma was also reminiscing but much farther back.

"What are Katie's plans, do you know?" Danny asked matter-of-factly, trying not to seem too interested. But Grandma knew him too well and eyed him with a slight grin of suspicion.

Did she see his mind was filled with dreams of a lovely angel with blonde hair and captivating green eyes?

"She planned to travel to her sister's house in San Francisco but this was as far as she felt she could afford to travel. Her sister's in-laws are high society and may not take to them butting in. Anyway, Katie is not the city type at heart."

"She mentioned that." His heart skipped a beat thinking she might leave. It was an awful feeling. "Perhaps they will stay. They are surely pleasant to have around but we can't have strangers milling about frightening them, can we?"

"Daniel, I nearly forgot. Jacob came by and said to tell you the man got on the train. Silas told him he bought a ticket to Bitter Springs but the man mumbled something about stopping in Riverdale. Jacob thought he probably wanted to stop there to gamble then he would most likely go on back to Bitter Springs."

"Wonderful. I assumed as much, about his leaving anyway." He swallowed his last bit of cake and took a swig of milk. "I think Tom was a bit overwhelming for him."

"Good. That unsightly man frightened Katie. I think she is still afraid her uncle will come and drag them all back."

Danny imagined Katie and the children cowering to a beast of a man and he felt his jaw clench.

"Daniel, I believe God brought them here for safekeeping. I hope this will not drive them on to San Francisco, as soon as she is able."

Danny felt a sick feeling wave over him at the thought of them leaving. The charming trio had quickly become embedded into their hearts. They were life to their lonesome spirits.

Grandma interrupted his thoughts. "I piled a few of my quilt projects and such in your room to make room for Katie and the children. After all I wasn't expecting you. You'll have to sleep in Katie's room tonight. I'll work on yours in the morning."

"That's fine. I will help you. I could have just slept in here."

"No, you need a good rest. It has been quite a day."

"Spoken as a true grandmother." He kissed her cheek and gave her a warm squeeze. A comfy bed sounded much better than the short, hard couch.

Later, Danny lay on Katie's bed, thinking about everything that had transpired since his return home. His mind flew from the scruffy stranger to the beautiful face of Katie, then the precious children and back to Katie again.

Father, show me what I can do to help. I need wisdom. How can we keep them from having to leave because of these heathen men?

He had barely prayed it and it came to him.

Thank you, Father.

He carefully plotted the plan the Lord had shown him and fell asleep.

When Danny woke, his first thoughts were of Katie. She had been sleeping in this room. He could smell a clean sweet scent. Was it just the lingering scent of Grandma's lavender stalks she removed last night? For a moment, he wondered what life would be married to such a woman. Wait a minute. What's gotten into him? The last time he took a woman into his arms was pure deception. But Katie was nothing like Gretch. No one was like Gretch. But then he'd never met anyone like Katie. Something about her seemed so...heavenly. He had never felt this way about anyone. He seemed to be in a fog—a beautiful golden fog.

A sunray came shimmering through the curtain, pointing in to a treasure on the bureau. He got up and took a closer look. It was several strands of Katie's hair laying near her brush on the dresser scarf. When he held it in his hand, it made him smile. His thoughts raced back to the celestial creature whose wispy curls fell across her cheek, lost in her music, and he had new joy in his heart to carry out God's plan.

His grandma promised him a wonderful ham and egg breakfast as soon as he brought the little family back to the cottage. "I will get it ready for all of you when you come back. Don't dillydally."

"Aye, aye, Captain. Be back with the goods right away." He saluted her making her laugh as she nudged him out the back door.

He made the trek up the hill in half time. He couldn't wait to see them and tell them the wretched man left town. But moreover, he couldn't wait to see Katie again.

The young woman who met Danny at the Overlook House door was refreshed and stunning and Danny stood still for a second to take in the heavenly picture. A golden curl fell across her cheek and he smiled. She frowned and tried to fix it back into the mass of hair she had arranged so becomingly on her head. He watched, fascinated.

"Good morning," she said sweetly, her eyes sparkling.

"Good morning. I trust you slept well. I have strict instructions from the Captain to bring her cargo back to the ship straight away."

"All is clear?"

"Yes, all clear."

"Yes, sir." She saluted playfully, while Sarah and Jeremy looked confused.

"Where's a ship?"

"Why, Grandma Gwen's house is our ship, dear." Katie

winked at the children.

"It's not a ship, it's a house." Jeremy scowled.

"It is pretend, Jer'my." Sarah jabbed him in the side.

"Ohhh. Yes, sir, Mr. Dandy." Jeremy straightened up and saluted.

"But I need to cover the chairs—" Katie found herself being gently escorted out the door and whisked away.

"Now, Princess Sarah, would you mind my hat for me? You know it just might save you from being put in the brig for I do believe you have stolen my dimples."

Sarah giggled, taking Danny's hat as if it were a prized possession, along with a handful of books he made sure they brought to the cottage. Jeremy was treated to a piggyback ride.

"Now, do you see the huge oak there? That was the one I loved the most. I used to climb up and hide in it and listen to my grandpa sing. He loved to go out into creation and praise God. Sometimes, he would sing so loud, I thought he would wake the whole town."

"Did he?" Sarah asked.

"I don't know. I never heard anyone complain. But his voice would echo sometimes."

"Can we sing something?" Sarah asked hopefully.

"Of course. What a great idea." And Danny burst into song.

I'm redeemed, I'm redeemed,
From the darkness of the night,
That so thickly enveloped my soul;
In my heart there have gleamed
Rays of wonderful light,
Where the waves of Thy glory do roll.

I'm redeemed, praise the Lord!
I'm redeemed by the blood of the Lamb;
I am saved from all sin,
And I'm walking in the light,
I'm redeemed by the blood of the Lamb.

Katie set down her packages and applauded."Well, you must have your grandfather's voice. I am impressed."

"Thank you. I didn't wake the townspeople, did I?" They shook their heads. "Good, then you should all join in this time."

"You should sing for Grandma Gwen like Little Tommy Tuckered and she will give you coconutted cake," Jeremy whispered loudly into Danny's ear.

"Jolly idea, little chap."

Singing came floating on clouds of glory coming from the garden. Her heart jumped at Danny's voice sounding so much like Samuel's. Someday she would join Samuel to sing with the heavenly chorus in heaven. She shook her head letting the memory go as the happy crew came home.

"We have come to sing for our coconutted cake, Grandma Gwen." Jeremy ducked his head as they entered through the side door.

"You have?" She looked at the precious troupe and all seemed well with the world. What a charming family they would make. They sang another chorus and she clapped.

"What lovely voices. But I haven't made any coconut cake."

"Ahhh..." Jeremy and Danny pouted together.

"But I might have some blueberry cobbler," Gwen said as she hugged every one of them.

"Is that good, Dandy?" Jeremy perked up.

Danny whispered in Jeremy's ear, "Trust me little chap, Grandma's blueberry cobbler is scrumptious."

"Booberry gobbler is scumplush," Jeremy sang.

Gwen chuckled. She was so glad to have them all back.

Katie sat down her packages. "We missed you terribly, Gwen."

"Well, this cottage was a tomb without you all, even with Danny here."

"The house on the hill is wonderful, Gwen, but we all wished you were with us."

"Hear, hear." Danny chimed in from the other room.

"We called it the Overlook House. It's a wonderful home, isn't it?"

"Heavenly. I hope it was all right I played the piano."

"Of course, child. I hope you enjoyed it. Danny said you played it beautifully."

"I was blessed to play. It had been so long. I loved everything about the house. And the portraits were so lovely. Your Samuel was a handsome man with such kind eyes."

"He was handsome and kind. When I heard Danny singing, I thought he'd come to visit me." She raised her hand to her heart and laughed at herself.

Father, please keep this little family with us. They are a joy to my heart.

After breakfast the children went outside and Danny told Katie how Jacob, Tom's young deputy, saw the unwelcome visitor leave town on the train.

"I am so relieved. He was one of the men Uncle Tyler hired from time to time. He used to stare at me and make me horribly uncomfortable. He is the type that would do anything for money and Tyler may have hired him to come and retrieve us."

"Well, he's gone and we will keep praying. We will go back to being a big happy family now," Gwen said.

"Aye, aye, Captain Grandma." Danny teased and gave her a kiss on the cheek.

"You are your grandpa's boy, full of blarney at times."

Leaving them to themselves, Gwen went out to see what great new discoveries the children were making in the garden.

"It is so comforting to know you are here with Grandma," Daniel said."She looks so cheery since you came to town. And children bring life. I always think on something my grandpa once said. He said, having a house with no children can be a sad place. But when a new baby is born to a family, new joy comes into the family. And so it is in the body of Christ, when someone is born again of the Spirit, it is like having a new babe and the whole body celebrates. My uncle and aunt spent many years hoping for a child and when cousin Audrey came, they were so full of life and joy. Come to think of it, her middle name is Joy. Perhaps that is why she is such a joyful little butterfly. When a man at the mission house accepts Christ as his savior, the place livens up and his joy is infectious. I see that kind of joy in Grandma right now and I am sure feeling it. You are a pleasure to have around and Sarah and Jeremy have brought life into our dreary abode."

"But we are the ones who have been given life; a new life and new hope. I am so thankful for your lovely grandmother. I have been afraid you might run us off for wearing her out."

He laughed lightly. "I don't believe that would ever happen. Would be more likely I'd beg you to stay. And from what I hear, you have given her relief from all the heavy work."

"What I have done is nothing compared to her care and blessings."

"Well, I doubt she would agree."

The thought of them leaving distressed him. He could imagine how distraught his grandma would be.

"May I ask you a couple of questions?" Danny asked Katie with an intensity she hadn't seen in him.

"Yes, of course." Katie looked up from the napkins she was folding.

"What does your uncle do for a living?"

"He owns a wagon repair shop."

"Is his shop in Bitter Springs? In the city?"

"Yes, on Main Street, although it isn't much of a city. Why do you ask?"

"I thought it might be a good idea to go and see if I can find out if he intends to keep looking for you."

Katie gasped. "Oh no, you have done enough already.

You mustn't talk to him. He can get terribly angry." She shuddered at the vision of Danny facing off with Tyler. Danny was big and strong to her but he was no match for Uncle Tyler.

"I am not doing anything God has not put in my heart to do. Don't worry; I have no intention of speaking with such a man, although the thought has occurred to me once or twice. This is God's idea. He will be with me. But I need you to do something for me. Will you write a letter to your Uncle Tyler and tell him you are well and if he wants to correspond with you, to do so at this address." He handed her a piece of paper with a law office address on it.

"All right."

"I intend to have him understand to go through this lawyer if he should choose to contact you."

"I see. Then he wouldn't know where we were living and it sounds more official for him to leave us alone."

"Yes."

"It's so kind of you to do this for us."

"I'll leave for Bitter Springs today and then must go back to Los Angeles before coming home."

Gwen came in the door as he spoke. "You are leaving us?"

"Yes, the Lord and I settled it last night. I will share it all when I get back. Katie, if you wouldn't mind writing the letter...I must catch the noon train."

"Of course."

"I'll get you what you need. You can let me know what this is all about later." Gwen scooted into a back bedroom and came back with supplies.

The children came in and wondered at Danny packing

his satchel.

"But Dandy, you will not get any booberry gobbler?" Jeremy's little voice sounded woeful. Danny stooped to give him a big hug.

"Perhaps you and Sarah can share my portion tomorrow."

"But what iffed the bad man comes—"

"Big Sheriff Tom is on the alert so you are in good hands, little chap."

"Danny, I wonder if—"

"Yes, Katie?"

His warm, tender eyes met hers and made her forget what she wanted. She would miss him—of that much she was sure. He seemed to sense it and grinned.

Does he know how much he makes my heart race?

Then she remembered. "I hate to ask you but I left several books at the hotel back in Bitter Springs. They were too heavy for us to carry. I wanted the children to have something left from their father."

"Just tell me where. I would be delighted to retrieve them."

She finished the letter and the women and children sent him off reluctantly with sandwiches and cookies for his trip. Katie knew they would be spending much time in prayer the next few days and wondered if the plan would do the job.

Bless his trip Father, and protect Danny from harm.

CHAPTER TEN

Worlds Apart

Danny surveyed Bitter Springs sweepingly from the train window. From what he could see, it seemed a good name for the miserable looking place. The trees were scrawny and weak-leaved. Winds blew about tumbleweeds and made funny little dust whirlwinds, never amounting to anything and dissipating quickly.

As he stepped off the train, he was hit by a suffocating dry gust of wind. He observed the people who milled around the station. Dreary lot, he thought. Perhaps a good rain might perk them up a bit. How could his beautiful Katie have lived in this desolation? It was certainly a wilderness.

The people were going to and fro like a normal town but at a slower pace. He kept comparing it to home. There were no cheery white rock walkways or picket fences with rosemary draping over the edges like a waterfall nor any roses, snapdragons, or any other colorful spots of God's creation. Only ugly brown raw wood fences framed his path. Fences that looked like someone broke off a tree branch, stuck it into the ground and tied them together with baling wire. What food gardens he did glimpse looked shriveled. He was so glad Katie was no longer in this desolate place. She must have been the single flower in a land of weeds and dust. No pristine little cottages nor big Victorian manses were within view and he doubted there would be any. He remembered visiting the Arizona Territory years ago and there were wonderful sights but this was surely not one of them.

Danny walked farther down the road, in the blistering heat. He wanted to hurry and get back on the train. He strained to read the business signs or at least what lettering had managed to save itself from the sun. Then it caught his eye, "Tyler's Wagon Repair" in faded letters above a barn-sized building. He walked by the open building, pretending to be a passerby.

A monstrous yell came traveling into the street, assaulting his nerves.

Is that him?

A huge man stepped out of the back shadows arguing with another smaller man. Danny backed away across the street and stood behind a wide post where he could not be easily seen.

"Whadya expect?" the voice boomed. "I ain't got no one to help at home no more since they left. Sent Markum after her. Figured since he liked her anyway, maybe he'd bring her back. But he probably just gambled my money and said he couldn't find her."

Danny could not hear the other man's part of the conversation but Tyler's angry tone was loud and clear to Danny's ears. He was talking about Katie. So Markum made it back here. Good. The thought of the vulgar man as a suitor to Katie made him cringe.

"She's a looker. Probably galavantin' around with some no-account somewheres."

Danny bristled. His fingers coiled into a fist. How dare he talk about Katie as if she were a hussy. She was sweet and innocent and pure—his sweet Katie. Danny's own thoughts grabbed at his heart, his sweet Katie. He had said it thrice now. The revelation of his own feelings was cut off as Tyler's voice boomed again.

"I'd like ta tell that girl what for. Got no sense, runnin' off like that with them kids—" His voice choked then he started to cough.

Danny wanted so much to go set the callous man straight. To walk over to this Goliath and tell him what he was and that he had better not try to come near Katie and the children ever again. However, he knew what he had promised God and he would be obedient to the plan. So he walked on, looking for the Bitter Springs post office. After getting the information he needed, he retrieved Katie's books and went back to the station to wait for the next train. He hoped he would never have to come back to this God-forsaken place again.

The train rumbled on back west until the sparse high desert houses turned into pure ugly hot desert, until eventually the landscape transformed from death to life. He sighed when he saw the fields of lush green produce. Is this how it had looked to Katie, when she left that awful place and saw the landscape change from death to life? Yet she must have been frightened coming into a new land and with no one to help her.

You brought her to White Rock, Father, and to us and to a safe place. I am so glad.

He opted not to get off at his beloved hometown. It was too short of a stop. He wanted to get this business taken care of quickly. As the train neared the big city, the building grew larger and less like home.

"LOS AN-GEL...EEZE!"

Danny disembarked and went on his way through the city as quickly as the bustling people allowed. It was growing fast. He looked out on the busy streets he traveled on a daily basis. Wouldn't Jeremy love to see the horseless carriages. It was all he could think of—being with them all. He wanted them with him always. He would love to take Katie and Grandma to the fine shops and Sarah and Jeremy to the beach. How much fun they all would have.

He stepped out of the carriage and came to the office building, where his old colleague worked. Although intent in purpose, he felt the slightest melancholy for days gone by. His short career as a lawyer was a difficult time in his life. He wondered what his life might have been had he stayed in the profession and fought as he had against the compromises of the whole system. Yet, he didn't seem to be able to stomach the memories. It was a hard lesson and he was glad he was far on the other side of it.

"Yes, Mr. Richards, I will let him know you are here." The secretary was young and pretty, dressed in modern garb, but no young woman could compare to Katie As she left her post, Danny surveyed the elaborately decorated office. The garish patterns on the drapes were not pleasing to the eye and strange paintings donned the walls. Aberrant animal statuary, which probably cost a pretty penny, looked ready to jump from table to table. None of it was at all appealing. He would rather be home with his cousin Audrey's beautiful paintings of God's creation in White Rock. He was sure Katie and Grandma would hate these gaudy adornments. He could see Sarah scrunch her cute freckled nose and what would his precocious little chap say about these statues? He could only imagine.

"Danny—so good to see you. Where have been keeping yourself? Come into my new office."

"Hello, John. Thank you for making time for me."

"Always time for you, old friend." The tall, impeccably dressed man grabbed him by the hand, shook it vigorously, and led him into his office. "I'll have some food brought in for us, just like old times, huh?" Danny looked around, amazed at more artifacts and fancy furnishings.

"Like it? It could have been yours, too, you know," his old friend said, waving his hand about the room. "Picked up these on a trip to San Francisco."

"Quite interesting, John. But my life is on track. You have been doing well for yourself, I see."

"Let me know and you can come and be a part of it, and wipe off that mission street dust," John offered with a twinkle in his eyes.

For a moment Danny felt as if Satan were making an offer of the kingdoms of the world again. He actually considered it for a split second as his job at the mission was closing. Then he looked around again and knew in his spirit this was no place for him. "No, thank you, but it is nice to be asked." He smiled pleasantly at his former colleague.

"I know," John drawled. "You would rather feed the hungry and sweep the streets." His friend shook his head in amused pity.

"I have been here, remember? I wasn't cut out for it, I am afraid."

"Well, it's a waste, I'd say." John sat down in his hand carved chair. "You were top of our class."

"Actually, I've come for some advice and service."

The two men talked all their business over sandwiches, chatted a bit about old times and then shook hands once more as they parted company.

"We'll get right on it. Give us a couple of days."

"Thank you, John. This will be a big help."

Danny walked out with a light step and breathing free. Not only was the plan set in motion, but also, any fleeting thought of going back into law was finished for good. Now he could go home.

"To the train depot, please," he directed with a smile, as he climbed into the carriage.

With his job accomplished, he could sit back and freely think of the little family at home in White Rock. Why was he claiming them like they were his? Going home was always wonderful, but now he had even more to look forward to. Charming people who shared his Grandma's roast beast and coconutted cake. He let out a small snort.

"What's that, sir?" the carriage driver asked.

"Nothing. Thank you."

What fun they would have. And Katie. Ah, Katie. He leaned back and closed his eyes and saw her standing at the door of the Overlook House, beautiful, sweet, gentle, kind and unselfish. Perfect. She was perfect. Startled, he sat up, his eyes opened.

But Father, what have I to offer her?

Working at the legal offices he had just come from left him with a bitter taste in his mouth and a miserable feeling in his gut. But what would he do?

Father, you know all of this. You must have a plan.

Hours later, he rested his head back again as darkness was framed by the train windows. He was tired but all he could think about was home and the wonderful conversations, the prayers, the songs, sweet Sarah and her mirrored dimples, Jeremy's adorable antics and Katie with her kind and loving ways. He found himself wanting to spend his whole life taking care of them. And I don't think Grandma will ever give them up either. He laughed to himself.

Can I feel love this soon? I don't know, Lord, that doesn't seem quite right and yet—

He laid his head back yet again and dozed. He smelled lavender, heard laughing, and was feeding coconutted cake to the sweetest most perfect lips.

CHAPTER ELEVEN

The Invitation

Katie had been given a delightful crash course on White Rock history: the people, the buildings and, of course, the Richards family. She loved hearing all about Gwen and Danny's family and the funny stories about Danny when he was small. He sounded just like Jeremy. No wonder Gwen enjoyed Jeremy so much.

"Who is this in this picture, Gwen?" Katie pulled a small daguerreotype off the mantle.

"That is Paul, my son, and his wife, Virginia, Danry's parents. Paul met Virginia back east on one of his many business trips."

"She is lovely."

"We call her Ginny. She was quite spoiled when Paul met her but she adapted and was a wonderful wife and mother. We tried to make her a Westerner but she had the East deeply imbedded in her heart. She learned to live out here quite well but she missed the East and other members of her family. I think we all knew they would go back one day. Paul's business drew him back East more and more.

When Victoria, Danny's sister, met her future husband, James, on one of their stays, that made it final. Danny and I went back for the wedding and took several things from the Overlook House they asked for and that was that. It was Danny and me from there on in. Paul and Ginny decided to give the house to Danny. They knew we would never want to leave it. I guess we're Westerners in our hearts, he and I and my Samuel who is now with the Lord."

"I grew up in New Hampshire," Katie said. "If all I knew of the West was Bitter Springs and those awful mining towns, I would hate the West. But I have seen such beauty along the way. And White Rock is perfect. I can't imagine why anyone would leave it."

"We thought so, too. When Samuel and I came here, we were sold. This cottage was our home. We owned the land and the hill and often went there on picnics and prayer times. We had given the land to Paul and Ginny as a wedding gift. When Paul's business prospered, he had the Overlook House built. After the children came along, they kept insisting we should be living there with them. We spent most of our time up there with the family so it seemed the thing to do. But we kept the cottage and I am glad we did."

"I can see you and Danny being stubborn about leaving this wonderful place, especially the Overlook House. It is a beautiful place."

"Vicky loved it, but she loved the East, too. Danny was ready to go on to law school. He loved it here and didn't want to go east. I was so glad. I would not have been happy back there. He really had no heart for law school but he tried to compromise with his parents' desires for him to have a profitable future and his desire to help others." She held the picture of the family, fondly. "Anyway, I miss them all." She pointed to Ginny." Can you see where Danny got his dimples?"

"Yes, they are...charming, like my Sarah. She got them from my father." She did remember Danny's smile. It seemed to be with her day and night.

"Where's Dandy? He goed away for a long time." Jeremy's sullen face peered up from the cache of books they brought back from the big house. His big brown eyes were another reminder of Danny. It made her long to see him again. His absence had left everyone a little out of sorts.

"He'll be home soon, Jeremy. He has important business to attend to," Grandma Gwen reached down and tussled his curly locks.

"Jer'my, look, it's a deer!" Sarah scrambled to her feet as the deer leaped happily across the yard.

"Come backed, deer. Wow! He can jump," he squealed as the two children sped out the door.

"They'll be back all right, when they decide my rosebushes need to be pruned." Gwen stood with her arms crossed, none too happy about the deer but she laughed at the antics of the children.

"Oh no, not those beautiful roses."

"Down to the nub. If I need a pruner, there is none better, but they never ask my permission about when to prune or how much."

Katie laughed. She never ceased to thank God for this lovely woman. Being with Gwen was like having her own special grandmother. Her family had told her she was too much like her Grandmother Farrell. She didn't like society, was creative, and full of love for God's creation. But Katie had only vague memories of her, being so young when she died. Grandma Gwen seemed a little like her and she had grown to love her in such a short time.

"Well, now that Danny's back for awhile, if we can keep him here, maybe I can get the back fence fixed."

"I can fix fences, Gwen. I had to in Bitter Springs."

"All the more reason you won't do it here. Danny will do it. You need to rest up for your new job."

Katie stood at the door. "Those are the most beautiful roses I have ever seen. I hope the deer don't eat them all up,"

"The pink ones? Yes, they are my favorites. They are a special bush called a Catherine Mermet. I planted those when Danny left for college. I called them—well—no matter. Why don't we all have a snack?"

Katie wondered why she didn't finish telling her what she called the roses but didn't feel right to ask her. How wonderful they were called Catherine. She turned to admire the roses just before Jeremy came bounding in.

"Crackers and cheesed?" Jeremy heard "snack" and was the first to peek his head in the door.

"No, little man, but something you will like." Grandma Gwen's eyes twinkled. "A piece of fresh peach pie." She held the plate before the children.

"Really?" Sarah's eyes brightened.

"A wholed piece?" Jeremy looked over at his mom in disbelief. She nodded and they quickly ran to wash up to get back to the table. Gwen leaned toward Katie. "Have they never had a whole piece of pie?"

"Only on the train stops at the Harvey House, on our way here."

Katie looked at the perfectly golden crust and the oozing peach filling set on charming burgundy, chintz plates, feeling as much a child as her little ones. "I haven't had fresh peach pie since I left home."

After thanking God for their treat, Grandma Gwen handed them forks and they ate like it was a treasure, thanking her repeatedly. Neither of the children could finish and so they saved theirs for later and went out to play again. Katie knew they were not used to having anything like the delicious food this wonderful grandmother put before them at every meal and in between.

"They saw the pies I made for our uncle but all I could do was save them some piecrust."

"Ah, the poor darlings. Well, the old life is surely over. You'll not be deprived again if I have anything to do with it."

"You'll spoil us. How will we ever go back to little again?"

The older woman's back straightened, her hands sat on her hips, her head cocked, slightly. "What makes you think you will ever go back to such a life?"

"Do you suppose I would impose on your generosity forever?"

"You'll not leave my house without a home of your own and all of your needs met." The older woman slapped her hands together and swiped her apron as if to dismiss such a thought. Katie thought better of trying to argue with her. Truly she felt loved. She never had any desire to leave this lovely cottage nor Grandma Gwen.

"Now, let's go pick roses before the deer devour them for their next meal, ornery little stinkers." Gwen and Katie went out the side door to the grassy area where the children ran in circles pretending to be birds and deer, giggling and squealing.

"I don't know when I have seen them so happy, except when I saw them just like this in my dreams. Gwen, how can I ever thank you?"

Tears trickled down Katie's face and she mopped at them constantly as they clipped off the roses. Gwen ushered her back inside and embraced her. Katie cried, sobbing uncontrollably on Gwen's shoulder. The roses lay haphazardly on the table while Gwen consoled her. Katie had not allowed for tears for so many long years, trying to be brave. Finally, she regained some composure.

"I am so sorry, I just couldn't seem to stop. I used to be able to keep myself from crying —now I seem so out of control."

"It's all a part of God's plan for your healing. You are releasing years of pent-up tears, child." Gwen slid some curls out of Katie's face.

"But—"

"I know, but it will heal."

"It has been so hard."

"Of course, but God is going to give you a new life, now —a good life. In this world there will be tribulation but he gives us wonderful times of refreshing and healing, too."

"I am afraid I will wake and this dream will be gone."

"No, child, this is real and I am not going anywhere and neither are you. Tell me about your family. Are they all gone?"

"Yes, all of them, except my sister, Charlotte, who I mentioned before. My mother died soon after Sarah was born, my father not long after. I couldn't get to them. It was awful. When my husband, Morgan, died in the mine accident, we were left alone and virtually penniless. My father's Uncle Tyler and his wife Nora were our only living relatives except Charlotte. She and her husband were in Europe, so I had no choice. Uncle Tyler came to get us. At first it wasn't too bad, but Nora's health grew worse. She was a sweet but tired woman and I was glad I was there to help her. Before she died, she asked me to stay with him."

Katie continued. "After Nora died, I hoped we would be of comfort to him but he took his comfort in the bottle. I prayed for him daily and tried to please him but he never responded. I felt like a failure. He grew hateful and angry, blaming us for her death. Yet I was constantly helping. I was afraid of him and could do nothing to please him. The letter I received from Charlotte just before I left pretty much said that her husband's family was her priority. She has her own life and I really don't belong. I felt she implied it between the lines. Maybe I am wrong about her letter but I don't think so. She sent money at times but I am pretty sure my uncle often got to the letters before I did and took it out as they had been opened. I guess I have no family, Gwen."

The reality of her own words hit her like a fist to her gut. Katie looked into her lap and Grandma Gwen lifted her chin back up, gently. "Will you let us be your family then?" she asked.

Katie looked at Gwen through her wet lashes. "To be a part of your family would be like heaven. Surely, I could never measure up."

"Oh, you sweet child." Gwen gave Katie a big hug to seal the contract.

At bedtime, Katie lay in her bed thinking about being a part of Gwen and Danny's little family. What a wonderful feeling to have someone dear like Gwen to love and care for them and how easy it was to love and care for her. Being a part of their family would include Danny, of course. Thinking about Danny made her heart race as she remembered his charming smile and kind ways. His handsome face seemed ever present in her thoughts lately. She told herself more than once, she must think about Danny more as a kind brother. He would find a sweet, young bride one day who wasn't a widow with children. And what a prize the young bride would have in such a man.

She settled her heart to pray not only for Danny but also his future wife, and when she was done, she settled into her comfy bed. What she saw when she closed her eyes was the charming, dimpled smile of a wonderful man with a heart of gold like his grandmother, holding out his hand toward her with a beautiful pink rose in it.

CHAPTER TWELVE

Sunday

"Mama, wake up, timed for fatjacks." Jeremy shook Katie's arm and woke her with a start.

"Okay, little buddy, I will be right there," but all she could see was a curly mop head flying out her bedroom door. What did he say? Time for what?

Katie popped out of bed, quickly got ready and came in to see Grandma Gwen cooking away.

"Good morning, sleepyhead. I made you a big breakfast before we go to church."

"How wonderful but if we are family, we shouldn't be spoiled like this every day."

"Nonsense. You have been on the other side a long time." Gwen handed Katie the most luscious looking flapjacks she had ever laid eyes on. They were piled up with peaches and a bit of pure cream on top.

"Grandma Gwen maked yummy peached fatjacks." Jeremy looked up from his plate with his peaches and cream spread from ear to ear.

Fatjacks, that's what he said.

Sarah nodded with cream peeking between her lips.

After eating and insisting on cleaning up, Katie suddenly realized they were really going to church.

Katie's face dropped. "Oh Gwen—my dress."

"It is all done, ironed and on my bed."

"No? You are a blessing, just like your name."

Katie shook her head. It was all too wonderful. "Those were the best flapjacks I have ever had."

"My favorite recipe. Samuel loved them. Danny inherited his grandfather's flapjack appetite. It was an easy thing to make and it held them for supper, probably because they ate so many of them."

"Gwen, when do you do all this? Do you ever sleep?"

"I wake in the wee hours. I have prayer and Bible study and then I get things ready for the day. But I don't know how I shall get any sleep thinking about fatjacks." They both had a good laugh.

"Well, you will spoil us all rotten and we'll be good for nothing."

"Spoiling is my business," she said with a wink at Sarah who smiled indulgently back at her, dimples and all. "Wait till you see what I have planned for supper." Her eyebrows raised in delight.

Katie threw up her arms in surrender and went back to Gwen's room. When she opened the door, she saw a lovely sweet blue dress with a white lace collar on the bed, but it certainly wasn't hers.

Katie held the simple but charming frock in her hand, returning to the dining room. "The only dress I found on your bed was this one. It isn't mine."

"It is now, if you like it. I found a dress my

granddaughter left behind and sort of reworked it.'

Katie pulled the dress into the light and looked at it.

"Oh, Gwen, it is lovely."

"You like it then?" The older woman's eyes lit up at Katie's response.

"Of course, dear one, how can I repay you?" Katie fell into her arms as if she were her own grandmother.

"What? You shall never even try. Does one repay family, child? My rewards come from heaven and seeing you and the children smile. Now is it stylish enough? I am a bit old for keeping up. Most around here don't bother with trying to keep up. It was a nice dress but needed a touch here and there, but I am afraid you will have to wear one of my hats."

"It is perfect—just like you and this peaceful cottage. I know little of today's style but from what I have seen on the train, it's just right." Katie's tears started to flow again.

"Mama, what's wronged?" Jeremy started to climb down from his chair.

"Not a thing." Grandma Gwen smiled sweetly and kissed his panic-stricken face.

"I am fine, son. I am just happy." Katie smiled.

"Happy maked you cry?" He was clearly puzzled.

"Sometimes, special things make us cry because God is so good to us like giving us Grandma Gwen." Katie wiped her tears and looked at Gwen. She was a blessing, more than she would have believed.

"I'm happy he gaved us Grandma Gwen with snowy hair and blued eyes. Our bery bestest Grandma Gwen."

Gwen reached down and cupped Jeremy's little face in her hands. "You and Sarah are the very, very bestest, too."

Katie got the children dressed and then put on her new

dress and quickly fixed her hair.

Grandma Gwen came to the bedroom door with shoes in hand. "I hope they fit." And they did.

"I am so blessed. You are so kind," Katie said, fighting back tears.

"You look lovely. All it needs is a little tuck here and there or we could wait and fatten you up a bit." She raised her brows, her eyes shone with a scheming twinkle then she left, chuckling all the way back down the hallway to get a hat for her.

Katie could only laugh and shake her head. She would be fattened up for certain.

They were all in the living room ready to leave, when the doorknob turned and Danny came in. His eyes caught sight of Katie and froze there.

She is as beautiful as I remembered.

Gwen walked over to hug him and whispered, "I know she is beautiful, but you mustn't stare, Daniel." It was like she read his mind as well as his countenance.

Katie must have heard what Grandma said. She was trying not to smile and it made him feel foolish.

Jeremy, coming from behind the two women, broke the embarrassing moment. "Dandy, Dandy! Sarrie, look it's our bestest Dandy."

Danny smiled and reached for Jeremy with one arm and lifted Sarah with the other.

"You are all a sight for sore eyes." He meant it for all of them but he lifted his eyes once again to Katie who would have soothed any man's eyes this morning.

"We sore missed you. We prayed for you every day."

"Well, God surely heard those prayers. Here I am. Did you gobble up my booberry gobbler?" The children nodded, giggling.

Then Danny looked over at Katie once again, and she was smiling like she had missed him, too. He caught himself staring and stuttered, "Oh, um, Katie I have your package." He sat the children down to give Katie the books.

"Daniel, thank you. I hope it wasn't much trouble?" She walked closer.

"Please, call me Danny, and no, not a bit of trouble."

Sarah caught sight of the books. "It's Poppa's books." She ran her hand along the top of one of them as if it were a treasure returned to her.

"Dandy did it," cheered Jeremy. "How did you doed it? Did you seed Uncle Tyler?" His eyes grew big. "Did he yelled at you?"

"No chap, it was easy to get them. Your mother left them in a special place."

"Oh, good, Uncle Tyler might hurted you."

"Little chap," Danny squatted face-to-face with Jeremy making sure he understood. "You never have to worry about Uncle Tyler. He won't frighten you anymore."

"That's right. Now, I hate to break up this homecoming, children, but we'll be late for service." Gwen grabbed her Bible.

Danny looked at the breakfast table and pouted. "Ah, no flapjacks for me."

"There is one left on my plate," Sarah offered.

Danny grabbed it like a kid, stuffing it in his mouth, making Sarah giggle. Then they scurried around and scooted out the door.

As they walked to church, Gwen engaged the children in singing games and Katie and Danny walked behind them.

"I hope you will stay, Katie. I have not seen Grandma this happy in years and I can't tell you what a joy it was to see you all here when I came home."

"I love your wonderful grandmother and this town and you have been so kind to us." Katie spoke quietly, wondering at all his attention. When she looked at him, his eyes were still on her. She could hardly breathe. He looked at her with such tenderness. Whatever reserve she might have had melted like a bar of chocolate in the hot sun. He wasn't saying anything either. They had slowed so much it took the church bell's peal of hur-ry, hur-ry to quicken their pace to the white stone steps.

They took a whole pew section to themselves and waited as a white-haired gentleman limped to the wooden pulpit.

"Good morning. It is wonderful to see you all here. I believe I see new faces in our midst, and Daniel, good to see you back. I hope you will soon share more of your mission stories and a sermon or two."

Danny nodded, smiling. "Yes, sir, of course."

Then Gwen stood and introduced Katie and the children. All eyes seemed fixed on them. Katie smiled shyly at the introduction and recognized a few townspeople that had been friendly to her and they smiled back. But across the aisle sat a striking black-haired beauty who glared at her in a dreadful manner. Perhaps she was looking at someone else. Katie looked back to the kind-hearted pastor and tried to forget her.

It was a wonderful service with wisdom-filled preaching and it blessed her. The pastor of the homey little church seemed to know all of his sheep. She watched as he called young and old by name and asked about their lives as if he knew each victory and struggle. It impressed Katie greatly for she had been brought up in a city church with much pomp in which the pastors were for show and held up as men to be honored and worshipped. In the huge crowds of people, the pastors knew very few of their parishioners and they barely knew each other. As she sat comparing the two, she could not deny that love filled this place.

"The congregation is full of committed people who have trials and need prayer and certainly a few backslidden and a few black sheep, too," Grandma Gwen had told Katie days ago. She told her Pastor Adkins had been injured badly in the Spanish-American War and yet, she said, he spends hours on his knees praying for them all. "He is in much pain but never speaks a word about it, knowing his flock prays for him. His wife is quiet and lovely," she added, "and is diligent to nurse and take care of many in time of need."

After the service, when Katie was introduced to Mrs. Adkins, she hugged Katie like a long-lost daughter, almost causing her to cry again. Walking home, Katie turned to Grandma Gwen as Danny was telling his funny stories of his childhood to the children.

"Gwen, am I dreaming? Could this all be real? You and

Danny and the beauty of White Rock, now the kind-hearted pastor and his wife."

"It is God's special blessing for you after all those hard years of suffering. Just receive it all as a gift from him."

"I am so afraid I will wake up and it will be like one of my dreams in Bitter Springs. Waking out of those wonderful dreams and still being in Bitter Springs was awful, but I must admit the dreams kept my hope alive. I think I may have been dreaming of White Rock."

"Perhaps you were. God was giving you hope for a new life, even in your dreams."

As they walked, Katie watched Danny with her little ones. They adored him. And he was so good with them. He would make a wonderful father.

"He'll make a great father, won't he?" Gwen observed.

Katie's eyes widened. Did she read my mind? "Yes he will." She found herself longing for him to be *her* children's father.

After a wonderful meal Gwen and Katie whipped up together, the family had songs and prayers and Bible reading. Then Katie readied the children for bed.

As she rocked Jeremy in the rocker, he looked up into her face and said, "I like being a family. I'm not scared here."

"Yes, this is the way a family is supposed to be, Jeremy," she said.

"We are a great family, aren't we, little chap?" Danny chimed in.

"Yes, Dandy, but what is a chap?"

"A chap is a very special young man."

"Oh, I'm a chap, Mama," Jeremy said, grinning proudly at her making her laugh.

"Well, I guess I better be heading up the hill," Danny said reluctantly.

"No, Daniel," Gwen said. "It is too dark and you know you cannot climb that hill in the dark. There's not even a moon out tonight. I fixed your room for you, I insist."

"Very well, Grandma, I know better than to argue with you." Danny rose and gave his grandma a kiss on her forehead.

Katie shook her head in agreement at him and she ushered the children off to bed. Gwen would not be thwarted when it came to taking care of everyone.

"I want Dandy to tucked me in," Jeremy whined.

"Jeremy, don't whine. You may ask him nicely."

Jeremy tugged on Danny's pants and asked Danny with a more humble tone.

"Why, I would be honored, master Jeremy."

"Me, too?" Sarah asked sweetly.

"Without a doubt, Princess Sarah." He bowed.

The children giggled and went off to bed, with Danny in tow.

"Goodnight, everyone," Katie said. She went into her room and watched through the adjoining door crack as Danny tucked the children into bed, telling a hilarious version of Jack and the Beanstalk. She hoped she could still hear after she closed her door. He was quite a story spinner. He would be a wonderful writer.

Father, please send me someone as wonderful as Danny. Are there any more like him?

CHAPTER THIRTEEN

The Nightmare

"No. No. It can't be. God, help me!"

The cries woke Danny and he realized it was Katie. He ran to her room and she was visibly shaking, though half asleep.

"Katie, are you all right?" He gently touched her arm.

She woke fully, gasping for air. "It was a...horrible nightmare but so real." She sat up in her bed. "Danny, I'm so sorry to wake you."

Grandma came in and shooed him away. He backed up to the door.

"What is it, Katie?"

"A nightmare. I'm so sorry to wake you. We were kidnapped."

"It is alright child," Gwen soothed, pushing back her hair.

Danny was still in the doorway looking at how beautiful Katie was, even in the night with her lovely hair all mussed and fallen. He was troubled by the fear in her eyes. He longed to take her in his arms and comfort her himself. But this was something foreign to him. He had never felt this way about anyone. There had been beautiful women around him but never anyone with the sweet and gentle spirit of Katie. She was more worried about waking them than her own trouble. Suddenly, Grandma stopped his stupor with an agitated, thin-lipped cock of her head and then the final gesture of her hand in dismissal. He backed into the hallway, peeked in on the slumbering children and went back to his room, feeling properly chastised.

Danny wrestled with God for hours both in and out of sleep, angry that anyone would frighten this lovely creature God had made so sweet and gentle. Then came the scripture he had preached to many:

"But I say unto you, Love your enemies, bless them that curse you, do good to them that hate you, and pray for them which despitefully use you, and persecute you."

He bowed his head and wrestled until he was able to pray even for Tyler.

Afterward, he thought of Katie and remembered how the long curls draped the pillow. He lingered on the picture of that moment for some time.

Gwen sat at Katie's bedside with her hand wrapped within her own. It was so comforting. And Danny had run to her room as soon as he heard. It made her feel so warm and protected.

"Remember, child the Bible says, 'There is no fear in the perfect love of God.'"

"But I love God. Why am I so afraid?"

"Because you have not grasped his love for you. Now, what have you done for your children these past difficult years? A great deal, I am sure. You have taught them to avoid the enemy in order to protect themselves. You have taught them to pray. You made sure they had all their needs taken care of to the best of your ability."

"Yes, I tried to."

"Well, think about how much you love them and want peace and joy for them and how you have protected them. Then you can see how much more your Father in heaven loves you. He has protected you and kept you, even in hard places. And now he has brought you out, just as he brought the people out of Egypt from the cruel taskmaster of slavery and misery."

Katie nodded, taking in all of Gwen's godly wisdom.

"God loves you and he parted your Red Sea. Now will you trust him to keep the enemy from harming you? Fear is not trusting or realizing how mighty God really is."

"I see. I never realized it was actually sin to fear man and to not believe how much God cares for me."

"Good, now let's pray for your sleep to be peaceful." Gwen kissed Katie on the forehead like a beloved child.

Gwen listened as Danny sat across the table from her, holding a steamy cup of tea and commiserating.

"I wanted so badly to comfort her. I...I felt so bad for her," he stuttered.

"Well, the Lord did his work. He used his word, hidden in my heart, to bring peace to her. She'll be fine."

Gwen looked into her grandson's eyes and saw more than just normal concern. She smiled ever so slightly on the outside but inside hope soared high.

She poured some cream and took a sip of her comforting warm tea. "Now, don't you think it is time for you to tell me what you have been up to?"

"I saw Tyler."

"Katie's uncle?" she gasped, setting down her teacup.

He nodded. "He is a huge man and offensively loud with a horrid disposition. He was ghastly. I caught a glimpse of what they had been under all these years. I wanted so much to face off with him."

"But you didn't?"

"Of course not. God would not allow it. I knew he set me on a different course, beside the fact that he most likely would have swatted me down like a fly." He chuckled and continued, "So after seeing him in all his ugliness from across the street, I traveled to Los Angeles to see an old colleague of mine. You remember me telling you about John."

Gwen listened, her hands folded on the table. "Yes, of course."

"John took the letter Katie had written to her uncle and promised to put a legal letter with it, stating all contact with her and the children has to be made through his office. We felt it would most likely deter him and the Markum fellow."

"What a blessing. We'll tell Katie as soon as she wakes."

"Tell me what?" Katie said as she entered the room.

Danny's eyes sparkled when he looked up. She was relieved, thinking something was wrong.

"I guess it is time." Danny winked at his grandmother.

"Is something wrong?" Her heart was back in her throat again. Could this perfect family last forever? She was living out a dream. Would she have to leave? She had callused herself to accept hardship too many times in the past years. She wasn't sure she had it in her to toughen again.

"My precious girl, has the fear come back so soon?" Gwen lifted her hands to her cheeks.

"Oh, I am sorry I—" Katie didn't know how to respond. She was a hopeless mess.

"Take it easy, Katie. Let me explain. Come sit down, please," Danny coaxed her into the chair.

"I'll get you some tea." Gwen went off to the kitchen.

"I went to see an old friend. He is the lawyer I mentioned. I went to law school with him. You see, I was a lawyer for a season. Anyway, I had prayed about your situation and this man coming to look for you. God directed me to go see my old colleague, John Fuller, to ask his legal advice. I felt he might put a legal stamp of sorts on your letter by adding a formal letter from his law office. He owes me—or so he thinks—for many favors through the years, so I left it in his hands. He is not a brother in the Lord but a man with some integrity and I trust him. Your uncle now can only contact you through John's legal office."

"I am so thankful. It was a wonderful thing to do for us."

"I also wanted to see what you have been up against and I did. God told me to go. Tyler is most assuredly an angry man."

"You saw him?" Her eyes widened.

"Now calm down, I didn't see him personally but across the way from his shop in town. I saw him arguing with a man. I got a clear view of what you must have suffered under his rage." His eyes spoke care and compassion right into hers.

"I wish you didn't have to see but at the same time, I guess I am glad to have someone understand."

"And I do." Danny sighed and reached to pat her hand.

Gwen stepped in with not only tea but a full breakfast.

"Gwen, you've finished it all and I haven't helped a bit."

Danny looked intently into her eyes. "Now listen, Katie, Grandma loves to cook and it is her joy to give. She says you do all sorts of wonderful things to help, so relax."

"I will try, but I have found so much rest and joy here, I feel like I am not pulling my load. I am utterly spoiled."

"After all you do?" Gwen said brows raised. "Well, here you can do this for me, then. I will send you two to the grocer's for several things after breakfast. I need a few extra things for a special supper and I'd rather not make the trip."

"Wonderful. Give us a list." Danny grinned at Katie like he had been given a gift. Did he sense the same elation she did?

"Give the girl a chance to finish her breakfast," Gwen said, hands on her hips.

"But the children—" Katie started.

"I have plans for them this morning. We have a job in the

side garden, I think they will enjoy."

Katie gave up, looked at Danny, and shrugged her shoulders. He was still smiling.

She ate hurriedly because of the eager expectation on Danny's face, then Gwen shooed them out the door.

CHAPTER FOURTEEN

Stolen Moments

"Good morning, Miss Ruby," Danny called out as they passed her in her beloved garden.

"Morning Dan'el, Katie. My, don't you make a right hamsome couple." Ruby's comment made the heat rush to Katie's face. Danny grinned. He was blushing, too.

"Need anything in town?" Danny offered.

"No, been to the post and all set here. Nice of you to ask."

They waved goodbye and walked slowly on to town.

"Her flower garden is second to none. Everyone comes to her for weddings, funerals, and seeds."

"It is beautiful. She was our first friend in White Rock."

"You don't say."

"She directed us to find lodging."

"Well, she has a good heart. She never has but kind words to say about people. She is kind of innocent, childlike in her ways. Says the wrong thing accidentally, if you understand what I mean."

"I do. My Aunt Nora was a little like that."

They walked on and Danny nodded to a quaint little grey house with pink trim, "This is where Mrs. Fraley lives. When I was little, I picked pansies for Grandma from her garden and she was furious. Then I let Mr. Thornton's milk cow out the gate of the brown house over there. I had help from my cohort in crime and best friend, Tom, who is now our fine upstanding sheriff. The cow trampled Doc Saunders' herb garden and oh boy, were we in trouble. After that we both toed the line until my nemesis took over."

"Nemesis?"

"Yes, a devious friend who created crimes and created me to blame for them."

"That doesn't sound like much of a friend."

"No, I think she was more like a recurring nightmare. My parents and grandparents saved me from her quite a few times. But it was a difficult thing to do when her father owned much of the town. I often suffered the consequences of her horrid ideas and sometimes I wasn't even there when they happened."

"How dreadful. You would have been following in the Lord's footsteps, then, by being accused of things that weren't true."

He turned to her, his head tilted. "Katie, sometimes you really amaze me with your wisdom. You certainly are like no young woman I have ever met."

"Well, I guess that is what the hard times do for us. It is just the Word of God, not me. Believe me, I have been just like you. I did nothing the easy way. I was far more rebellious than I realized, and terribly smug when I left home to marry Morgan. I thought I knew everything and I was going to live happily ever after, my way."

"Hmm, yes, when I went off to college it was the same thing. I was going off to be a successful lawyer for God but it was my idea, not God's."

"In the book of Isaiah, it says God's thoughts and ways are higher than ours."

"Well, I learned that soon enough. I went through plenty of hard times. And I nearly married that devious girl."

"No? How could that be?" Katie couldn't believe it. He was so good and kind.

He looked down, almost looking ashamed, kicking a little at the dirt as he walked.

"She pretended to be a believer when she grew up and I was swayed by the hope that she had changed. I soon found out she was just as selfish and heartless as ever. She wanted to use me as a way to gain a higher place in her high society crowd. She kept pushing me in the legal profession at the same time God was drawing me away from it. I would have spent my entire life working myself to death to keep her in luxury. It was the devil's ploy to keep me from God's work. She never once set foot in the mission, though I begged her to meet some of the wonderful men who had overcome. She said it would lower her standing to do such a thing. That was when I finally woke up."

"How awful. I would love to meet those men you helped. What a wonderful testimony of God's love, grace, and power. Personally, I have an aversion to high society. My sister Charlotte fit right into Mother's mold and is involved to this day but I avoided it like a plague. I knew it was not for me. I would just as soon traipse through your grandma's garden and wander the hills out back."

Danny laughed. "That sounds just like Grandma. That's

the way she used to be. She loved to go to the hills, sit on the big white rocks, and pray and sing to the Lord, where no one could hear her. I know she misses it."

"She told me she can't make it up the hill now. Why couldn't she stay in the big house?"

"When I left, it was just too hard for her to be there alone. It was her idea to stay at the cottage. I really think she just wanted to save money by not having to hire people to see to the horses and keep the whole house and grounds. I know she misses it though and so do I."

"You miss hiding in the oak tree?" Katie teased playfully.

He laughed. "No, but they were grand memories."

"Even though you weren't supposed to be spying." Katie shook her finger in amusing accusation.

"Yes, but she knew I was there and I thought I was so cleverly disguised in that tree."

"Your family seem like a fairy tale to me, I will have to watch myself with envy." Her steps lightened as their friendship grew.

"I never thought of it that way. You think so much like Grandma. I like that."

She watched as his smile grew and his slight dimples appeared. How handsome he was.

"How nice to be compared to your beloved grandmother. I am not sure I have had a better compliment."

Danny smiled again, stopped abruptly and stared intently at her. "I can think of many compliments to give you, Katie."

She was overwhelmed by his unexpected comment. She finally finished the breath she held the moment he stopped to address her. She took the lovely words to heart, wrapping them up to be remembered always.

"You know, the house is my inheritance and everything in it. But of course, Grandma is also my inheritance."

"What a wonderful inheritance, especially your precious grandmother. She is a treasure."

"She is, isn't she? Just about the time I was to go off to college, my father's business was having trouble. He had no recourse but to go back East and straighten things out. My mother and my sister, Vicky, went with him. Vicky met James and then they had two strong reasons to stay. I think my mother knew they were not coming back, because she gave instructions to Grandma about the house and the things in it. They have a new beautiful home back East but it cannot compare to the Overlook House in my eyes. Determined to stay here, Grandma and I eventually moved down to the cottage and I finished college."

"She must have been lonely, poor dear."

"I am sure of it, but she kept busy taking care of others who needed her. But I must tell you, she has come alive since you and the children arrived. You have brought joy back into her life in a special way."

Danny looked at her as if she were due some sort of honor just by being here. Their eyes met and her stomach tightened and the breath caught in her chest.

Would she ever be able to think of this man as just a brother?

After a moment of uncomfortable silence, Katie spoke, "Why did you choose the legal profession?"

"I had to head in some sort of direction. I wanted to help people somehow but I didn't have the stomach for doctoring. I would faint dead away at the sight of blood."

His eyes glazed, his mouth dropped open, and they laughed together. "I went to college at what is now officially the USC Gould School of Law–the first of its kind in the West. It was awfully hard work but I did well. I became a fairly persuasive lawyer for a season and I won cases. I suppose if I'd never known the deals that happened behind the scenes, I could have fervently fought for the downtrodden. But I was appalled at the deception and compromise. I am afraid I don't fare well with compromise. I battled against it but it was too big for me and my heart was not in it. It made for losses that upset people."

"It isn't right that people would compromise concerning the lives of others."

"No it isn't and I saw a great deal of it. It was a hard place for me but I learned a great deal and gained in strength of spirit by depending on God. My parents insisted I go to college and I thought perhaps I could serve God as a lawyer. I needed a job to provide for Grandma and me and someday my own family."

He hesitated and then quietly continued. "I felt the tug from the Lord to write but I believe now that he wanted me to grow more to be able to write with any passion. The job grieved me and I knew it was the Holy Spirit in me that was grieved. God opened an opportunity at the mission so I took it. I had been helping out for some time and they needed a full-time director, so I accepted."

"Did you do any writing at the mission?"

"Yes, but it was a long season of my life. I wrote about a few of the men that came through the home. There has been much victory but much heartache and loneliness, as well."

Katie could see that he had suffered as she had but in a

different way. She wanted to encourage him without sounding like a schoolgirl.

"I think writing would be wonderful. Perhaps that was what God had in mind. He allowed you to go in both directions to gain knowledge about different lives and people. You must have fascinating stories. I would love to read them and I am sure others would, too. Perhaps you will be published and work in your own beautiful library at the top of the hill. It is such a beautiful place."

His gentle face turned to her, seeming to take in what she said. Then he tenderly smiled.

"And you, Katie, what is in your heart?"

"Me? I am not entirely sure. I guess I was just trying to escape my awful life and raise my children in peace. I dreamt of a beautiful place and people who were kind. I craved peace and beauty. White Rock is like that. I am afraid I could just sit among Gwen's garden roses and just while away my time. God made the most beautiful things. But I suppose having my music back again would be a huge desire. Maybe write more music. I guess that sounds frivolous."

"Not at all. You must use the gifts God gave to you. You have quite the romantic heart, Katie. It fits your sweet disposition perfectly. And from what I have heard, you could be creating masterpieces."

"Thank you." She took his words as another spark of hope in her heart.

"How difficult it must have been for you under the hard hand of that uncle in that utterly desolate place." Danny shook his head at the memory of it.

"Yes, but it was good in that I know what it did in my

heart."

Danny looked astonished. "I don't understand."

"It brought me to the end of myself and brought me to see that God's ways are not always our ways, in fact, most often not."

"Ah, I see, like my work as a lawyer and my work even at the mission. It was a huge learning experience for me. A place of being broken."

"Yes, he has his ways of molding us and conforming us into the image of his son. That is a hard thing but beautiful in his sight."

"I understand perfectly. The 'us' has to go and we become more like Christ. As John the Baptist said, 'I must decrease, He must increase.'"

"Yes, it's true. I know someday I will be more thankful for my wilderness in Bitter Springs but it might take time. I am not sure I understand my time in the gold fields, fully, except the time to grow in the study of the Bible."

He gave a little laugh. "He was making you as pure gold." His eyes searched her face. "You are, you know."

"Oh no, not me." She shook her head. Morgan never said things like this to her. In fact she never felt this way with Morgan. Morgan said little in general. Her discourse with Danny was delightful, intelligent, and compatible. She felt a tinge of guilt that maybe she should have felt more like this with Morgan but he wasn't like Danny. She and Morgan had little in common.

They continued on happily lost in conversation. Then as they rounded the corner, there on the far hill between two huge oak trees was the beautiful Overlook House, in the distance. Not visible from the cottage, it was the first time she had seen it since that day—the day she had escaped Markum and hid there. The day she met Danny.

"Oh, it is lovely. I was so afraid to go there, not knowing whose house it was," Katie said.

"My legacy. What glorious memories I had there." Danny stared longingly toward the old homestead.

"And they really should be written. They should be in print." Katie was adamant. She believed in him and believed in his stories.

"I never thought to write them." He blinked, seemingly lost in the thought.

"But you must. They simply cannot be lost. You could call them Tales from Overlook House." She was lost in a vision of a series of beautifully bound, leather volumes.

"What a great encourager you are, Katie." His eyes met hers again with a depth she could not explain.

"Perhaps your grandma is rubbing off onto me." She looked back at the house and they stood for a long moment.

"Someday, I will marry and bring Grandma back there to live."

Katie frowned at the thought of Danny having a wife. It seemed to prick her heart but what claim could she have on him? Of course, he would marry a younger woman and settle down. Yet it seemed so right being with him. If he did marry someone else, would she be able to love them both as sister and brother? Perhaps, but it was not what the deepest recesses of her heart were hoping at all.

Danny looked toward the Overlook House on the hill in all its glory, envisioning Katie and the children when they were staying there. It seemed so natural. He couldn't imagine anyone else there with him. He remembered her standing with childlike awe in the library, loving every painting, every story, enamored by everything he held dear. He could have stayed forever in that moment. He could see them all on a brisk winter's evening in the library. He would be at the desk writing and Katie at the piano, bringing the sounds of heaven into the room. The children would be playing games on the big rug in front of a toasty fire and Grandma in her chair, with Bible open, blessed again.

A horse galloped by and broke the trance. He smiled and offered his arm to go on into town.

"I am so pleased you enjoyed the house."

"I did. I have seen many fine homes but none as beautiful and charming as yours."

"It was a wonderful place to grow up. When I used to hide behind the big oak tree or in its branches and listen to Grandma pray, she would pray that God would bless her adorable grandchildren who needed to be obedient and not spy on others."

Katie laughed. "How glorious to have people constantly praying for you. My life was not like that. I cannot even imagine such a thing."

"I ran off on those days, horrified that God might not be too pleased with me, but I always came back for more. I could not resist Grandma's prayers or Grandpa's voice. He sang incredibly when he sang just for God. It was like the Holy Spirit empowered him and all the angels in heaven joined in. I know my heritage is a blessing. I can only praise God for the blessings I have had. Please, Katie, tell me about your family."

"I grew up quite well off in the city. My mother was quite the socialite and Father busied himself making money to keep us in high standards. Eventually he became mayor. They were good to me but I seemed to be the ugly duckling, never fitting in."

"Ah, but remember, the ugly duckling turned out to be the beautiful swan."

Katie smiled bashfully and went on. "My sister Charlotte took to my parents' way of life, busying herself with friends, luncheons, and parties. Her friends would cajole me to play the crass new tunes on the piano but I wanted to play my own songs—hymns and classical pieces and pieces I wrote myself. Their way of life seemed superficial to me. I loved to read and they never wanted to talk about books or the Bible. I once asked to go to a little country church I found and they refused to allow it. I guess it was horrifying to them someone in my class would attend anything but the great cathedral where our family worshipped. So I obeyed, grudgingly."

"I remember the big city churches. They did seem rather stoic and cold from what I was accustomed to."

"Do you have plans now that your mission job is over? I'm sorry, it's none of my business."

"Don't be," he said gently. "The Lord hasn't made it clear yet. I have saved a great deal but I can't flounder long or I will put Grandma and me in a bad position. I never wanted to ask my father for money as I am supposed to be a prominent big city lawyer now." He sighed heavily. He wished he did know. God was not sharing his plan, or more likely he wasn't hearing God's voice.

"Where did you go after you were married?" he asked

Katie.

"At first we went to the Dakotas but work was scarce and then Morgan heard the stories about the gold mining in the west. I had great hopes when I married but I went from one extreme to another: from wealth to poverty and from the social calendar to an empty, lonely life. But let's not talk of that on such a lovely walk," Katie said with a sweeping look at all her lovely surroundings. "I feel as if I have come to paradise now."

She was smiling. He loved her smile. She was like a breath of fresh air. Her kind, sweet voice of godly wisdom and encouragement, those brilliant green eyes, and the golden curls that snuck over her ear never ceased to fascinate him. He had never met any young woman like Katie. Something in him wanted to pick her up in his arms and twirl her around. Even the wilderness could not spoil her. She sees every flower, every cloud, and is thankful for it all.

Once in town, Katie was captivated with the charming shops and the lovely fashions and goods they stocked. The windows were clear with freshly painted panes and window boxes of zinnias, calendula, and snapdragons of various colors. There were charming cottage-like buildings that invited you in and the streets were well kept. A shopkeeper swept his porch in his big apron and smiled and nodded at them.

She lingered at every shop window. "I am afraid I have been in a dungeon too long. I must seem like a silly schoolgirl."

"Never. Your joy is infectious. I have seen your dungeon, fair princess. It was an exceedingly dreadful place. It makes me see how I have taken all this for granted."

When they came to a dress shop, she stopped abruptly. An exquisite green dress in the window enchanted her and she couldn't seem to pull herself from it.

"This is Mrs. Finnegan's shop," Danny told her. "Grandma said she came from Boston and has been taken in by our happy little town and she is quite pleasant. Shall we go in?"

"Oh, no." Katie backed away a few steps. "It would be ghastly to go in looking like this." She looked at her faded dress. He was reminded that Jeremy's berry cobbler had accosted her nicer dress last night. Or was that gobbler? He laughed to himself. But she still looked wonderful to him.

The dress held her captive and she couldn't seem to draw herself away. "There is even a hat to match. It is so beautiful. Perfectly designed," she mumbled.

He watched her, completely charmed by her childlike sweetness.

"It matches your eyes, you know."

She looked at him, her eyes wide and pink waved over her cheeks.

"I guess we should go get the groceries," she said, turning from the shop.

As Danny paid for the groceries, Katie was lured away by a side shop with children's things and dishes of fine china. As she looked around, there seemed to be no end of wonders: amazing music boxes, elegant clocks, and brilliant white linens. It had been so long. She admired the intricate roses on the china platter painted so delicately. She remembered the exquisite china in Danny's house when they had their first meal together. He seemed so elated when she complimented the china, she wondered why. Most men could care less, and then there were those who chose to throw it on the floor. No. She wouldn't think about her uncle. She continued to look as her feminine heart soared. She meandered on to another section and spied a cherub-faced baby doll.

"Ah, for Sarah," she whispered.

Then a hand reached around her and picked up the doll. Her heart sank until she realized it was Danny.

"I say, wouldn't little Sarah like this? And what about this little train car for Jeremy?" He produced a wooden train engine from behind his back and rolled the wheels with his finger, his eyes all a-twinkle.

"Oh no, you mustn't spend any money on us. You have all done so much already. Maybe I can buy them when I have worked for a while."

"We can talk about that later. We need to get them now or they may be gone." His big puppy dog eyes pleaded for agreement.

She could not resist him. She consented and his face lightened. It was worth the joy it brought to give in to him.

When he left to pay, Katie turned to see a set of raven's eyes glaring at her. The black-haired beauty who had stared her down in the church service stood facing her.

Katie nodded politely to her.

"Hello, I am Miss Corbeau. I am sure Danny has mentioned me to you. I heard darling Grandma Gwen had taken you in. What a benevolent soul she is, taking in the poor and needy." Her eyes took a vertical assessment of Katie. "She has always been that way, even when Danny and I were young. We grew up together, you know—two peas in a pod. Everyone knew we would marry someday." She brushed her perfect dress as she spoke as if to wash off any degrading dust from her surroundings.

Katie stood in horror as this sickeningly sweet-mouthed vixen made her into a charity case and made sure she knew about the relationship between her and Danny. She went on and on about her lifelong attachment to Danny. Her eyes were dark and void of the slightest light to warm her demeanor. The richly adorned female had a sinister air about her making Katie wonder at the relationship she insisted was between her and Danny. She wanted desperately to flee but waited her out as she continued violating her with her ugly spirit.

"Well, it was nice to see you at church. After all, most of the poverty cases and vagrants don't come to Sunday morning service, you know. Well, it was nice to meet you...what was your name?"

"Katie," she spoke demurely.

"Kay-tee." She parroted it as if it were something foul.

Katie watched the cold-hearted serpent slink away. Her expensive skirts swished at Katie as if to say, "you have been cut down to size." Then she turned in profile, knowing Katie was still watching, and closed her dark lashes with an impudent smile as a final insult.

A few moments later, Danny walked up to Katie with the purchased toys in hand. Feeling full of shame and humiliation, she stood numb finding it difficult to speak.

"Katie, what is it? Are you okay?" he prodded.

"Yes, yes, I'm sorry." Katie forced a smile and tried to regain her composure. The feline had stolen her joy, just as cruelly as if she had been a small child who had a baby doll ripped out of her hands and thrown to the floor, breaking it into pieces.

"Is it something I have done? Do you want me to take the toys back?"

"No, of course not. I guess I am just getting tired." She tried to be cheery as it was obvious Danny was confused and saddened to see her so downcast. It was difficult to come out of the scene she had just experienced. Her mind was spinning. Am I a vagrant? Was the evil female Danny's betrothed?

Their conversation was quiet and pleasant but it was not the same as they journeyed back to the cottage. It was as if the voluptuous tormentor had stolen her voice as well as her joy.

CHAPTER FIFTEEN

Surprises

"Do *we* have a surprise for you." Danny waved the packages in the air with a big childlike grin on his face.

Katie followed him but she didn't smile until she saw their faces lighten and look at each other excitedly. Gwen and the children had been happily eating peaches and cream until now.

Jeremy was so excited that his bowl took a spill off the table. "Uh oh, my peaches."

"Oh dear. Jeremy, you've spilled it all over Grandma Gwen's chair."

"It's all right." Gwen reached for a cleanup rag and wiped it up, along with Jeremy's shirt. "See, all taken care of, and I'll get you more."

"Mmm, peaches and cream. When we are all through, then we will see what's in the packages." Danny winked.

But she knew there would be no savoring of peaches and cream today. The children hurried and sat on the rug next to Danny who handed them their gifts with childlike delight.

"A train! Look, Sarrie a train." Jeremy's response made Danny look at Katie in triumph.

"It's so cute and a blanket and clothes, too." Sarah sat cuddling her little doll close to her heart.

The children gave their ardent thank-yous, then were lost in their own imaginative world.

Grandma Gwen went over to see Sarah's doll, while Danny and Jeremy ran the train around the rungs of the circular rug, tooting like a train whistle.

"Look at that sweet-faced baby doll. Why, she looks just like her little mama. I think I may even have a cradle somewhere for her. Now let me think."

"Really?" Sarah looked up in wonder.

Later, when Danny took the little ones out back for a short hike, Gwen and Katie sat on the couch to rest.

"What ails you, child? You're not upset with Danny, are you?"

"How could anyone be upset with Danny?"

"Oh, I don't know. I have been known to be upset with him now and again." She chuckled her eyes bright with mischief.

Katie wondered whether to say anything but it was so pent up inside, she broke down. "Are we a charity case for you? Am I a...a...vagrant?"

"A what?" Gwen scowled. "Why would you think such a thing? Did someone say that?"

"A Miss Corbeau in the store, when Danny went to pay for the toys."

"Gretchen." Gwen's eyelids closed in recognition and she took a deep breath. "She would say that, yes, that is just like her."

"I first saw her boring holes in me at the service on Sunday."

"She had her mind set on Danny for years and she does not give up easily," Gwen said. "Though I can't believe she could still think she has one iota of a chance with him. You must have disturbed her terribly. As lovely as you are, she must be rather jealous."

"Of me? But she is gorgeous."

"Yes, but her heart is not I am afraid. When Danny was younger, her beauty fascinated him and he felt sorry for her because her mother ran away back to France, deserting her. But eventually her cold heart wore him out of his stupor, which was an answer to our prayers. She would get him into trouble and finagle her way out by blaming him for every sordid deed she devised. Also, she would not let one girl close to him to be his friend. He soon grew tired of her evil ways. He was a good boy and everyone knew it, but she was malicious. There didn't seem to be a kind bone in her body. I had never met one like her. What exactly did she say to you?"

The pieces fit together in Katie's mind. She was the one Danny almost married. The one who was terribly evil as a child and beguiled him as an adult.

"She said it was kind of you to take us in. And that most charity cases and vagrants are too embarrassed to come to the morning service."

Gwen's jaw dropped. "Well, I'll be. She is not worth the effort to tell her what for but I have a mind to." Gwen was fit to be tied. She stood up from the couch, steaming like her own little teakettle.

"No, Gwen. I don't want to make trouble for you and

Danny. This has been paradise for me."

"She *is* trouble. I suppose if Daniel had an Uncle Tyler it would be Gretchen."

"I suppose if I can pray for Tyler, I can pray for her." Katie sighed as she looked off out the window, knowing it might not be an easy task.

Gwen sat back down. "You gentle-hearted child. She is the most in need of prayer of anyone I know. I guess we'll let our Father in heaven take care of her. She has an evil spirit and a selfish heart. Don't take anything she says to heart." Gwen turned Katie's head to face her. "You are a part of our family, not a charity case. You couldn't be a vagrant if you tried. Outward beauty, wealth, and expensive garments cannot stand against you sweet loveliness and precious spirit.

The chatter of happy voices cut short their talk. Danny popped in with Jeremy on his back and Sarah with her apron filled with wildflowers.

"We had a great little hike. It was so clear and we could see all the back mountain ranges today."

"Ah, I remember those days." Gwen put her handkerchiefed hand to her heart. "When we were young, my beloved Samuel and I would have picnics and enjoy the lovely view. Then when he and Danny's father built the house, we had many happy times up there. What a glorious place it was, to pray and sing and picnic." She stared out the window, lost somewhere in her happy memories.

Katie envisioned Grandma Gwen at the big house in her garden singing. She wished there were a way for her to go home to the Overlook House.

Sarah gathered the wildflowers together and presented

them to her mother and Gwen. "Danny said you would like them." She smiled at Danny.

"I told the children about my exploits in the old oak tree, Grandma."

"You did?" She chuckled. "He was the cutest little stinker," she told the others, "but I knew he was there because he admired our prayers and Samuel's singing. It was a happy memory for us to share for many years."

"So many wonderful memories that should be written." Katie looked at Danny affirming what she had told him.

"I have thought so for years. Amen, Katie girl, we'll get him writing yet."

A supper of chicken and dumplings and boysenberry pie courtesy of Katie's hand caused Danny to moan in blessed misery as he reclined on the couch.

"You two ladies will make me an elephant."

Jeremy giggled and Danny went after him to wrestle on the floor.

"Sarrie, help!" Jeremy squealed between giggles.

She did and everyone was laughing before long.

When they settled in for the night, and the children were ready for bed, Danny told them his special version of David and Goliath, acting the whole story out and making them all laugh again.

With the playacting over and the bedtime prayers spoken with the children, the adults rested quietly in the living room.

Feeling a bit forlorn, Katie said, "I guess the holiday is over. Tomorrow I must go to work."

"That's right. You go to work for Mrs. Perkins. How do

you think it will go?" Danny asked.

"Well, I hope I will do well. I am trained for the position although a bit rusty. It will all come back to me, I am sure. I never wanted to do any of it. Now here I am—a real social secretary after all."

"You will do fine," Gwen said.

"And if she isn't pleased, or it doesn't suit you, then you just come back home." The words were out of Danny's mouth as easily as if she were his sister.

"Yes, this is home," Gwen said.

Katie smiled at these two wonderful people who had become like a new family.

"Are you sure you can handle the children? I don't want you to overdo."

"Bosh. They are little angels."

"And I must be back at work soon, too," Danny said, "but I must say my heart isn't in it. My job at the mission is winding down. I sensed leaving was the right thing. I have been feeling it for some time."

"Yes, Daniel," his grandma said. "That's what I have been getting in prayer. God must be changing directions for your life."

Katie's heart raced at the thought of him coming home for good.

"I have been thinking about it continually but I haven't a clue what I am to do. I just can't quit and sit at the desk in the library and write, much as I would love to."

"If it's God's will, he will make a way," Gwen said.

"Wouldn't that be wonderful." Katie was thrilled. Having someone live his dream and vision was like doing it herself—especially someone as wonderful as Danny.

"He will bring stories to life and with the truth of God's Word, which is deeply embedded in him," Gwen said.

"Yes, he would, and I have noticed his well-worn Bible," Katie said.

Gwen winked.

"Hmm....now why is it that I feel as though I have left the cottage already?" Danny faked a scowl.

They spent the rest of the evening talking about what each had been learning in their devotions. It was hard to go to bed for the fellowship was so pleasant.

Katie thought about the day as she sat on her bed, brushing out her long spiral curls. Their conversation had been so wonderful. Despite the disturbing interlude with Gretchen, she had a glorious time with many special moments. The way Danny stopped and looked at her when he said he had many compliments for her. She wondered what he might have told her. And the surprised look when she spoke about him writing the stories of his childhood. He called her wise and like his grandma. It was wonderful to be likened to Grandma Gwen. Danny was so perfect. How could she ever find anyone so wonderful? He wouldn't want a widow with children to start out his life, would he? Would any man care for her children, as he has? He has absorbed them into his heart so quickly.

He is faithful to you, Lord, servant-hearted and generous, kind and gentle yet a man of strength and honor.

She sighed, laying down her brush. If only I had met him first. But of course, Sarah and Jeremy would never have been born. She crawled into her comfy quilted bed but could not sleep, her thoughts went back to the incident with Gretchen. What an awful woman. She must have been a horrid child. Poor Danny. She was like a beautiful poisonous plant. Katie pieced together all Danny had told her as they walked to town, adding what Gwen had said about Gretchen, and lastly her own confrontation with her and it all seemed to fit. Does she still believe Danny will come back to her? What had Danny called her...a nightmare—yes that's it.

How do I pray for this nightmare of a woman with her heart of stone and eyes of a serpent, Lord?

CHAPTER SIXTEEN

Prayer for Enemies

Gwen sent Katie off the next morning well fed and with a box lunch just in case her new employer did not provide it for her. The children were playing happily in the garden when Gwen felt it was appropriate to speak to Danny about Katie's experience with Gretchen.

"No—she didn't? She shouldn't be able to get away with such things," Danny seethed, his jaw clenched.

"Don't get excited, we don't want the children to hear. Gretchen has always managed to weasel her way out of everything, but someday God will judge her for her behavior and her parents for never chastising her. We can only—"

"I know—pray." Danny raised his hand to stop the obvious words coming next. "She is so cruel. Sometimes it's too hard to pray for our enemies, Grandma."

"Surely these two that have come to our attention are the dregs of the earth but we must obey the words of our Lord."

"I wonder which one is worse? I thought Gretchen was finally done with me and now she speaks all this rubbish to

Katie—kind, sweet Katie. It makes me so angry." His fist clenched and released.

"It is always harder to forgive the offense toward innocent loved ones than it is for yourself. Don't think I haven't had to fight this one out, for I have. Katie is the epitome of a true child of God and her little ones a delight to me. I think she was ready to leave to keep from causing us any embarrassment. She did not get angry, she threw it all back on herself."

"She would do that. You don't think she'll leave, do you?" He looked at her like a frightened child.

"I don't think so. She really has nowhere to go. But Daniel, you must not take offense and get angry, even with Gretchen. You must set to prayer."

"I know. I have been through this before at the mission with some of the young boys who came through our doors, whose parents cared nothing about them. It was heartbreaking. I wanted to shake those parents. Right now, I want to shake Gretchen—shake the evil heart right out of her. I wish she would just move on to the big city where she desires to be and stay away from us. I never told you all that transpired between us, but she has a far more sinister heart than you may know."

"I may know more than you think. She has always concerned me. I watched the evil grow in that girl year after year and I spent many nights praying for her and for you because of her, not to mention the other little ones in school. She needs salvation or she will go on to harm others."

They bowed their heads and prayed for Katie and the children, and then for the salvation of Gretchen and Tyler and then remembered to mention Markum as well. The words did not come easy when their enemies were mentioned but they knew the Lord's commands and would obey until God's love would help them pray more in earnest.

"I think it best to leave day after tomorrow to go back to the mission. Best to get things settled and ready to leave. I can have a bit of special time with the men before I leave. Is God giving you any directions? I do need to provide for us somehow."

"Now Daniel, remember God is our source, not you. You will find his direction. Rest in him."

"When I was in Los Angeles, John offered me a job. I even thought about it on the way there, thinking maybe God wanted me to go back into the legal world but as I walked around his office, it seemed so foreign and worldly. I never did fit into that way of life and I am just not cut out for the compromise. They seem to have a different way of thinking than I do."

"I know. God has a perfect way for you. And one day a wife and family."

She hesitated saying it, but she knew it was on his mind. His eyes widened. She saw these two young people as a match made in heaven but didn't want to say anything. It was God's work, not hers, to put it all together. She noted the way Danny looked at Katie and the way she blushed when he did, many times. She remembered the look on his face as he stood at the door when Katie had the nightmare. She was such a beautiful young life, lying there with her golden tresses hanging and her delicate face overwhelmed with fear. He could not draw himself away. Gwen had also noted their laughter and the gentle caring tones of their voices sharing the wonders of the Bible and their lives. And how the children adored Danny and he them. Everything added up to a perfect match but she would wait and see how God did this.

Danny interrupted her reflections, "I can't even think of anything until I can provide for us. Why doesn't God just tell me?"

"Well, how much time have you spent listening lately?"

"Not enough, I suppose. Pray for me, Grandma."

Gwen reached up and cupped his handsome square jaw, looked into his big brown eyes and smiled. "Of course, Daniel. God has given you special gifts and talents. You must ask him how to use them for his glory and for provision. You will have lots of train time to pray."

"True. Do you think Katie will be all right? You don't think she would run off because of Gretch, do you?"

"No. She knows what Gretchen is all about, now. I don't know everything Gretchen has said to her but I imagine it wasn't pleasant."

"We both know Gretch does what she pleases. Why does she have to pick on Katie?"

"I know. Our sweet Katie has been through quite enough, I would say."

Danny was quiet for a moment or two, then jumped up. "I need to go to town to pick up a few things. Do you need anything?"

She cocked her head. "Just the mail."

Danny walked to town deep in thought. This was all his fault. If only he had not fallen for one more of Gretch's evil tricks. That woman was completely incapable of love. He knew it now. She didn't want him anymore than she wanted anyone. Gretchen had played the coquette, so sweet like syrup, but filled with lies and deceit. She only wanted him because she could never lose a battle. She couldn't stand to lose. Ever. Gretchen had cheated and threatened and hurt others all through Danny's childhood and it frightened him when it came to her attack on Katie. What was Gretchen up to and what would she do to accomplish her goals? It was unnerving him to think about it. He hated to leave but he knew he must go and part with the Men's Street Mission season of his life. God would open a new way.

He must have faith to entrust Katie and the children and Grandma to the Lord's care and get this done. He smiled, thinking about the reason he came to town and it wasn't just to get the mail.

CHAPTER SEVENTEEN

Properly Attired

Danny sat down to rest after fixing the fence and cleaning up.

"When does Mama comed home?" Jeremy was getting impatient. His bottom lip was starting to take over in a pout. He was not used to being so long without his beloved mother. But it would be hours before she came home.

"Well, let's see," Grandma said taking him over to the cuckoo clock. She tried to show him on the clock but when she looked at his perplexed face, she just soothed. "Soon, little one, soon."

"Jer'my, this Sunday, we get to go to Sunday school," Sarah said.

All of a sudden Grandma Gwen shrieked, making all of them jump. "Land sakes, Daniel, I forgot. Okay, troops we're off to town."

Danny and the children all shrugged at each other and moved toward the door.

"Where'd we going, Grandma Gwen?" Jeremy finally asked partway down the road.

"Children need proper attire," she answered, walking like a soldier on a mission.

Jeremy looked at her with squinted eyes and wrinkled brow, making Danny smile and wonder what great things were going on in his little mind.

Danny picked up a little shirt from the store table. "What about this one, little chap?"

Grandma was sizing up dresses for Sarah. Danny noted Sarah's apprehension. She nodded politely at each one Grandma picked out for her. Finally, he observed his beloved grandmother's wisdom take over.

"If these were all in your mother's size, which one would you choose for her?" Grandma said.

Instantly Sarah perked up and picked a blue calico and green flower print and a dark pink one with ruffles, which she seemed to admire most of all.

They found socks and other items the children needed.

"They need bedclothes," Danny said out of the side of his mouth.

"Oh my, yes, they are threadbare," she whispered.

So they found new nightclothes and Gwen picked out a lovely gown for Katie as well, similar to Sarah's.

"She'll fuss about it, but no matter," Gwen said.

"This has been such fun. It reminds me of the years when you were just a wee little fellow."

The joy on Grandma's face warmed his heart. The new life at the cottage was making her young again.

"Grandma Gwen?" Jeremy tugged at her skirt. "Are we tired yet?"

Danny burst out laughing and the whole store

wondered at the great joke that was spoken.

Partway down the street, his grandma ventured, "What did I miss, Daniel?"

But it only set him laughing again and the children giggling at him.

He could barely get it out. "Jeremy asked you if we were tired yet. You had told him on the way to town, 'Children needed to be properly attired' and I guess he was properly tired." Then he laughed all over again, with Grandma cackling beside him and the children laughing at them.

Danny looked at the big grin on Sarah's face, "You stole my dimples again."

Sarah smiled. "No I didn't. They are still right there on your cheeks."

"You are too smart for me." Danny pulled gently on her pigtail and she smiled.

He saw Ruby pull her curtains back and smile as the foursome walked home in high spirits.

"Oh, dear, I can never repay you." Katie looked astounded by the nice selection of things they showed her when she came home.

She plopped on the couch overwhelmed and started to protest.

"Now, Katie, wouldn't you want to be able to give to others?" Gwen chided.

"Of course I would. If I could I would bless you and Danny so you could live back in the Overlook House."

"You precious child. Now, you listen up." She scooted next to her with her lips firm. "If you want God to bless you in giving to others, you must first learn how it feels to receive from others. You need to feel what it is to be on the receiving end when you are in need. You feel uncomfortable right now, don't you?"

"Of course. It's completely humiliating."

"Yes, and right now we are in a higher place above you as you are on the receiving end. When Danny goes to the Men's Street Mission, those men will not receive because they feel the same way. Danny had to learn to be wise and gentle in the way he gave to them. They were already in a humiliating position."

"As I am." Katie's head dropped.

"Yes, but it's temporary. Soon you will be on the giving end."

Danny sat watching these women in admiration and quietly listening.

"I see. If I were always giving then I would be in a high position and not a humble one."

"Yes, if you learn how to receive graciously then you will give graciously as well. Besides, I can't tell you how much you and the children have given me."

Sarah interrupted the women as she came from the bedroom in her new pink ruffled dress

They all clapped for her. Katie felt a little tear on her cheek. She barely choked out, "You look so pretty."

Gwen whispered, "You will soon be bringing them home blessings from your own hand. Let us enjoy giving this time." A smile crinkled his dear grandmother's eyes and Katie acquiesced.

"Howd about me?" Jeremy came bounding in with his buttons all askew and his mop of curls bobbing about, but looking the well-dressed boy in his white shirt and short pants.

"You look wonderful, darling. Now you know, Jeremy, they are only letting you go to Sunday school on trial. You are still rather young for the class," Katie said, while she rebuttoned his shirt.

"We haven't had much time to ask about your day. How was it?" Danny asked.

"There were lists, and more lists and lists of lists. I think Mrs. Perkins needed them all to keep her on track." Katie shook her head. "I was oriented with the mansion and servants and I am not sure I remember a single thing. I shall be making lists in my sleep, no doubt. The Perkins Mansion is lovely but stiff and cold. It's not at all like your lovely home on the hill, as big as it is."

"It's a warm house, isn't it? But it is really people who make it cozy," Gwen said.

Danny could not keep his eyes off of Katie. He thought about the memories they had already been making together. But it was time for a new one.

"Excuse me, ladies, but I have one more gift." He jumped from his chair and started toward the back bedrooms.

Katie was admiring the lovely nightgown she had been given and the bedclothes for the children when Danny came back with his huge package. "This is my gift and it's actually something you will need."

Katie took it and opened her mouth to protest, but Gwen's sermonette was still in the air. She gasped when she pulled the green dress from the wrapping. Then from behind his back, he produced the hat. She bit her upper lip trying to hold back but the tears cascaded down her cheeks. Gwen offered her handkerchief and Katie dabbed away.

"Oh, Danny, it's the dress in the window."

He waited, wishing she wouldn't cry and hoping she would accept it. Had he made a mistake? He couldn't stand to see her cry.

His grandma grabbed Katie and the dress and hat and drew her back into the bedroom.

When they walked back into the living room, Danny was voiceless and his heart skipped a few beats at the sight of her. She was beautiful even in her worn dress but this was made for her. He was enchanted. She was breathtakingly radiant, dressed as she should have always been, a true lady but without pretense. Her wet red cheeks only made her more glorious.

"Mama, it matches your eyes. You look so pretty." Sarah fawned over her.

Jeremy followed Sarah and for once was speechless, too.

"My, oh my. You are absolutely stunning," Grandma agreed, pulling the wrinkles out of the back of the dress.

Katie blushed when she looked at Danny. Their eyes met. Sarah was right, he thought. Her eyes were made brilliant by the green dress. Her golden curls cascaded from the back of the elegantly dipped hat and he imagined her painted in all her glory above the mantle in the Overlook House.

"You know, Mrs. Perkins said I would have to get something suitable to wear for the big teas and such. I thought I would have to buy fabric and make something quickly but now—I feel like a princess."

"I saw your eyes light up when you saw it. It seemed perfect for you. It is." He could barely say anything more without giving his whole heart away.

"Thank you both so much for everything. We are so blessed."

He basked in the beauty before him and in the grand idea he had to make sure that Katie looked like the daughter of a king next time she faced Gretchen. She would not call Katie a vagrant again.

Sarah twirled in her new little dress and curtsied to Katie. "Mama, you are a princess and Grandma Gwen is the queen and...." Sarah thought hard for a second. "Okay, then Danny must be the prince."

Katie glanced up, wide-eyed. She looked at him. All he could do was smile at her. He was entirely happy with that remark and he wanted her to know it.

Jeremy scowled. "But I'm the princed, Sarrie."

"You are the little prince, silly. Mama can't marry *you*."

Eyebrows rose and the room got pin-drop quiet. Danny watched trying to hold back a full grin while Katie's cheeks blazed. He caught his grandma smile ever so slightly, as Katie abruptly turned to head back toward her room.

The vision of the green dress on Katie, the way her curls fell from the hat and her fleeing blushed pink face from Sarah's innocent remark would stay with him in the days ahead. It would be another wonderful memory of happy times and a lovely vision he could not get out of his mind— nor did he have any desire to do so.

CHAPTER EIGHTEEN

Cat Claws

Katie could tell he hated to leave. Danny waved one last goodbye as he left to go back to the Men's Street Mission, leaving behind all their somber faces. The train whistled at him in urgency and he sprinted to its call. He had tarried too long at the happy cottage, with lingering goodbyes.

Gwen wrapped lunches for Katie and Danny. Katie hugged, kissed, and gave a multitude of instructions to her little ones and then flew out the door to the Perkins Mansion.

At the end of their day, the children were little chattering magpies telling about their experiences with Grandma Gwen. Katie and Gwen exchanged happy glances.

"We are planning some gardening, a trip to the store and maybe we'll create some delicious treats in the kitchen," Gwen said, winking at the children. Then she whispered to Katie, "This could be a good thing. They won't miss Daniel so much."

"How true. They absolutely adore him."

"My Daniel *is* rather wonderful."

Katie nodded in agreement, feeling a little sheepish about all the feelings stirring inside of her whenever he was mentioned. She was already missing him terribly and could barely concentrate at work. Surely this ache would go away in a day or so.

"I guess it is time for me to write to my sister and let her know where we are and that we are doing well."

"You may use the pen and paper in Danny's room on his desk, anytime. The ink is in the drawer."

Katie wrote the letter to Charlotte, saying as little as possible from a heart filled with so much. It proved to be a challenge, but she managed to tell her they had moved to White Rock, California, and she had secured a position with a woman who often held grand teas and needed assistance with all the planning and arrangements. She told her sister they were boarding with a kind elderly widow. She left out mentioning Danny for now. She didn't want any questions she might not know how to answer. The life that lay between the lines was way beyond the simple missive but it was hers to hold in her own heart. She thanked Charlotte for her monetary help through the time spent in Bitter Springs, and told her someday she would tell her all about it, but for now all was well.

When Sunday came, Gwen suggested Katie wear her new green dress. Katie had wanted to wear it, but she had to search her heart to make sure she was not wearing it just to stop the humiliating remarks of that wretched Gretchen. She wanted her motives to be pure.

All down the street and at the church, she felt eyes on her and heads turning. She attributed it to the lovely dress and hat Danny had purchased. As she looked toward the door of the church she could not help but see the eyes of the enemy seething. Gretchen looked her up and down as if she had stolen the dress from her. Katie turned her eyes away and attended to the children.

Gretchen watched Katie and Gwen study their Bibles intently as the preacher preached. But she ignored him as usual as meaningless drivel. That despicable girl was going to be real competition in such a costume—exactly the one she had thought to buy for herself. Gretchen assured herself she would have been far more alluring in it than the blonde waif. She wondered where her Danny was. He was supposed to be back. She only came for Danny's benefit, not to have to see the vagrant charlatan and her little imps and his stuffy old grandmother. She relished the day the old woman would be carted off to an asylum. His grandmother had always been in her way. But she went too far this time, taking in the little blonde intruder. That was inexcusable.

And who does she think she is—walking into Danny's life and taking over the whole family? She could not have had the money to buy the window dress. He must have bought it. Ah, of course—the store woman said it was sold to a man. She glared over at Katie and her nostrils drew breath like a horse ready for battle. She'd won many battles and would not lose this one—no matter what it took.

She smiled as she fanned herself and felt her confidence gaining ground for the destruction of her enemy.

After the service, Gretchen waited inside, peeking out the door for an opportune time to get Katie alone. When

Katie was alone she hurried out to her. She stole close. "You know, no man wants to purchase used merchandise."

Katie looked at her with a confused expression and it made Gretchen smile. She took off as if what was said was a perfectly regular greeting, and she—a perfectly normal person. She climbed into her elegant carriage and sneered back at Katie.

Reaching her mansion in an exhilarated state, Gretchen hurried past the servants as if they didn't exist, and flighted up the staircase. She went directly to her room and started flinging her clothes out of the closet as her maid—who had followed her—watched stoically.

"These are all worthless. Nothing I want. I must make a trip. Moira, go arrange a trip for the city. I want to leave first thing in the morning."

"But your father is due back tomor—" the servant started.

"So." Gretchen said, piercing the maid with her black squinted eyes. "And don't you dare contradict me. I'll be back soon enough. He can wait." I have more important things to do than listen to his boring business tales, and what new lawyer he bought off now, she grumbled to herself.

After getting her directions, the maid went off to make arrangements.

"I'll show Miss Ka-tee how to turn heads," Gretchen hissed, admiring her perfect shape and striking face in the mirror. Something in her eyes made her shudder for a moment. Something diabolical lurked down deep as she stared into the recesses of her heart, showing her she was capable of darker things than she had ever imagined and when she blinked she felt no shame.

Katie felt as if she had been slapped and had no idea why. The scent of strong perfume lingered and it made her nose wrinkle.

Gwen meandered over. "I saw Gretchen sweep by. What did she say?"

Katie hesitated." To tell you the truth, I am not really sure. It was odd, she seemed rude but what she spoke didn't make sense."

"Just remember, Katie, anything she might say wouldn't be worth thinking about it. She is one of a kind and the likes of which most never see in a lifetime."

"Hmm...but I knew someone when I was a girl at home. It seemed she had no conscience. She tried to lure me into doing awful things. She was exceedingly cruel and heartless, almost murderous."

"Maybe they are related, if not in flesh, in spirit. Gretchen lured Danny at every turn. He suffered greatly under her spell."

Katie felt a little spellbound herself by the strange words Gretchen had spoken.

Gwen and the children did most of the talking on the walk home. Katie could see the concern in Gwen's countenance, but she knew she had to sort this out for herself.

At home, they all felt the loss of their beloved Danny. He was so much a part of their happy times. Katie could see it in every face and her own heart longed for his presence. She hadn't realized how much of an impact he had made on their lives, especially on hers.

Before bed, they spent time praying for him.

"Keep our Dandy safe and bringed him back to us in a hurry."

"We miss him," Sarah added.

Katie smiled at their prayer, and secretly added a big amen. Then she sent Jeremy off to get ready for bed.

"Sarah, how are things going with Jeremy here with Grandma Gwen?" Katie asked.

"He has been really good, Mama. Sometimes he wants you but he gets over it and finds something new to do. I miss you, too."

"I miss you, too, my little princess, very much."

And she missed another besides her little ones. It seemed like he'd been gone for weeks. She thought about the grin Danny wore when Sarah said he was the prince, as if he were happily taken with the idea. It made her smile.

"Mama, why are you smiling?"

"It's nothing, dear."

But it wasn't.

CHAPTER NINETEEN

Saying Goodbye

"It is good to see you, Brother Danny." The wrinkled face lit with joy as Danny brought his satchel in through the Mission door.

"Good to see you, too, Henry."

"Brother Danny!" More enthusiastic voices echoed around him.

"How are you fellows?" He shook hands and exchanged brotherly hugs.

He smiled as he looked on the faces of these beloved men, old and young, but all of them brought to salvation and learning to live again. These were the precious fruit of his hard labors. He grieved over those who left without a new life in Christ; those who decided to go back like dogs to their vomit rather than let God change them. Many souls had gone on and were doing well but this group was his last crop. He was melancholy and they were heavyhearted, but they all knew it was God's will. Most of them would be strong enough to face life again soon. The ones who were not ready would stay with the new missionaries who were coming. Change was uncomfortable for the freshly delivered men but in their wisdom, the board sent the new missionaries ahead of time on and off to get acquainted and it would ease Danny's exit from the men somewhat. The couple coming in to replace him was seasoned and would be like parents to the young ones. A woman's touch would be good. The thought danced in his heart. Yes, a woman's touch would be good for him, too. He smiled.

The men scrambled to scoop him up a meal like a king had come home. It was an honor he received from them as an act of love and concern. He treated them as brothers and they respected him greatly. They fellowshipped and he told them all about his amazing homecoming with Jeremy and his antics being a highlight to share.

"What about his mother? Is she pretty?" one asked.

"Well, to be perfectly honest, she is quite beautiful and the sweetest Christian woman outside of my family I have ever met."

"Uh oh, I think he's in trouble, fellas," Henry said, winking at the others.

"Well, if this is trouble I wish it on all of you," Danny said making them all laugh.

After more teasing and sharing, Danny visited with the man who temporarily stayed until the couple came to take his place. They had gone to retrieve their belongings. At dinner, he told the fellows about being properly attired and they laughed heartily.

Danny walked upstairs to bed. He would be leaving this "family" and going back to Grandma and the precious family at the cottage. He had missed them terribly from that first hour on the train.

As he closed his eyes, memories flashed from picture to picture of Katie. The first time he saw her standing at the Overlook House, wondering if he was friend or foe. Then when she looked admiringly at the portraits and library. She was so taken by his world. Then he saw her at the piano like a heavenly soul who had come to earth. And how beautiful she was, the night she had the nightmare, when her spun gold curls trailed down her pillow. And lastly, a vision of a princess in green made him sigh.

He opened his eyes. She was so beautiful in the dress and hat. *I am so glad I got them.*

I adore them all, Father. If only we could all be together always. But I must take care of Grandma and this precious family, too, if it is your will and I have no idea how to accomplish it. Please keep the discouragement from rising up in me. I know you will make a way. I know, Father . . . "be anxious for nothing."

The days and nights seemed dreadfully long, waiting to go home but the new missionaries finally arrived and he made them comfortable, showing them how things worked. But mostly he shared more details about the hearts of the men he had known there, even filling them in on a few who had left in hope they might come back.

The day came to say goodbye and there stood a small group of watery-eyed men. He was a brother to them but also a spiritual father, even at his young age. They loved him and thanked him and he went on his way.

He stopped and looked back and waved once more before going on to the train station. When he turned, he knew he faced an unknown course ahead but he—just like those men—would trust in God for every step for God was faithful.

"Mornin', Mr. Daniel," the porter said recognizing Danny.

"Morning, Sampson. It's so good to see you. A beautiful day today, brother."

Sampson chuckled. "Mussa been somethin' good happen today, huh, sir?"

"Yes, Sampson, I am headed home for good."

"You is leavin' the Mission, Mr. Daniel?"

"Yes, new helpers have come and it is time for me to go on back home and find out what the Lord wants me to do now."

"Well, that is good, sir, vera good. God bless you. The Good Lord will show you, yes sir, he sure will. Bein' home is the best place for sure." Sampson took Danny's satchel and made sure his trunk was loaded.

"God bless you, and your family, too." Danny put a hefty bill into Sampson's hand. "Here, brother, make sure you have a big turkey for Thanksgiving."

"Oh, thank you, sir. That is so genrus, so genrus."

"It is just a gift from the Lord, brother."

As Danny started up the steps, he heard a familiar voice grating above the crowd at the other end of the train platform. She was shouting orders abrasively to all who were trying to assist her. He cringed, pulled his hat down, and barely peeked to see the all-too-familiar female. He quickly snuck into the train car and found his seat as fast as he could. She hadn't seen him. He sighed in relief. Slumped at his window, he watched her entourage of servants carry all manner of things as they scurried to find a suitable carriage. He analyzed Gretchen in all her garb. She was a multifaceted crystal glass filled with arsenic, beautiful on the outside and lethal inside. Men were gawking and women admiring, but she was dazzling only to those who did not know her. He knew her all too well and she held no splendor in his eyes. To him, she was pure poison and her black heart dulled any false radiance the fancy glass might have. He shuddered at the thought that he was once so close to her. He would be glad to be back where true beauty waited at the cottage.

He nestled into his seat and by the time the first town surfaced, he was left to himself in another world that brought back a cavalcade of memories, one right after another pertaining to that arsenic filled glass.

CHAPTER TWENTY

Gretchen

"But you shouldn't do that," young Danny choked out in a forced whisper.

"Why shouldn't I?" The coal-eyed girl challenged with an impudent scowl that spoke volumes to the young boy. She often acted the part of a caged animal when confronted —one he did not want to tangle with because she scratched hard.

"Mrs. Milner said I was a spoiled brat. I heard her tell Daddy." She flipped her raven braid and turned back to the task at hand. At Gretchen's vindictive hand, books and papers flew out the schoolhouse window where the wind played havoc with them, the loose papers taking to flight.

The boy's sense of decency made him cringe. "But Gretch, that's mean."

"I don't care. Nobody better say anything about me and think they can get away with it," she spewed back, her eyes afire. He knew that look and he hated it, always wondering how she could be pleasant one minute, then be so hateful the next, pulling stunts like this.

"I am not doing this," Danny protested as courage mounted in him.

"You better not go, Danny, or I will tell them you did it all and made me stay to watch," she vowed. And he knew she meant it.

Fear stung him and for a moment he was paralyzed as he had been so many times before by her threats. He felt the cowardice chastising him. He was trapped yet again by the crafty black spider and he knew how adept she was at spinning her webs.

He watched as she did as she always did—whatever she pleased without consequence. She was utterly spoiled, undisciplined, and babied. Their schoolmates, whom she duped often to get her way, kowtowed to her out of fear. But Danny finally could take no more. Taking his chances, he flew away from her sticky web of vengeance.

As he bolted, she screamed after him. "You did this, Danny. Danny did it. Danny did it ALL!"

Her words rung in his ears as he ran home. His parents weren't there.

Grandma will listen. She will know what to do.

He ran to her prayer spot on the hill and heard her singing. He tried to wait patiently but couldn't any longer.

"Grandma," he spoke softly.

"Daniel, what is it?" she asked, wrapping herself tighter in her shawl.

"Grandma, I need help. I was at the schoolhouse with, uh, Gretch. "His eyes dropped to his feet, expecting a lecture.

"Oh, I see," she said with a heavy sigh.

"Grandma, she's mad at Mrs. Milner and she's throwing

all her books and papers out the window into the wind."

"And?" Her eyebrows rose.

"And she said if I left she'd tell everyone I did it."

"Did you do any of it?"

"No, of course not. I like Mrs. Milner. You know I wouldn't. I told her she was being mean."

"Good. When are you ever going to learn to stay far away from that child?" The lecture began.

"She said she found something really cool behind the schoolhouse, so I went." He stood slumped over in disgrace. Gretch had trapped him, again.

"Don't you believe anything she tells you. Do you understand? You have been told over and over. It is such a battle for your parents and Grandpa and me, too, when these things happen. She manipulates her parents just as she does you young ones. I cannot imagine what the girl will be capable of when she grows up."

I cannot imagine what the girl will be capable of when she grows up.

His grandmother's words rang through his mind for years. They would come back to him over and over as she spun her webs in the future—and she would spin plenty. As the years passed, her manipulation went somewhat underground as she found sneakier ways to get people to do her bidding. He saw them manipulated by her as money and gifts became her bait. He stayed away, as far away as he could.

Then Gretchen came home after a tour of Europe at 18. She was captivating. She was dressed in splendor but moreover, she had grown into the most beguiling beauty. Her skin was flawless and her dark lashes and full lips tantalized all the local young men. The once-striking girl had been transformed into a bewitching and ravishing young woman. For weeks, the town folks watched as suitors arrived from every city she had toured. Bored with their attentions, she sought after the only one she ever really wanted—him. He wondered why at the time, but now he knew. It was because she couldn't have him.

As alluring as she was, his focus was in another place and he was growing in his commitment to God and he had pursued his law degree.

"Danny, how perfect for you. Think of all the people you could help," Gretchen encouraged. "I have been helping the poor by putting things together for the shut-ins. It is so rewarding."

He was mesmerized by her sugary sweet dialogue and captivating beauty. But had she really changed? He asked himself that question more than once while away at college.

But her scheme worked and she lured him into her good graces. They spent much time writing letters back and forth and on holidays they spent time together.

"Gretch, I have been thinking. I am not sure I am cut out for being a lawyer."

"What?" For a second, her eyes sparked, then her demeanor changed. "It is a perfect job for you. You can help people and earn money to provide for a wife someday and even for your Grandma." She toyed with his collar, sounding so sweet—too sweet.

"But I see too much compromise. You help one and another one is hurt. I have seen wheeling and dealing behind the scenes and it troubles me greatly."

"I am sure Gawd has this all figured out, Danny. It will

all work out," she soothed. She gave him a look, which drew out every carnal manly desire in him and he momentarily forgot the strange way she said God.

"I suppose." He patted her hand. But he wasn't fully convinced.

He left to go back to college compelled to do the right thing and finish and they continued to write.

Dear Gretch,

My studies have been difficult this semester but I am almost finished. My schoolmate John has already secured a position in a law firm here and expects they will want me as well. I know this will please you.

I have been going with a friend to help out at the Men's Street Mission House here. It is so rewarding. There were many who needed care and counseling and it felt good to help them with even the little I had to offer. I have wonderful stories of salvation and deliverance to share on my return.

Graduation is coming up. I hope you will be able to attend.

Yours truly,

Danny

When her letter arrived, he smiled to himself. She was the most beautiful woman he'd ever seen. He stared at the envelope. Was she truly God's choice? It seemed right. After all she had changed and they had much in common, now. He sat on the edge of his bed as he read the long-awaited reply.

My Darling Danny,

I was elated to hear of the possible position for you. What a glorious opportunity. It surely must be God's way.

Danny darling, a man in your position must be careful of where he frequents. Please keep it in mind in the future.

I was wondering if you would take me to the big cathedral when I come. I have always longed to see it. I suppose you attend there now since you are involved with more reputable society in the legal profession. The city life certainly suits me. I love the feel of business and society. I believe I was destined for it.

I will be coming to your graduation, of course. I am so looking forward to seeing you and spending time with you and meeting your high society friends and colleagues.

Yours devotedly,

Gretchen

p.s. I believe it would be best to call me Gretchen now. After all, we are adults now. Perhaps even Miss Corbeau would be appropriate when I am introduced. It is so important to make a good impression.

Danny was a mass of confusion. He was excited to show Gretch off to all his school friends but ghosts of the old Gretch were hiding somewhere between the lines. He couldn't quite pinpoint what it was, but something continued to gnaw at him. What did she mean, "be careful where you frequent"?

Perhaps, I will feel more at peace when she arrives, he thought. If she could see the mission, she couldn't help but be touched. He realized she would not fit in at the mission but other well-situated Christians came to visit from time to time. He made up his mind it would all be fine.

He also wondered if his grandma would ever accept Gretch. Somehow she was not convinced of any change in her in any way, but she said little.

The train whistle blew and Danny stirred in his seat. He rested his head back again only to exchange the last memories for newer ones, as he relived the specter called Gretch.

"Danny, look. That is the kind of home I want. Let's stop and look. I simply must see it. Stop the carriage."

Gretchen would not be thwarted and so they got out of the carriage and walked to the three-story brownstone.

"It is perfect, so grand for entertaining. Don't you think so?"

"But don't you think it is a bit pretentious? Entertaining who?"

"Not for a big city lawyer. We'll be doing oodles of entertaining: all my friends from Europe and all the prominent people in the city. My father knows plenty of them. We will make White Rock a mere pebble in our memory." She sneered, wrinkling her nose and waving her hand to dismiss their hometown.

For a split second, he saw the old childhood twinkle deep in her onyx eyes that told him she would have her way. When he flinched, she softened, touching his arm and drawing him close to her. She looked into his eyes; her pouting lips luring him back into her web.

"Gretch—en, a young lawyer cannot afford this house," he spoke gently.

"But you will be extremely successful, of course. And with my inheritance we shall have it." She let go of his arm and searched out the front ground a bit.

As he stood in front of the expensive house, an old memory came back like a cattle prod.

A young Gretch stood at the candy counter, her eyes burning, her lips tight and her nose pinched.

"I will buy all the candy I want when I get my inheritance. I will have everything I want."

Little Danny was horrified. "But that would mean your parents would be dead."

"So? I don't care." She snapped her pigtails around, took some candy, and stuffed it in her mouth.

The heartless words never left him. He loved his family so much. How could she say such horrid words?

He came back to face an adult Gretchen with a stabbing in the pit of his stomach. "There is the Overlook House, you know." He found himself testing her.

"We'll sell it. What a wonderful idea. We won't be living in that pathetic little town. Your house is awfully provincial, not modern at all, you know. We certainly cannot entertain there." She laughed mockingly and continued her diatribe. "None of my things would fit in, and that awful china. You really should start ridding the house of all that old stuff. And put those archaic paintings in the basement. Nobody would want to purchase it with all those old holy people staring from the wall. This house is more to my liking." She turned to stare again at the upper-class home, narrowing her eyes and smiling premeditatedly.

Danny was beginning to get a sick feeling in his gut. He tried to shake it off and they continued their tour of the city. He thought about the Overlook House, his beautiful family home. She hated all of it. But he wanted to be there, not here, and wanted no part of entertaining her society friends, as she called them. Oh, he must think. He tried to picture her there. He couldn't do it. She hated books and wanted the piano only for her friends to provide dance music, talking incessantly of some woman named Isadora who performed in Europe. She hated his house. How could anyone not love it? Would all women feel the same way about it?

He looked over at her face. It was contorted. He had seen it before. She was calculating how to accomplish what she wanted. It was beginning to unnerve him.

She turned to him and softened her face. "Oh, Danny darling, you look so serious." She fluttered her lashes and smiled.

He stirred in the train seat, as the train horn blew, wondering why all these memories were coming at him, one scene after another. It was as if he needed to see it all. Then another rose up. The final one.

He was finally going to take her to the mission. She had heard about several elegant dress shops downtown, so he catered to her whims and when she was finally done shopping, he directed the carriage toward the mission. As they came close to the entrance, the streets were dank and little shoeless children waded in puddles, squealing happily. The children stopped playing and stared wide-eyed as the fancy carriage slowed before them.

Gretchen's eyes turned stormy. He remembered that look. It made the hairs on the back of his neck rise.

"Danny, this is a dreadful area for a lady to be seen in. How dare you bring me to this wretched place? I am a lady and I do not belong here." She glared at him with a sparking flame.

Her horror at the mission and ministry crushed him. Wasn't she helping the poor herself at home in White Rock? Or was she? Grandma never saw her. Grandma didn't believe it. Was it all a lie?

"It is hideous and vile here. Look at those urchins in the street. A man of your position should not set foot in this part of the city. I warned you about it in my letter. Don't you ever bring me here again," she demanded.

"But Gretchen, it is the Men's Street Mission where I have been working when I can. God has done so much for these men. They have been looking forward to meeting you." He stood at the side of the carriage now, compelling her to come.

"I told you, I didn't want to come." Her voice was livid, her eyes burning, and her nostrils flaring. "I will soil my dress. This is a extremely expensive frock I'll have you know." She was livid. Her perfectly chiseled face contorted into an ugly almost sinister shape.

All at once, Danny's eyes were opened to the truth. It was as if the old Gretch was transported into the present and he was no longer blinded by her beauty nor deceived by her coquettish ways.

Again, she changed her demeanor as he gave in and turned the carriage back. She chatted on and on about the city and Europe and how perfect their new life would be but he found he barely heard a word she said. So that was what she meant about being careful where he frequents. She was talking about the Men's Street Mission.

"Danny, I am famished. Let's go to the restaurant Daddy told me about."

He conceded. His jaw was clenched and his face stoic. He was not ashamed of the mission or the men back there waiting. No—he realized he was ashamed of Gretchen. He wanted to take her back to her hotel and go back to the mission and apologize to the men. Across the street at the mission was precious real life and here was a nightmare right before his eyes. She had not changed at all. She had succeeded in deceiving him one more time—one last time. She was what she had always been—spoiled, selfish, cruel, and malicious. Grandma knew. She always knew. Grandma —wise, sweet Grandma. Forgive me, Grandma. He would never sell the Overlook House. It would break her heart. For that matter it would break his.

After taking Gretchen to her hotel and telling her it was over, he hopped back into the carriage relieved, determined to not go anywhere near any young females any time soon.

Father, I need a wife more like Grandma, my mother, and my sister. I need a godly mate, sweet, unselfish, and kindhearted, who loves you as I do. I will wait until you bring her to me. Oh, Lord, I've been such a fool. You taught me all about this in Proverbs and I still didn't see. I could have lived the rest of my life in bondage to her. Forgive my foolishness and thank you for letting me see the truth before it was too late.

Breaking out in a sweat, Danny pulled out his handkerchief, mopped his forehead, and straightened in his seat. After rehashing much of the Gretchen scenario of his life, he was exceedingly relieved that she was no longer a part of it. Those years had been a long, deceitful ordeal for him.

He reached for a tasty treasure from home and happily shut off the awful memories. A sweet face, laden with long, yellow tresses, swept away the ugly memories. Joy swelled in his heart as he realized Katie was the perfect answer to his prayer in that moment of deliverance from Gretchen so long ago. Where hell's fiery torment once vied for his affections, now was heaven's glory waiting in humility and meekness. He couldn't wait to get home.

CHAPTER TWENTY-ONE

Homecoming and the Tea

It was late and Gwen and Katie were up, mending and talking. When they heard a soft knock and the handle rattle, they both stood.

"It's me, Danny," he said peeking in through the door.

"Danny Boy—you are back sooner than we thought." Gwen's face lightened.

"Here to stay." He dropped his satchel and hugged his grandma warmly. "The trunk will be delivered in the morning. You are up late. I expected you to be in bed."

Katie was elated to see Danny, her heart doing somersaults. His eyes met hers and he stepped closer. She wished she could run over and hug him. Did he want to do the same? If only they could hug like sister and brother as in the Song of Solomon. But he was home and she was overjoyed. The missing piece to their puzzle was in his place and they would be a happy family again.

He walked toward Katie. "Katie, you are a sight for sore eyes. Those scruffy old fellows at the mission were wonderful but not so easy on the eyes as you."

"Well, I call that a roughshod compliment, Daniel." Gwen stood with her arms folded, amused.

His face dropped. "But I didn't mean it that way."

His face started to turn red and the whole scene made Katie start laughing. He looked so pathetic, a big-eyed puppy that didn't know what he'd done wrong. "It's all right. It is good to see you, too. I—we—have missed you a great deal."

It was enough to make him stop and sigh. "It is so good to be home and for good."

That sounded so good to Katie. She hoped he would never leave again.

They settled in and Gwen prepared him a little of their leftover dinner. "Was it hard to go?" she asked Danny, setting a plate at the table.

"Yes, Grandma. The men were so good, so kind, and I saw tears welling up. I felt I had done well with many of them but you always hurt for the ones who left too soon."

"Of course, but you must look at the lives of the ones who had victory and pray for them as well as the others."

"Yes, they all have a special place in my heart."

"We have all been praying for you," Gwen said.

"Yes, especially Jeremy," Katie started, then the women laughed and chorused, "God answered his prayers."

"And just what did our little chap pray?"

"That you would come home in a hurry." Katie smiled, thinking it had been her prayer as well.

"Ah, the little fellow. I missed him so. I told the troops at the mission all about him. I got them to laughing and promised to write and tell them more of his antics."

"Well, we are all glad to have you home."

"I saw Sampson this trip. He was well."

"Sampson? The porter?" Katie asked. "Do you know Sampson?"

"Why, yes, the children mentioned him when you all shared your train stories."

Light dawned for Katie. "Why, it has just come to me. He mentioned your name before we ever came to White Rock. He said a nice gentleman lived in White Rock whose name was Mr. Daniel. I never put it all together."

"Yes, that's what he calls me and here we are."

How wonderful Sampson was and if he only knew she and the children would be staying with Mr. Daniel's own grandmother.

"Tomorrow, Katie will be working her first big Grand Tea for Mrs. Perkins. She has put the entire thing together and will be greeting all the guests and placing them," Gwen said.

"How impressive. Will you be wearing your new dress?"

"Of course, thank you again. But I am nervous."

"You will do wonderfully. How could anyone resist your sweetness?" Gwen said.

"Hear, hear. And when they see how beautiful you look all dressed in green, oh my."

The way he sighed after he said it took Katie aback. He looked embarrassed but it made her feel wonderful. She had not forgotten the look on his face when she first put it on.

They called it a day and as she readied herself for bed, she realized all the anticipation about the Grand Tea tomorrow had been swept away. Katie's thoughts were now focused on Danny: the moment when their eyes met, his calling her beautiful, and when he said it was so good to come home to *his* family.

The next morning joy prevailed in the house again.

"Dandy, Dandy...he's back, Sarrie."

"God really hears your prayers, Jer'my." Sarah ran to Danny and reached for his arm.

After hugs, the happy family ate breakfast, chattering like magpies. Katie excused herself to change from her housedress into the exquisite dress Danny had purchased for her. When she tucked the last curl into her hat she noticed her cheeks no longer looked hollow, thanks to Gwen's good cooking. Even the dress fit better now. She felt young and pretty.

There were grand cheers again when she appeared—all except Danny. It wasn't like him to not say anything. But then his face became one huge grin and she knew he was pleased.

"Dandy's taking us to town." Jeremy jumped around jackrabbit style until Katie captured him.

"Jeremy, settle down, please. We are all happy to have Danny home but we don't want to drive him away, or have Grandma Gwen tell us to find a new place to stay."

Danny started to object but Gwen tugged him back, wagging her head slightly.

"Let's go, little chap, and you and Sarah can tell me all you have been doing while I was away."

"I had better go now, too," Katie said. "There is still so much to do. I am so glad you came home last night. It distracted me from my anxiety about the Grand Tea today."

"I think that is good, to be a distraction." Danny winked at his grandma.

"Well, I didn't mean—" Katie started. She wanted to say it was much more than that.

"All right, we don't want Katie to be late today." Gwen scooted them all out the door. "Danny," she added, "pick up the butter and eggs last from the Sawyers' but don't wait too long. She is going to the orchard today."

"Yes, Captain," he said saluting, making the children giggle.

The happy group made their way to the corner where Katie would take her leave. She kissed the children, thanked Danny, and headed for the Perkins Mansion. She turned once to look back and Danny was still watching her go. She sucked in her cheeks trying not to smile.

The Perkins Mansion was impeccably decorated with flowers and ribbons and extra marble statuary set in grand array. The smell of lemon cake and buttery pastries permeated the hallway as Katie walked through the manse. From the banquet hall she could hear the string quartet practicing. The cello thump-thumped and the violins struck up a waltz. It made her sway merrily as she made her way to her table just outside the open double doors leading to the hall. It reminded her of home. These were the things her mother loved to do and it brought a short stop to her sway. But she would relish the good memories and not the bad. The tables were set with delicate china and teapots on the most pristine white lace tablecloths Katie had ever seen. Waitresses and waiters popped about to put everything in place. It was wonderful having music to work by. She wished she and Gwen could have attended it together.

All was ready and Katie stood gazing the room in her lovely dress—feeling a grand sense of accomplishment, but still a bit nervous that all would go as planned.

From behind her she heard footsteps. "I don't know how you did it, but you are a treasure, Katherine. It is perfect, absolutely perfect. The grandest of Grand Teas I believe I have ever had. You look quite elegant yourself, I might add." Mrs. Perkins and Katie surveyed the ballroom-turned-banquet room in all its grandeur.

"Thank you, Mrs. Perkins."

"Well, I think it is time now for the guests to arrive."

The two women went to their posts. Katie was ready with small program cards all written in her perfect hand, corsages, and her seating list.

Then the woman started to arrive. Those from the city came in exquisite dresses and hats. Then the townswomen arrived and she recognized a few faces from church and around town. It was nice to begin to know some of them. Then another familiar face stood out in the small group that had come in late. A face Katie did not care to see.

Katie felt the cold eyes appraise her disdainfully and heard her snicker to the young woman beside her. "Help is worthless if you overdress them, you know."

The young woman with Gretchen appeared embarrassed by her remark, but Gretchen just snatched her program and chose her own seat as if Katie was not there.

Katie wondered if Gretchen often came in late, commanding an entrance. She was dressed in a deep burgundy gown with black lace edging showing her perfect figure. Her shiny black hair was pulled into an elaborate bun and her hat was tipped just slightly to reveal more black lace and feathers.

Katie watched as she chose whatever chair suited her

and ordered the waitress around. The city ladies were so enthralled with her beauty and costume, they barely noticed her rude behavior. However, the ladies from White Rock purposely ignored her and spoke among themselves.

"Is everything going well?" Mrs. Perkins peered around the corner as most all the ladies had now arrived.

"Yes, perfectly except for one who refused to be seated."

"Ah, let me guess. Miss Gretchen Corbeau?"

"Why, yes, it was."

"It is expected after all these years. If it weren't for her father and business...well, anyway, don't let it bother you." The kind woman smiled and went into the luncheon.

Katie assumed Gretchen had to be invited, although she hadn't seen her name on the list. But there were a few invitations Mrs. Perkins attended to personally. She felt a little sorry about Gwen not being able to attend because of keeping Sarah and Jeremy but she said she had been to more than her share of Grand Teas.

The Tea was truly grand, and when it was over, Mrs. Perkins could not praise Katie's efforts enough. Katie was elated. Being badgered for so long, the praise was a soothing balm to her soul.

She had her back turned away from the doors, as she picked up her lists and cards. From behind her, she heard Gretchen's voice as she passed by, laughing. "She wore that thing to church last Sunday. Well, I guess it is better than her rags. She has certainly taken advantage of Gwen's hospitality."

Again the girl was silent at Gretchen's comment and she glanced back at Katie with a decided frown. Katie once again had her joy drowned in a river of hurtful words.

"She's as nasty as they cum, that one Miss. She is the scourge o' White Rock, I dare say," Molly, the little maid, said, coming from behind her. "Pay her no never mind. She's not worth it. She's as cruel as the devil hisself. Been a torment to every lass who ever was taken with Mr. Daniel. He was under her spell for a season, but his grandmither prayed 'im out, she did. She's a wicked one, that Gretchen." Her eyes sparked and squinted as she shook her little head.

Katie listened intently and wondered at all Molly had said. Gretchen must be worse than she thought and not just a lot of talk. She had spent no little time pondering the comment Gretchen had spoken after church when she said Katie was "used merchandise." It came to her, finally. She didn't mean her *dress*. She meant *Katie* was used merchandise because she had been married. What an appalling thing to say. She had thought that Danny might rather have a woman who had never been married but why did the spiteful beauty make her feel so unworthy of him?

Katie came home tired and not so elated as she had been. Changing into her housedress, she didn't want to eat and yet she was hungry. Gwen coaxed her with fresh hot bread out of the oven with fresh creamy butter and a slice of cheese from the farm nearby. It tasted heavenly and brought her out of her stupor a bit.

Danny wasn't there and she was glad for the moment. Gwen told him it was more appropriate for him to settle back into the Overlook House. But Katie did not much care right at the moment, still dwelling on the "used merchandise" comment.

After dinner, Katie did the dishes and put the food away. Gwen reached for her arm and said, "I'll put the children to bed. You go climb into bed yourself."

"Thank you, Gwen. I am tired."

Gwen always knew. She always knew what was needed.

In, bed, Katie cried out in a tired prayer.

Oh, Father, it is so lovely here and I do love it and I thank you for Gwen and Danny and Mrs. Perkins but I miss my children and I feel so attacked by that heartless Gretchen. What is wrong with her? I haven't done a thing to her.

She didn't pray with a lot of conviction but when she stopped speaking, she heard a still small voice, say,

I never did, either.

CHAPTER TWENTY-TWO

The Picnic

Caught. Katie and Grandma stood looking at Danny as if he were a criminal, as he stuffed the bread in his mouth.

"Got hungry, did you?" Grandma stood with her arms crossed and eyebrows raised.

"I didn't mean to wake you. I just couldn't wait to see everyone this morning." Danny grinned sheepishly, hoping for sympathy.

"You didn't wake me, the sun did," Katie said, smiling at him.

You are the sunshine, he thought as he returned her smile.

Before long a pleasant breakfast of sausage and eggs and Katie's amazing biscuits sat before him.

"Umm...these are so good, Katie." Danny was emphatic. This perfect woman made the best biscuits in the world. He could just sit and look at her and eat biscuits all day.

He noticed she seemed to be elsewhere with her thoughts.

"Is everything alright, Katie?"

"I'm sorry. I guess I just have to sort some things out."

Danny wondered if he was one of the things she had to sort out. He hoped she wouldn't want to sort him out of her life. Maybe she just needed a distraction.

"Say, it's Saturday. Let's go on a picnic," Danny said.

"Oh, boy." Jeremy jumped from his chair ready to go. He whispered to his all-knowing sister. "What is a pig nick?"

Sarah shrugged. "I think it is where you eat out of doors."

"Well, that sounds pleasant for you young folk. I'll stay and do some letter writing," Grandma said.

"Bosh, as you would say. Do you think I would suggest a place you could not go easily? I know just the spot."

"Well, it does sound pleasant. Are you sure?"

"Sure as rain."

"Is it going to rain?" Jeremy looked disappointed.

"No, no little chap, just an expression. Look at all the sunshine."

"Katie, let's see what we can whip out here in the kitchen." Grandma was excited now.

They put together a wonderful lunch and the happy group set out for Danny's special spot. They walked into the backcountry and settled close to the creek bed area, which elated the children. Danny and Jeremy caught crawdads and sent the females backing away. They all waded but when they got too wild Katie and Gwen retreated to the quilt.

"They are having so much fun. I think Danny is the

biggest kid of all," Katie said, listening to the laughter coming from the creek with splashing and occasional squeals.

Katie was finally resting but all the week's events began jumping into her head.

As they sat on the big quilt resting, Gwen asked, "Is anything bothering you, child?"

"Gwen, am I always so easy to detect? I'm afraid you'll think me foolish."

"Nonsense, what is eating at you? Something has been troubling you since the tea. Didn't it go well?"

"No—yes. The tea was perfect. Mrs. Perkins was elated. But Gretchen showed up. I hadn't noticed her name on the list. Maybe Mrs. Perkins was hoping she would be out of town. She was horribly rude and said some ugly things again. But I think I am beginning to understand what she meant by what she said outside the church. I thought she was talking about my dress, that maybe she had bought it and taken it back. I think she was talking about Danny and she was talking about me. I was used merchandise. No man wants used merchandise."

Gwen's mouth dropped. "Oh, how horrid. What a lie that is—right from the fire of hell. It is a heartless thing to say and so untrue. Certainly you don't believe it?"

"I don't know, maybe she's right. I hadn't thought much about it before."

"That is absurd. That may be so of a floozy but never of anyone as precious and pure as you are. Tell me, child, do you think Boaz felt that way about Ruth?"

"Of course not. He must have loved her a great deal to even take a Moabitess. He was so kind and caring."

"I believe that, too. He married both a widow and a Moabitess. You are a beautiful treasure as she was in his eyes. It is no wonder that Gretchen spews her hate so viciously at you. Don't you see all the men who look your way when we go to town? Not to mention Danny. He is enamored with you."

Katie was surprised. "I never noticed the men. Danny? With me?"

"Child, are you blind?"

"Well, I guess I have seen or felt there might be something there. I was afraid I was imagining it."

"He is overly cautious when it comes to women. Gretchen would make any man walk in trepidation having been beguiled by her."

Katie wanted to know more but didn't ask, besides the giggling trio made their way to the little picnic spot.

He is enamored with me?

"We don't have to eat the crawdads do we, Danny?" Sarah held her tongue out in disgust.

"Heavens no, princess, we will enjoy the wonderful fare of Grandma Gwen and Lady Katherine, your mother, who live by yonder castle." Danny waved his chivalrous arms, making them all laugh.

"That looks yummy, I am sammiched," Jeremy said.

"I believe that would be a colloquialism for, 'I am famished and I will be wanting a sandwich,'" Danny translated.

"Jer'my, you are a little piglet," Sarah scolded.

"Yes, indeed and I am a big fat hog." Danny blew his cheeks out and the children giggled.

"Well, I do believe we have a couple of silly fellows here

with us today. Perhaps they would better qualify for court jesters," Katie retorted back, feeling a little of her joy return after her talk with Gwen.

"No doubt. Perhaps we should stop their chatter with some food."

Jeremy giggled as his mother dried his feet and tickled them as she helped put his socks and shoes back on.

"So little princess, do you want help with your socks?" Danny's eyes twinkled with mischief.

Obviously, Sarah knew better than to get her feet tickled. She shook her head and quickly put her shoes and socks on, but she giggled anyway.

"Foiled." Danny sat back and folded his arms.

"Let's pray and eat," Gwen said.

They were well fed and reclining, finding elephants and big white angels and all manner of things in the clouds.

Then Katie shared about the wonderful Gethsemane cloud experience they had before they left Bitter Springs. "That was no fairy story. It was so real and perfect. I was overwhelmed. I still am."

"It sounds glorious," Danny said.

"A real gift from the Father," Gwen added.

"We saw it, too. Then it disappeared." Sarah looked up, remembering.

"It dist-appeared." Jeremy shook his little mop head and lifted his animated arms in the air.

After more stories and much laughter, the sun was sinking in the sky and they all knew it was time to head back to the cottage.

But it was Gwen who got things afoot. "I am sorry to spoil the fun, but it is getting late and I don't want to be too tired to make it home. I don't want you to send a mule after me."

"Of course." Katie laughed at the thought and jumped up quickly to put everything together.

Danny gently pulled his grandmother to her feet. "My arm, fair lady, shall we reclaim the castle?" And with one arm for Grandma Gwen, the picnic basket on the other, and Jeremy on his back they headed home. Katie and Sarah came alongside with the quilt and odds and ends from the day's adventures.

"Dandy, we didn't climbed any trees."

"We sure didn't, little chap. But we will search for Robin Hood next time and climb the lookout trees."

What a wonderful family you sent us to, Lord. Gwen and Danny are such a joy. He is such a gentleman, always taking care of all of us. He is a delight without being a fool or lazy. And Gwen is the perfect grandmother. I don't ever want to leave this comfort. I have never been so happy.

When they reached the cottage, Danny put the children down with some books. His grandma decided to take a short nap at Katie's insistence and Katie said she would clean up the picnic basket.

Danny didn't want to miss a second of a chance to visit with Katie. When he came out from tending the children, she had made tea and unwrapped tea biscuits for the two of them.

"I'm afraid they are worse for wear. Not a peep left in them."

"Thank you for settling them down. You made it a

wonderful day for them."

"They are wonderful. What a fun picnic, or should I say pig nick?"

As Katie curled up in the chair with her hair in disarray and her cheeks pink from the sun, Danny sighed. Her hair was sunshine itself and her eyes glistening stars. He dared not look much more for if he looked at her lips he would be inclined to kiss them. He looked away momentarily, sipping at his tea, in hopes of recapturing some sanity. Never had anyone had such an effect on him.

"It was a perfect day, thanks to you."

"I surely did not make those delicious popovers. But it was a great day, wasn't it? The children seem to be in their glory. You have raised wonderful little ones, despite all your obstacles. They have made me laugh so much my jaws hurt. It is such a contrast to the last few years for me." He rubbed his sore jaw.

"Was it hard at the mission?"

"Yes and no. When the men responded to the love of Christ, it was so rewarding. But those who went back to their derelict life grieved me. I learned to continue to hope and pray for them and yet let go of them and work with the ones at hand. In the last few months, I sensed God was calling me on. Then a letter came to confirm it. They had a couple to be a permanent fixture. By the time the letter came, I was prepared and ready. It is interesting how God does that."

"Yes, I sensed it, too, before I left. I kept thinking it would come in the form of money from my sister but it came in a much different way. I guess the Lord had to do something to push me all the way out. But I am so glad to be here. I feel I have gone from darkness into sunshine."

"You look like sunshine," Danny slipped out, looking intently at her sun-tinged face.

"My father used to call me that when I was little. It was very endearing."

"It fits you perfectly."

She blushed and quickly asked, "Will you write now? Perhaps the wonderful stories of the mission men?"

"I would love to but I must also earn a living for us." He had intended to say for Grandma and me but he could not bring himself to exclude Katie and the children. To him it would have been a lie.

"God will put it all together. Look at what he did for me? I should never have worried for a moment, but of course I did."

"We all do. Maybe someday we will learn this lesson of faith. Right now, I have faith that some of Grandma's cake is still in the pantry."

"Do we dare?" She smiled in conspiracy. They both jumped up and took their teacups into the kitchen.

"And what is she going to do, spank us with her wooden spoon?" He grinned as he turned to face her.

Katie laughed. "I can see you as a bad little boy, getting a wooden spoon spanking."

"Can you? Well, it happened once or twice."

"Must have been hard."

"The spanking?"

"No, I meant spanking such an adorable little boy."

He reached to push back a curl from her face. He drew closer unable to breathe and he felt her breathing grow stronger.

She feels it, too.

"Katie, you are the loveliest woman I have ever met and you have a sweet and pure heart. I never want to be away from you ever again."

He could feel the warmth of her cheek close to his. A sudden catch in her breath when he spoke the words gave him hope. He wanted to hold her passionately and kiss her and restrained himself but she nearly melted into his arms and he held her gently for a long moment. It was enough. It was an acknowledgement that she felt the same. Cne could live with this memory for some time. They gently backed away and looked at each other.

"Oh, Katie..." he whispered but the household was stirring and the sounds brought them out of their daze.

Out of the corner of his eye, Danny caught a glimpse of his grandma down the hall, as she popped out and saw them. She backed into her bedroom. Was that a smile he saw on her face?

CHAPTER TWENTY-THREE

Vindicated

The little family sat contentedly in the pew. Jeremy sat between his beloved Dandy and Katie, his busy legs dangling from the bench and Sarah sat on Katie's other side snuggled next to Grandma Gwen. Then Katie saw Gretchen come from a different pew to sit directly behind them. She could feel those piercing eyes penetrating her back. The pastor preached on the book of Ruth and Gwen leaned forward and winked at Katie. She smiled back, remembering their earlier talk about Boaz and Ruth. Strange, how her used merchandise accuser sat directly behind them during this particular sermon. She hoped Gretchen would listen to the message but somehow she felt it would not be the case.

When the service was over, Danny stood and turned to exit the pew.

"Why, Danny darling, it's so good to see you home again. We have missed our favored boy," Gretchen drawled. She tried to grab his arm as he exited the pew but he pulled it down to pick up Jeremy and offered the other affectionately to Katie. Giving Gretchen a short unemotional "thank you," he turned his eyes toward his real friends who had gathered to say hello.

Gretchen would not be thwarted, her eyes smoldered. "Well, aren't you going to introduce me?" she asked, nodding toward Katie.

Quite matter-of-factly, Danny said, "I do believe you have already met." His eyebrows rose at her audacity and he turned again to his friends.

Katie watched Gretchen's dark eyes broaden at Danny's words, then contort into beady accusers as she stared Katie into oblivion. Katie saw a darker depth in her raven eyes than she had seen previously and she looked away. She knew Gretchen had been expecting to draw Danny away and she had been highly slighted. Somehow, Katie sensed this would scarcely be the end of Gretchen's attentions and it made her uneasy.

As they walked toward the cottage, Katie felt thoroughly vindicated by Danny. Gwen chattered happily with the children who had been bribed with helping her make dinner, leaving the two of them to meander home.

Katie did not want to let go of Danny's arm. It was so strong and protective and comforting. Suddenly he stopped.

"There's the house." Danny looked toward the Overlook House peeking out between the trees.

"It is the most beautiful house I have ever seen. Someone should paint it."

"Audrey, my cousin, was always going to do it but put it off waiting for a perfect time and suddenly we left it. It stood in its soft, spring-green glory with the Live Oaks seeming to call to them with their welcoming arms."

"You really do like it, don't you?" He turned to look at her.

"Oh, yes, Danny, it's heavenly—like being home only better. The library, the gardens, the lovely furnishings, I don't think one could dream of anything more wonderful."

"Yes, it is special place I cannot let go of—"

"Oh, you must never give it up." She was distressed at such a thoughts. But she caught herself quickly, looking down. "I'm sorry. It's none of my business. It is just so wonderful and a part of your heritage."

He smiled, looking pleased instead of upset at her intrusion. "I have no desire to give it up. I hope it will always be in my family. You know, you can see both the sunrise and the sunset from there. The family was careful not to plant any trees that would block the view."

"I remember the sunset when you were there. You made us all feel so at home."

"I'm so glad. That reminds me. I had a dream last night." He hesitated.

"A dream?"

"Yes, I was sitting in the library and we had been reading and talking about what we had read. I was watching as you started playing the piano, then you left the piano and we had a waltz together around the library. The funny thing was the piano kept playing the waltz while we danced and we thought nothing of it."

They laughed together. "What a lovely dream and funny, too. I did so enjoy playing the piano. I am afraid I was quite lost in the music. It was so restful for me after all those hard years." She was not about to mention her own dreams like the latest one where he was holding her close and they were watching the sunset from outside the Overlook House, but it made her smile that he was having dreams of her as well.

"You know, your tunes stayed with me. They helped me through the last days until I came home."

"Really? How nice."

They walked a few steps then they turned again to look at the house. "I can't wait to show you the things you missed. I think we should go up there soon"

"That sounds wonderful. Could we take your grandma, too?"

"Of course. I will borrow a wagon or carriage."

Excited with their new plans, the couple walked home at a quicker pace. Then he paused and looked down. "Katie?"

"Yes?"

"Do you mind if I ask you something?"

"Of course not." He sounded serious and it made her a little nervous. They continued at a slower pace.

"Your husband, do you miss him a great deal? Perhaps it's wrong of me to ask."

She thought for a moment. It was a hard question for her. She didn't know quite how to say what she felt.

"Death and loss are always a shock. It seems when you lose one person in your life and you have lost others in the past, they all come toppling down on you. I had already lost my parents. I barely knew Morgan even after five years of marriage. He was always gone, searching for the moon or rather the elusive gold. When he came home, the children didn't even know him. He was like a character in a book. You know them but they are intangible and unreal. To be honest, Danny, I saw so little of him in those last years, I only missed the hope of what could have been and never really was. He wasn't a bad man, just...absent. The Lord became my husband. My life has been spent in his Word and on my children. I tried to tell them good things about their father and teach them about their heavenly Father."

"Your life must have been so difficult." His kind tone blessed her and his eyes radiated compassion, making her lose her composure.

"Yes, but God carried me and taught me a lifetime of lessons that, hopefully, I can teach my children."

"Sarah and Jeremy are the most delightful children I have ever encountered. They have surely won our hearts Katie, as you have done." He looked straight at her. She took the genuine expression of his feelings into her lonely heart. She felt she never wanted to be without him. But was this even possible? "Used merchandise" ran through her head and she bowed her head as the enemy continued to strike at her through the words of a raven-haired messenger.

"I hope Grandma and I can make your lives a little better."

"But you already have." She looked up into his tender brown eyes, hoping she could make him see how much she meant it. His lips thinned into a smile making her smile back.

They finally made it to the cottage to a frustrated Jeremy, who had been watching for them. He lit up as they approached the door. The Dutch door was closed at the bottom and he stood on a stool behind it, his arms folded.

"Kind sir, may we enter? The fair princess is famished, I believe." Danny bowed to the doorkeeper.

"But you are lated and all the gin-gin bread has been

ated." Jeremy shook his head seriously, his little lips firm but twisting, trying not to smile.

"Ah, a poet watchman. You don't say. We missed the royal gingerbread?" Danny frowned.

"Did you eat it all yourself, Little Prince?" Katie played along.

"Of coursed. You are too lated and I think you will have to stay outside now."

"Do have mercy, kindly little prince. You wouldn't leave us out in the cold tonight." Danny pleaded in all earnest.

"It's not cold."

Sarah giggled and came to open the door.

"Ah, Sarrie, they will eat all the gin-gin bread." Jeremy grimaced at his sister.

"Aha, it isn't really gone." Danny pursed his lips and ran after Jeremy, swinging him in the air after he caught him, his giggles making everyone laugh.

"Grandma Gwen said she was making a bit of gin gin bread."

"So that explains why you were being so selfish. But that is not like you, son. Perhaps you shouldn't have any." Katie's reprimand produced the shamed face she had hoped for.

"He has been busy helping me cook, maybe just this once?" Gwen said, "after supper of course."

"I'm sorry we took so long, I should have been here helping you," Katie said.

"Nonsense. You need to have some time to enjoy yourself. I had plenty of help."

They chatted about the sermon, the Overlook House, and the meal Gwen and the children were preparing. Danny helped Katie set the table.

"Fried chicken's my favorite. I got to help maked the tatoes," Jeremy touted.

"Everything is your favorite, silly."

"No, Sarrie, I don't like sparegust." Sarah nodded, remembering.

Danny raised one questioning eyebrow at Katie.

"Well, Jeremy, I think even asparagus might taste wonderful if Grandma Gwen made it." Katie winked at Danny.

"Indeed. We are truly blessed with two amazing cooks in the same household. Asparagus—of course." He rolled his eyes.

"Well, I don't think I could be compared with your grandma. But I do want to learn all her wonderful recipes. The chicken smells delicious."

Later the little company was trying out Jeremy's new favorite and the visiting was nil as they were completely absorbed in the mouthwatering fare. Their plates were full of crunchy fried chicken, mashed potatoes, and garden picked green beans.

"Gwen, I have never had fried chicken this good and when I was young I went to many fine restaurants."

"The secret is cream." Gwen winked.

With barely any of the perfectly crusted chicken left, they rested and decided the gingerbread would have to wait until later.

Danny and Katie insisted on cleaning up and the children played in the side yard. Gwen went back to lie down. Again the two of them were left alone to talk.

Katie noticed he was deep in thought. "You seem a little troubled."

"Yes, a little, I suppose. I haven't clear directions from the Lord about what I am to do next. I guess it is time to climb the hill and have a good long talk with him."

"I find the hardest time to hear is when you're overwhelmed. You can make the body sit still but the mind just keeps running."

"You are a woman of much wisdom for one so young. And when you are overwhelmed, it is the very time you need to hear. I know I must lay all my ideas before the Lord, and generally, he will have his own ideas."

"Better ones. He directed me here but not because I was fully listening. Had I listened, perhaps it would have been easier. Nonetheless, God still directed my steps."

"I am so glad he brought you to us."

"So am I. I don't think I have ever been happier.'

"Nor I." For a moment their eyes connected and neither said a word until the children came charging in with adventurous tales from the yard.

Gwen came into the kitchen looking chipper.

"Is it timed for gin-gin bread, now?" Jeremy asked wide-eyed.

"With whipped cream on top," Sarah added, licking her lips.

Soon they sat around the table thoroughly enjoying their plates of warm gingerbread with fresh whipped cream. The happy family spent the rest of their evening in song and stories of their lives.

"We had singing chickens once," Sarah said giggling.

"But Sarrie, you tolded me they weren't singing,' Jeremy said scowling.

"They really weren't singing. But Jeremy was sure they

were because their mouths were open so big," Sarah said.

"They were panting and needed water," Katie explained.

"They looked like they were singing."

"Ah, well I am sure they did," Grandma Gwen said gently.

"I think chickens sing like this. And Danny started to cluck and the children joined in."

As the laughter wore down and the family rested quietly, sleepiness took hold of the little ones.

Jeremy fell asleep on Danny's lap and he finally put him to bed and Gwen read to Sarah out of her Bible storybook at her bedside. Katie cleaned up the gingerbread dishes.

Danny came back into the living room just as Katie had finished in the kitchen.

"Well, I suppose it is time to go up the hill. I think I shall have a good long listen. Looks as if I still enough light out if I hurry. I will be back when God sends me." He got up, gathered a few things together, and stood facing her.

"I will be praying for you," she said, her eyes unable to pull away from his.

He took her hand and held it to his lips, kissing it softly. Her heart stirred.

"Would you please tell Grandma not to expect me as I will be praying and will be back as soon as possible? I will stay until he tells me to come back."

"Of course."

"Good night, sweet Katie." He gently brushed her cheek with his warm hand. She watched as his tender eyes danced all over her face, then picked up his things and left for the hill. She almost wished he would turn around and run to her and take her into his arms.

Gwen came into the room as Katie stood at the side door and toward the back hills. "Has he gone for the night?"

"Yes, he said not expect him, that he must go and have a long listen, as he put it."

"Ah." She nodded in understanding. "We must pray for him then."

As the two women stood at the door looking after the trek of a determined beloved young man, they prayed for divine wisdom and the answers he needed.

When they finished their prayer, Katie turned her head toward the garden. "Gwen look—the rosebush."

"Ah, the bridal bush. It must have happened overnight. What a lovely sight. I don't believe they have ever bloomed quite like that. If we cut a few, they will keep on blooming."

"Is that what you call the bush, the bridal bush?"

"Well, yes, sort of. When I first saw the blooms on the bush, I said to myself, that is Danny's Bride. She will be like those roses, sweet and gentle, beautiful at every stage of bloom, soft and delicate. I felt his bride should carry them on her wedding day." Gwen went after the trimmer and vase.

"Oh," Katie barely spoke. She was embarrassed by the fact that they were her favorite roses. Why hadn't Gwen told her before?

Danny's Bride. Her heart jumped. How blessed it would be to be Danny's bride.

Gwen returned and clipped them off while Katie held the vase. Gwen took a bud and placed it near Katie's face. "They suit you, you know. They match your skin tone and your lovely pure heart."

CHAPTER TWENTY-FOUR

Bittersweet Bribery

"Sooo, Miss Ruby, tell me about this Katie who is staying with Grandma Gwen?" Gretchen made her voice as sickeningly sweet as the elaborate table she had set before Miss Ruby.

The two unlikely diners sat at Ruby's table filled with all manner of chocolates and pastries prepared exhaustively by Gretchen's cook at her command. Gretchen offered them generously trying to squeeze all the information she could get out of Ruby like a sponge.

It was thoroughly offensive to her to visit with one so beneath her in social rank and breeding. She knew sitting in the foolish old woman's kitchen would be a difficult task, but she had no choice.

"Umm, these is so good," Ruby mumbled while packing the queen's dainties into her mouth.

"So do tell," Gretchen prodded, tapping her fingers.

"Well, I was told she lived with a mean uncle what treated her real bad and he was a lookin' for her and the youngens and we was not to say nothin' 'bout her and the youngens to this stranger fella who came to town. You didn't know that? Anyways, seems he was sent by the uncle. Oh, mercy, I am wantin' to try one more of them crunchty ones, them is good." She giggled and reached for more.

Gretchen shooed them toward Ruby, her lip curled and nausea welling up. How long could she endure the woman's vulgar mannerisms and language. Looking about the kitchen, she was concerned her dress might be soiled just sitting on the woman's chair, as everything in her kitchen looked as though it was an extension of her garden, soil and all. Gretchen wanted to wring out every detail to take her revenge. She had always succeeded in the past. Danny would finally be hers to rule over. He wasn't going to run from her as he had done in the past. Not this time. He would come back to her begging for her and those blonde curls could fry in the desert for all she cared.

Grabbing a few chocolates Ruby hadn't touched, she popped them in her mouth and pretended to be socializing with Ruby. Acting her part well, she casually interrogated the old gossip, "How interesting. Is there more? Where did she...they... come from?"

"Uh, Sour River, Bitter Creek, nah." She pressed her fingertips to her head, leaving spots of chocolate. "But somethin' like that. I'll 'member it in a minute. That allus happens when you just go on to somethin' else." She chuckled and pulled at a popover, her hands glued with sugar crystals and cherries.

Eventually Ruby did remember and Gretchen took note. Bitter Springs.

"Ya know, I been thinkin' Dan'el's kind a sweet on her. About time he settled down—had some youngens. Don't ya think, Mith Greshen?"

Ruby's words started to slur, her mouth filled with chocolate and pastry. Ruby looked up with her big grey eyes and her smile revealed chocolate between every visible tooth in her mouth, where there were teeth.

Gretchen's eyes flamed when it dawned on her what Ruby had just said. Danny sweet on that little no account blonde? It was hard enough to stomach Ruby with chocolate coated teeth and sugar-crusted lips but to say such words! Demented old fool. The rage boiled but she bit her lip until it hurt. She could have thrown every drop of her bakery cuisine in the uncouth woman's face, but she thought better of it. She may need her later.

Having drawn all the information out of her that seemed plausible, she took a few chocolates from the untouched area of the lavish spread. She left Miss Ruby to gorge herself, begging an important appointment and was off.

Her mind was spinning like a black spindly spider that spins her web, fooling her prey with her tiny threads, unseen to the unsuspecting. She thought how nice it would be to arrange a nice little family reunion for Katie and her uncle. The blonde vixen would go back to a place of suffering and hardship. The thought exhilarated her. She breathed a deep breath of victory. But she couldn't celebrate yet. There was work to be done.

Glad to reach her stately mansion she threw the doors open. "She'll not take Danny from me," she mumbled under her breath. "No one takes what is mine." The more she thought of Ruby's last comment, the more the fury stirred within her. Jealousy flamed hotter with every step she took up the long opulent staircase to her room and it would push her to procure her plan.

She removed her black hat with its fine white feathers, tossing it for the maid to pick up and admired herself from head to toe in her massive gilded mirror. Gretchen knew full well most men idolized her and she could easily lure someone to do her dirty work with a little help from daddy's bank account. But this time she might have to do some things on her own. For a split second the rebuff Danny had given her flashed before her. Her eyes pinched. Danny will never escape me. Her glare turned back to the mirror. It changed to a smile at the vision she saw looking back at her. A woman so tantalizing, no man could resist.

No one except Danny, her inner enemy derided.

Her eyes burned with rage turning her smile into a sinister smirk. She ripped the pins out of her hair and let the shiny obsidian mass slither across her shoulders until it reached her hips.

"He is just distracted. That will soon be remedied," she answered the enemy in her head.

"Knock, knock," said Gwen peeking through Ruby's back door, which had been left ajar.

"Oh, come on in, Gwennie. Look at all my sweets." She motioned with her arms across the table. Gwen's mouth dropped open at the array of baked goods and chocolates set in front of her friend. It was like a full city bakery at one place setting.

"I was just returning your rake, Ruby."

"Have a seat and try some of these. I just love them crunchty chocolates. Oh, and them popovers is best I ever had."

"Where did all this come from?" Gwen asked, slipping into a chair in shock.

"Well, it was Miss Gretchen. She just come over and brung all this. Just left a bit ago."

"Gretchen? What did she want?" Gwen's brows furrowed.

"Oh, she was chattin' with me. Here, Gwenie, have a clare, I think she called them. I better quit. My tummy's feeling kind of queasy."

"I believe they call it an éclair, Ruby. I should think you would be miserable. Gretchen has that effect on people," Gwen grumbled.

"Huh?"

"Oh, nothing. So, what were you two chatting about?" she asked as nonchalantly as she could.

"Well, let's see. We was talkin' about Katie and where she come from. Then she up and run off. Said she had a 'pointment. Didn't mention it aforehand. Just got up all the sudden."

"What were you talking about just before she left?"

"I was sayin' how it looks like Danny is taken with Katie."

"Oh my," Gwen said under her breath.

"Don't ya think so, Gwennie? They make a right handsome couple."

"Yes, I suppose they do." So Ruby had indulged more than sweets with the vindictive young woman.

"Where is your bicarb, Ruby?" Gwen went to the cupboard Ruby pointed to and pulled it out.

"Thank you, Gwennie. I guess I overdone it." She looked a little green but happy.

"Someone sure worked awful hard making all these delicacies." She shook her head.

Ruby offered for her to take them home, but the thought of anything coming from the home of Gretchen made them highly unpalatable. Ruby was oblivious. But that was Ruby. She was an innocent sort and kind-hearted, rarely seeing evil for what it was. God seemed to protect her.

Gwen fed her friend her medicine, wrapped some of the treats for Ruby and left when she felt Ruby was better. As she walked back to the cottage, her head was in a spin. Would Gretchen have had her servants create this feast just to find out about Katie? She wouldn't have come near Ruby's house unless she was serious about something and why would she want to know where Katie came from?

What was Gretchen up to?

CHAPTER TWENTY-FIVE

Down from the Hill

Two days came and went and Danny had not come back from the Overlook House. Jeremy was moping around and none of them was particularly cheerful. They all seemed to be waiting for their beloved Danny.

Gwen piddled in the kitchen after supper and Sarah and Jeremy played quietly on the rug. Katie tidied the living room and picked up the vase of precious pink roses. She pulled them to her face soaking in their fragrance and thinking about what Gwen had said, that they matched her lovely heart. What a sweet thing to say.

The side door rattled, and Katie turned around to see Danny staring at her. He looked at her, then at the roses, and then he stepped backwards out the door, craning to see something. Was it his rosebush, which they had been cutting from all week? When he stepped back in, his smile broadened.

Her eyes magnified. He knew—he knew the name of these roses—Danny's Bride. She nearly dropped them. Danny stood, looking elated at the sight of her holding the vase of roses.

Jeremy ran for him. "Dandy, Dandy, did you seed God like Moses?"

Danny laughed, shaking his head as he lifted Jeremy up, setting his Bible on the table.

"No, not quite like Moses, little chap but he does speak to me."

"Did God tolded you to be my daddy?" Jeremy looked up at him with big brown hopeful eyes.

Katie nearly choked trying to get her mouth to work. "Jeremy! You shouldn't say things like that." She was glad she had set the roses down.

"Why not? I love Dandy. He is a bestest daddy for me and Sarrie. We think so, huh Sarrie?" Jeremy looked over at Sarah who was trying to hide behind a book.

Katie swallowed hard, struggling to find words. "Well, darling, we must not ask him such things. He is our special friend. Isn't that a nice thing?"

"Yes," he answered quietly.

"Then, let's just enjoy his company for now, okay?"

"Okayed." A little satisfied, he hugged Danny.

"Perhaps the children have had their own talk with the Lord," Danny said, winking at Sarah and Gwen. Gwen raised her brows and suppressed a smile and Sarah brightened, dropping her book down.

Gwen cut in, trying to relieve the situation. "Well, I do hope you have heard some good things in prayer."

"I certainly have but not all I need yet. God seems to speak what he wants me to know for now and not necessarily what I think I need to know." His smile disappeared as he finished the sentence and he appeared lost in thought.

"Then you shouldn't worry for he will show you in due time," Gwen said as if it were old hat for her. "I have something for you to eat if you are ready."

"Yes, I am hungry. I have missed my two extraordinary cooks."

Danny mentioned a few of the things in his prayer time that God encouraged him about but Katie could tell he held back much. She wondered at what he didn't share.

The family seemed back to normal by evening with Bible reading and songs and a quick game of dominoes with the children.

"Well, it has been fun but it is time for bed. I must be up early as Mrs. Perkins has new household arrivals coming in tomorrow. I can't imagine what will come. She has so many already. I suppose she must enjoy them, but most of them are hideous."

"Idols from other countries," Danny said. "That is why they look hideous. I saw some at the legal office. John seemed enamored by the ugly things. People just don't realize some of these things are images of ancient gods that people worshipped and some worship even today."

"It seems people really go in for these things from the Orient and elsewhere. I heard the ladies from the city talking at the Grand Tea. I much prefer the way you have decorated the cottage and the house on the hill. They are inviting and warm and yet elegant."

"I guess we all think alike around this house," Gwen said.

"I remember when I went to John's office, I kept thinking about how you would all hate the grotesque decorations."

"I suppose if I have a home one day, then I will decorate it just like you have," Katie said, hating even the thought of ever having to leave them.

She caught Danny look at Gwen and she smiled back at him. He winked and Katie wondered at it.

"Yes, I do believe we are a perfectly agreed little family. Now come on, little chap and I will tuck you in." He got down on all fours to give Jeremy a ride.

"Me, too?" Sarah asked shyly.

"That goes without saying, little princess. Hop on." Danny the horse hobbled all the way to bed with squealing children on his back. Gwen went to the kitchen with Katie following.

"Can I do anything to help for tomorrow, Gwen?"

"No, child, it is all done and ready. Go on to bed. I guess we kept our boy too long for him to go back up the hill, but he can bunk on the couch tonight."

"Good night." Katie yawned and gave her a kiss on the cheek.

"Good night, angel. Sweet dreams."

Katie smiled to herself. I have surely had a great deal of those lately.

Danny came back into the kitchen with the children delivered happily to their room.

"Is it just the two us?" he asked.

"Yes, Katie had a hard day at work today."

"I wish she didn't have to work. It seems odd her

working so hard and me doing nothing."

"Trust in the Lord. He has this all figured out. You know even if you were working, you wouldn't be able to persuade her to stop. She doesn't belong to you, son."

"I know but we seem like such a happy little brood."

"Did our Father have anything to say about that?" She hoped he would tell her.

"Yes, I believe he has, Grandma. But you know I must have a job to provide for us. I guess I don't understand why he hasn't shown me what to do yet."

"He will. Don't get anxious. I can see what is happening here and what is between your two hearts. If God is in it, all will come to fruition and he will show you soon, I am sure of it."

"You love her, too, don't you?" His big brown eyes looked hopeful.

She smiled at him and brushed his jaw with her little hand. "From the day she came to stay."

They hugged and she went on to bed, with prayers for the little ones, and the lovestruck ones and for protection for them from other ones who would seek to harm them.

CHAPTER TWENTY-SIX

Plans Set in Motion

Gretchen took a deep breath, wishing she could hold it until she left town. But she had business—important business—so she disembarked the train at Bitter Springs. People gawked in every direction. She paid her meager tip reluctantly to the porter and made her way to the tasteless hotel. Securing herself a room, she went to the closest grouping of people who hung around listlessly by the door of the dry goods shop.

Gretchen had worn her cheapest dress but they still stared. A few people loitered inside the dusty store. She could feel them following her every move. She was uncomfortable but not intimidated. No one intimidated her. But she didn't relish being in this crude little town.

She stepped inside. "Does anyone know a Katie who lives around here?" she asked scanning the room, holding her skirts close to keep from touching anything or anyone.

Silence answered her, until the droll voice of the proprietress responded. "Used to be a Katie. Never much saw her, but a time or two. Took over for her aunt when she passed. I heard tell she skipped town on the rails."

"Where did she live?"

"Out to the haller."

"Is her uncle still here?"

"Yup."

"Know where I can find him?" Her teeth clenched.

"Yup."

"Is he around?" Her eyes blazed and her foot tapping in irritation.

"Nope."

She was fuming. She glared at the obnoxious people and set her jaw but took a deep breath and finally asked the right question, the right way, "Tell me, just where does her uncle work and where can I find the place?" She was fit to be tied and they knew it and it didn't rattle them in the least. They looked at her with blank, emotionless eyes except a few younger fellows who nosed into the store and grinned at each other a time or two, jabbing each other in the ribs.

"Down to the repair shop." The proprietress pointed at the road.

"I'll 'scort you, miss," a tall gangly bumpkin offered. She gave a short nod. He offered his arm but she backed away, picked up her skirts, and followed him out. The hoots and hollers started and the half-dead crew came to life tripping out the door and craning out the windows as their friend walked with Gretchen down the street.

Fools, she thought, as if it meant anything that this ill-bred, tree-sized idiot escorted her to the shop.

She quickened her pace, hoping to get her business done and get out of this pigsty.

"There 'tis," the boy said pointing to the uncle's shop.

Not bothering to say thank you, Gretchen rushed in.

She stood before a huge rough sort of man but it didn't deter her for a second. She didn't mince words.

"Are you Katie's uncle?"

"Who wants to know?" His voice bellowed and then he bent over coughing.

"You do, if you are," she snapped back. "I came to tell you that I know where she is."

"And why should I care?" He squinted at her suspiciously.

"You were looking for her, weren't you?" she persisted, but was beginning to worry.

"Yup, when she run off." He kept on hammering, between coughs.

"Well, I know exactly where you can find her."

"Well, I got papers sayin' she's fine and only to contact her through a lawyar."

"What?" She was stunned. She had to think fast. Legal papers? Ah, of course, Danny must have done this.

She changed her tactics. "Surely, you want her back?" She dug up all the sweet sounding inflection she could muster, her old tactics, which had worked well on her father.

"Maybe. Who are you and what do you want?" He was getting irritable. She sensed he was going to cut the conversation off soon.

"I just want you to come and get her."

"Can't." He coughed deeply and she backed away.

"Get someone else to do it."

"Don't think so." He kept working.

"I'll pay. You arrange it."

He spied her with narrowed eyes. "So what's it to you?"

"She is in my way."

He continued to hammer on the wagon wheel. She was losing patience.

"How'll the fella get paid?"

"I'll be at the hotel. But I leave in the morning. Ask for Miss Corbeau—er, uh—Corbit. He will be quite happy with the amount, I assure you."

Tyler grunted.

With that much arranged, Gretchen wasted no time. She did not want this barbarian to change his mind. She had to be rid of Katie and she would stop at nothing. The slip-up with her name made her angry with herself and she hoped the coughing man didn't catch it. She also hoped she didn't catch some nasty disease from the man.

Gretchen pampered herself with her stash of chocolates and pastries she made the cook produce for the trip and waited for a message. She waited all evening, frustrated that no one came. It was deplorable being without a maid or boy to do her errands but she didn't want to take any chances to bring anyone along. If Moira had been here, Gretchen could have thrown off her dress and petticoats and had her burn them. She struggled to undress, something she had barely done by herself before. She ended up sleeping in her dress, afraid she couldn't get her corset back on or get herself buttoned back up and she didn't want any of the vile people here to touch her.

The next morning the message came. Someone was downstairs to see her.

She met him at the bottom of the stairs. He looked evil, disgusting. Perfect—he will do. She had him eating out of her hand. He was enamored with her and she loved it. He would be an easy pawn.

"Okay. It's a deal. Here is half now and you'll get half when the job is done. Here is an address to send me a letter. I will send it then. But you must follow my directions." His eyes bulged when he saw the amount, almost as much as they did when he saw her coming down the stairs.

She was pleased. She knew the scum would do it for less but she didn't want him backing out and having to go through this repulsive experience all over again.

With all going according to plan, she immediately left for the train. As she walked the street, she felt all eyes on her. Normally, she would glory in it but not among these savages. They were filthy and beneath her like so many back in White Rock. She wanted to be out of this town and on the train back to her pampered life and wait for the outcome of her lovely scheme. She nearly waved at the people as the train pulled away, so elated at her plan being executed but she didn't. She turned and began ordering the porter about.

Tickled with herself, she indulged herself with a stopover in the city at a grand hotel, where she luxuriated in baths and wine and pastries and a new frock—and a maid to help her in and out of it, of course.

On the train home she fancied Katie being kidnapped and taken back to her uncle. She imagined her in tears as she cried for help. It thrilled her. She felt the blood pumping through her as she felt so many times before when she plotted revenge. She would not only have Danny back but also revel in getting her revenge on the little blonde trollop. She would make her sorry she ever came to White Rock.

CHAPTER TWENTY-SEVEN

Mercy & Faith

"It's a letter for Mr. Daniel, Mrs. Richards—Special Delivery."

"Oh, my. Thank you, Amos."

Gwen shut the door and handed it to Danny.

He turned it over in his hand. "It's from my old colleague, John Fuller. I wonder why he would send something special delivery?" He hoped it wasn't another lure to come back to the legal world he left. But certainly he wouldn't send something special delivery.

He looked up, after reading the letter, wondering what to say. Katie's Uncle Tyler was supposedly on his deathbed and wanted to talk to the lawyer. He said it was a life-and-death matter in regards to Katie. Danny didn't want to alarm anyone and, not knowing if this was a trick, thought it best to keep it to himself. John suggested Danny might be able to handle the situation better.

"It is a legal matter that I need to see to. I must leave right away. Can I do anything for you before I leave? I won't be too long, I don't think. But it might be several days."

"No nothing, I can think of right now. We'll manage. I hope it is nothing serious."

"It is somewhat but I can't get into it right now. Do pray."

"Always."

He kissed her, gave the children a hug, and went for his things. Most of them were at the Overlook House but he knew he didn't have to dress for Bitter Springs, so he grabbed his Bible, a little food, and headed for the train station.

"Silas, I need a ticket to Bitter Springs, Arizona Territory, please."

"Sure thing, Danny, here you are. Popular place lately. Gretchen just came back from there herself. Better hurry, they are loading."

Danny hurried to the train and jumped aboard. When he finally settled, he wondered at the strange thing Silas had said. Why would Gretch go to Bitter Springs, of all places?

The conductor interrupted him and it reset his thoughts to the challenge at hand. Facing Tyler was not something he wanted to do but there seemed to be no real choice in the matter.

Father, I really need your help. I am not sure of what is happening here. If the man is truly dying then I need you to help me give him the gospel.

He continued to pray and read his Bible, searching for spiritual strength and wisdom. Occasionally he would think of the happy little cottage he left so abruptly. He lingered on one incident in particular: a vision of Katie holding his roses —the bridal roses. It was a sign to him when he came down the hill from his prayer and fasting. The Lord told him that this young woman was sent to him to be blessed and to bless his life. He thought deeply about the word at the time and wondered if it were temporary or permanent. Then, when he came off the hill anxious to see everyone, there she was with a whole vase full of his roses. His heart soared at the sight. He felt it was an endorsement from the Lord to his hope of permanence. Being Danny's bride is certainly permanent. She had won his heart so completely but he must have God's approval as he had gone his own way almost to the point of destruction with Gretch. Katie was what he had been waiting for. And of course there was Jeremy's little voice reminding him, "He is a bestest daddy for me and Sarrie."

"Bitter Springs, Ashfork and Sycamore Cannyonnn...."

He finally arrived. It had been a long trip. He surely had not planned to be back to this town so soon, if ever.

He hopped off the train, and watched as women fanned themselves to no avail and men milled about looking as miserable as he felt. Big puffy clouds loomed above but did nothing except making him breathless. Katie had talked about the monsoons. It sounded good right about now. He set himself to search quickly for the place he had been directed to go.

Give me strength, Lord and put your words in my mouth and if this is a ruse, protect me.

For a split second the thought of Gretch being in this place flitted through his mind but he had a job to do so he suppressed it. The last thing he wanted to do was to think about her. He was to face Tyler, Katie's tormentor, not a man who would listen to reason. Only God could take hold of this meeting.

Danny came to an old rickety shack close to the doctor's little place in town. The doctor was just walking out the door.

Seeing Danny he said, "He hasn't much time, son. Better make it to the point."

Danny blinked. It was true. The old man was dying. Danny knew the doctor's comment was a message from God. He must not waste any time.

An old scruffy woman was taking up a dish from Tyler's bed stand and nodded at Danny as he came in. Odors of sickness and medicine lingered. Looking at Tyler, he tried to focus on the meeting at hand. The huge booming-voiced monster had been reduced to an ashen-faced, weak, old man. He had his hand on his heart as if it hurt him and his breathing labored. His eyes were hollow with fear.

"I'm the lawyer you asked to see," Danny said, looking down at the feeble man. Every angry thought toward Tyler diminished as he saw death waiting to take him.

"Listen," he croaked desperately, trying to lift his head.

"Take it easy, I am right here." Danny moved closer to the head of the bed.

"Listen, gotta stop him—Markum...sent to get Katie. She done it—that black-haired woman—she paid him. I weren't thinkin'. Wasn't gonna do it but thought if Katie came back I could give her...but gotta save Katie." He pointed to a box near the bed stand. "Get that."

Danny was trying to decipher the broken message. Nothing was making any sense. He reached for the box.

"Take it. Ain't mine. The bottle it stirs the anger..."

Danny was not concerned with the box. He was intent on finding out what this was all about regarding Katie's safety.

"I don't understand. Katie is in danger?"

Tyler nodded as tears coursed his cheeks.

Danny felt it would be best to do most of the talking. "Someone was paid to kidnap Katie?"

The old man nodded again. "Markum. Works for me some. I told him I didn't want to go fetch her, but he did. He wants to get back at her for puttin' him off." He coughed and tried hard to get his breath.

"What was this about the black-haired woman? Someone you know?"

"No she was a stranger—highfalutin' city gal. Black eyes. I never seen nothin' like her."

"Did she give a name?"

"Yes, but she was lyin'. I don't remember it. But she stayed at the hotel. You gotta hurry. Ida said Markum left yesterday on the train. Hurry."

Danny wanted to hurry. He was tormented, trying to decide between running off to keep Katie safe or staying to deal with the sick man's soul. His flesh fought hard but he knew he could not leave this man to eternity. He would leave Katie in God's hands.

Father, protect Katie. Don't let these evil people harm her.

He had seen Markum and that was disconcerting but Gretch—Gretch he knew all too well. What was she capable of? His grandmother's words came back to him again; I cannot imagine what the girl will be capable of when she grows up.

"Ya need to go. I am dyin'. I ain't no good. I shoulda stopped it. Pa told me I was no good. He was right. Always beat me."

He was trying to hang on. Danny could see it. Compassion touched him as he looked at the tormented man.

"Tyler, God loves you."

"Nah—not me. I am not worth lovin'. My pa sa_d so.' He coughed for a spell, then continued, "I didn't do nothing bad then, but he never believed me. I tried to tell him but he jus' beat me, over and over. My Nora, oh my poor Nora..."

Tears poured down his tortured face.

"Your wife?"

He nodded, coughing, "She was good, like Ma. I started to drinkin' and wore her out with my anger. Nora...Nora...I am so sorry," he called to her.

Danny knew he must share the gospel with this man before it was too late but he had a peace to hear him out.

"I hit the youngun'. I never hurt no little one before. I was so drunk. After Nora died, I kept to the bottle day and night. Katie was good. I knew it but I couldn't tell her. I never knowed how. I ain't done nothing good ever. I deserve this but I am scared." The fear was evident in the old man's eyes that bulged like a dog in pain.

"Tyler, you didn't hit Jeremy. You only scared him." Danny watched as Tyler sighed heavily. "God really does love you. He made you and he sent his only begotten Son to die for all those things you say you did," Danny shared tenderly.

"Naw, not for me. I am too bad. Pa said it...said God hated me. Said I was goin' to hell with him. Said not to listen to Ma."

"But at first you didn't believe that, did you?"

"No. I did everything he said. I don't know why he kept

beatin' me. Why Pa, why?" He cried out to the cruel father like a little boy, looking away.

Give me your words that will break through to this man, Lord.

"Tyler, your father was wrong. The things he did were his own sin. God is your real Father. He would never say things like that to you. He created you. You must ask God for forgiveness for the things you have done and forgive your pa for his sin against you."

As Tyler lay still, thinking and wondering, Danny continued to pray. A peace came over the room and over his breathing.

"Tyler, no man can say his sin was worse than what God himself bore on that cross. It is like saying the suffering of the Savior wasn't good enough to take care of your sin."

It was like a light went on. His eyes cleared and they were fixed on Danny.

"Ma knew it. She told me but I was so confused."

"You can go to be with your ma and Nora. And someday see Katie and me and the little ones again."

"You know where she is...Katie?" His eyes widened.

"Yes, she is safe." He spoke it at that moment in faith believing God would protect her. But he wished Katie were with him. How sweet and forgiving she would be.

The old man started to convulse. Danny prayed for him and he calmed again. Then he gave him a quick rendition about the thief on the cross as quickly and powerfully as he could.

The old man lay still, listening intently.

"What do I do?" His breathing labored.

"Just tell God you believe he sent his Son to die for your sins and ask him to forgive you. Just like the man being crucified next to him, you want to be with him."

"I do, oh, God I do believe. I do believe. You took my sins. Forgive me, Lord, I been a really bad man. I hope you won't send me away. I want to be like that thief." Then he bawled like a child. Danny's cheeks were wet with tears as he watched the transformation of this man before his eyes. His countenance was completely changed and the hard features turned soft and gentle.

"Tyler, you know God forgave you. You must now forgive your pa because God forgave you."

"Yes. I forgive you, Pa. I don't know why you was so...mean but I forgive you."

Danny felt his quaking heart rest as Tyler was forgiven and forgave as well.

The woman of the house stood in the doorway, her hands all wrapped up in her apron, her eyes wide. Danny wondered if she had been there during the prayer. She couldn't help see the change in Tyler's face. Her mouth dropped and she stared at him in silence.

"I believe, Ida, God loves me, Ida. God save Ida," the sick man cried out. Ida looked like she'd seen a ghost. She bolted out the door and out of the house. Danny saw her run by the window.

"Thank you, boy, for tellin' me I will see my ma and my Nora. Do you think they will be happy to see me, though?"

"Yes, they will be elated to see you. And I will tell Katie and the children. You know she prayed, they all prayed for you a great deal and they have never stopped."

"You go and take care of them for me. Tell them I am sorry—so sorry." His eyes fell in shame. "You take the box. It's hers and it's important. And all I have here is hers—the land, the business, and the house—all of it."

"I will tell her. She will be so happy to know you found the Savior." He reached for the hand of the pale man to say goodbye but the huge hand fell to his side. He could honestly tell Katie the man died in true peace. Peace was all over the room, like heavenly sunlight.

He did not wait for anyone to come back but headed straight for the hotel. He overheard two women talking over the fence as he left.

"I don't know what got into her. She ran to the church fast as a rabbit."

"Ya don't say. Ya suppose she's 'fessin her sins?" cackled the older lady.

Danny wondered if it was Ida they were talking about and if she would be Tyler's reward. He wiped the tears again from his face, and walked steadily toward the shabby little hotel.

"Yes sir, we had a right fancy lady come to stay. She was as spoiled as they come. Like to drive us plum crazy. Signed her name Miss Corbit." The hotel clerk rolled her eyes.

It was Gretchen, no doubt. Corbit—a lot like Corbeau, he thought. But what has she to do with all of this?

Danny turned back to the woman at the desk. "I wonder, do you happen to know a man named Markum?"

"Yep, sure do, he's a bad 'un. Dodged a few bullets and hangings I heard tell. Cut throat, he is. No good."

Danny swallowed. "Can you tell me what he looks like?"

"Tall, chunky, brown-haired. Wears a grey hat. Hair's kinda scraggly."

"Thank you." That was the man who was in White Rock, all right. "Is that his first name?"

"Don't know." She shrugged. "Come ta think of it, she met him—the fancy gal. The morning she left. Gave him something. He sure looked happy, so did she, in a strange sorta way."

After getting her name and thanking her, he took off for the train. He had to wait an agonizing hour, on top of the fact that the telegraph was down. He was surely being tested. He had to trust in God's care of Katie. Finally the whistle blew and he hopped aboard, sat back. His hands were tied except to pray and wait. He was both blessed and distressed. What a strange turn of events.

If only the train had wings. It was going to be a dreadfully long trip. Oh Lord, if I ever needed your peace, it is now.

CHAPTER TWENTY-EIGHT

Captivity

Katie shut the huge door of the Perkins Mansion behind her. It had been a long day and she was anxious to get home. As she reached the corner, she heard footsteps behind her—stopping when she stopped. Something wasn't right. She turned left towards town instead of right towards the cottage, afraid to turn around. She headed as quickly as she could move toward Millie's restaurant. The more people the better and the sheriff was often there. She felt a sense of relief just reaching for the door. As she stepped in, her eyes caught Millie's. Katie was ready to open her mouth when she felt a big hand in the middle of her back and felt hot breath on her neck. She started to scream.

"Now, Katie, it would be best to not make a sound so the young'uns won't come to no harm."

She froze. Markum?

Oh, God—the children? I can't scream, not now. Does he have them? What do I do?

Thoughts and questions swam in her head. She had no choice but to back out of the restaurant with him. She searched for Millie with her eyes, hoping she would see the fear in them. His hand on her back made her cringe.

Father help me.

Katie glared at Millie. Then Millie ran towards the back door. Did she see? Will she do anything?

"Tom, something's wrong." Millie was breathless when she opened the door to the sheriff's office. "Katie, the gal at Grandma Gwen's. She was scared stiff. It was all over her face. Something's not right, Tom."

"Take it easy, Millie. Slowly tell me what happened." He tried to offer her a seat but she just popped right back up.

"Katie started through the restaurant door and a man came up behind her. Didn't get a good look at him—kept his head down. She looked terrified and she backed out with him. I know that look. Like looking down the end of a gun barrel."

"Which way they headed?" he asked, strapping on his gun belt.

"I don't know. I came over here. Gotta find her. I'll look around the shops."

Tom searched the area around the restaurant quickly and then headed down the street, frustrated with himself that he didn't ask more questions.

His deputy met him coming down the street. Jacob eyed his gun belt. "What's up, Sheriff?"

"Katie—Mrs. Jensen, have you seen her?"

"The perty gal from Grandma Gwen's place? Yeah, just seen her. She was walking with some fella toward the station."

"C'mon." Tom directed his deputy back up the street. "Did he look like the same man that was here before?"

"Come to think of it, he did a little. I think it was him but he was all duded up. Why would she be walking with him?"

"I don't know but Millie said she looked scared. Could be a kidnapping. You run the back way and make sure they don't get on the train."

Jacob sprinted the back way towards the train station as the sheriff continued up Center Street, keeping an eye out. What would his best friend say if he came back to find Katie kidnapped? He shook his head.

Need your help here Lord. Keep her safe and help us find her!

The train wasn't due yet so Markum took Katie off to a treed area nearby.

"Where are my children?" Katie looked her captor straight in the eye.

"They'll be fine iffen you just do as you are told." His lip curled into a sickening smile. "You always was a real looker, Katie." He pawed at her face and she stiffened. "Now, maybe you'll come live with me."

"You're taking me to Bitter Springs? What about my children? Please, just let me go to my children," she pleaded.

"C'mon now, Katie, I'll be havin' a big spread and a nice house real soon." He drew close to her again and tried to kiss her. His breath reeked of alcohol. She evaded him and pushed him away.

A deep red burned across his face at her rebuff. "Course, I don't have to take you back to Bitter Springs at all. Been told I could just dump ya off in the middle a nowheres."

"What?"

"Not my idea. Got paid real good fer it."

"Tyler paid you to get rid of me?"

"That's a laugh. Old miser don't pay nothin' to nobody."

"Then who?" Katie was shocked. Who would do such a thing? Nothing made sense.

"Never you mind. Been dealin' with higher class than you. You is my ticket to bein' a rich man." He looked into the sky as if he were dreaming about it.

That is why his clothes were different. He had money from somewhere. But why would anyone want to harm my children and me.

Oh, Father, help us, please!

"Please, leave my children with Gwen in White Rock. I will go anywhere you say."

"Well, now ain't that a right nice offer. But I can get better n' you, now. I got money. Tired of your snubbin' me. Yer too holy for my likes, anyhow." He stuck his grisly face in hers with his eyes pinched. "I'll be finding someone who'll warm up to me. You is as cold as ice."

She shrank from him. All the things Gwen had shared about fear came flooding back like a river of love from God's throne. God would protect her and God would protect the children. She felt a peace that seemed almost ludicrous. A peace she should not be feeling but she stood her ground and glared at Markum.

He glared back. "You might be goin' back to Tyler's or maybe I will just push you out on one of them desert train stops on the way. Where you wanna go, Katie? Maybe a nice deserted place where you can beg for your train fare back? Nah, I'd have ta just push you off the train where there ain't no people. Can't have you comin' back till I get my money. Maybe some Injuns will take you in." He laughed and grabbed at her hair, pulling until it hurt. "Pretty scalp fer sure."

His threats did not concern her except in regard to her children. No matter what, Gwen and Danny would love them if it were time for her to leave this world.

"You shouldn't make enemies where you go, Katie." He raised his brows. "Look to where it's got ya." His evil laugh was cut short by the train whistle in the distance.

Enemies? She couldn't think. All she could do was pray. Sorting all this out seemed impossible. *Father?*

No weapon formed against you shall prosper.

Oh, Lord, it doesn't say there won't be an attack but that it won't prosper. Get me through this fire and keep my children safe. You are our deliverer. You have delivered us before.

I am your rock and fortress, and deliverer: your God, your strength.

She found strength of spirit against fear, remembering who her God was and a little one's voice deep in her heart said, "God will provide."

"Let's go 'n keep your mouth shut." He shoved her back toward the train.

The train whistle sounded and Danny hung onto the rail by the steps so he could jump off as soon as possible. He looked toward the waiting area as it approached. There's

Katie—what a relief. But how did she know I was coming? Who is that man with her?

Oh, God, please don't let it be that man.

But it is—it's Markum—but he looks different. He's dressed well. Ah, Gretch gave him money.

The train was still moving when he saw Jacob in the distance approaching. But when Danny turned his eyes back to Katie, she was gone. Markum was standing at the eastbound train steps and started to get on. Did she get on the train? JACOB! HURRY! The train slowed and Danny jumped off, nearly tripping, and ran toward the eastbound train. He watched as it started to move.

NO, FATHER, NO!

He looked for Jacob and saw him coming toward him.

"Danny, what happened to Katie? Is she with you?" Danny shook his head. "Did you know she was kidnapped?"

"Yes," Danny said. "She must be on the train." He grabbed Jacob's arm and ran for the moving train.

The two men ran with everything they had to catch it as it slowly gained speed. They both jumped for the caboose with all they had but only Jacob with his youth, long legs and reaching arms was able to grasp it and hang on. Danny missed it by inches and went flying and rolling on the ground.

Danny rose from the dirt, horrified that he could do nothing.

Lord, am I being tested again to trust you? Please keep my Katie safe. Use Jacob to bring her back and protect Jacob.

He watched, holding his hat and raking his hair over and over as the train grew smaller and smaller until the oaks obscured it from sight. Involuntary tears started and stopped as numbness took over and despair tried to eat away at him.

He turned, dragging himself back to the station.

"Danny." The voice of his old friend, Tom, drew his head up. "Jacob, did you see him?"

"Yes, we both tried to run for the train. He made it." He looked back at the long space the train had just occupied.

"Katie and the man on it?"

"Yes, Tom, I am pretty sure."

"I'll go wire ahead to the next stop."

Danny nodded and then turned back to look at the empty tracks that carried Katie away, his fingers tightening as he clung to her hat.

Katie watched as Markum's bulbous, bloodshot eyes roamed the station platform. His haughty manner had turned fearful. Had he heard someone call "deputy" as she had? He turned to Katie, grabbed her arm, squeezing hard and pushed her toward the steps. "Go hide somewheres so I look like I am alone. I'll look fer you later."

Katie ran up the steps and turned left toward the back of the train, hurrying. She glanced out the passenger windows. Danny? Could it be? Does he know I am here? But it was the last call and the train would start moving. What could she do? Would he find her? Perhaps she could keep hidden from Markum until Danny came and found her and made Markum lead them to the children. She made her way back farther looking for a place, a compartment—something to hide her from Markum until Danny came. And then she heard a still small voice tell her what to do.

Jacob stood at the back of the caboose. He brushed himself off and made sure his deputy badge was still there. He looked back to see Danny looking completely forlorn on the tracks. He wanted to yell back to him that he would get Markum and save Katie but he found he could only wave at his friend to tell him so, as the train moved speedily on.

He made his way through the railroad cars searching for Markum. He would just love to take him by the throat and —but knowing he must be careful on account of Katie, he slowed and looked more carefully. Better

put his badge away until it was needed. Ah, there he was but she was not with him. What did he do with her? He felt to wait and watch him for a while and see if Markum would lead him to her.

Markum kept looking around suspiciously like a

trapped rat. Not much of a poker face on that weasel. Bet he never won one game. Jacob lowered his hat so he wouldn't be noticed as Markum scanned around him.

Where's he going? Maybe he'll lead me to Katie. Jacob was as stealthy as his big frame would allow him to be, following behind the fidgety kidnapper. When they came to the last car, it was empty. Markum looked side to side and under things frantically. Doesn't he know where she is? Did she get away from him and come here to hide?

Then Markum turned and saw him. Nothing to do now

except confront him—if he remembers me. Jacob stood acting like he was looking for a package in the car, which was filled with trunks and freight. Remaining calm, he sized the lout up and waited to see what he would do next.

"Seen a gal back here anywheres, got yellow hair?"

"No," Jacob said. "She belong to you?"

"Um, yup."

As the culprit turned to look around the car, Jacob pulled his gun. When Markum turned back his eyes grew large and he pulled at his gun but Jacob was already there and they wrestled. Jacob forced him to drop the gun. He didn't want to shoot him without knowing where Katie was. When Jacob reached for his handcuffs, Markum broke free and stumbled to the back of the train but Jacob knew he was far too cowardly to jump even though the train was slowing for the next stop. Jacob kicked Markum's gun between two trunks and went after him. He reached for Markum's flabby arm and twisted it behind his back, causing the man to yelp and click—he was cuffed to the hand rail. He wouldn't be jumping for certain now. Jacob checked the kidnapper for hidden weapons and drew out a pouch stuffed with bills.

"So Mister, best to fess up now." He wagged the pouch at him. "Want to tell me about the kidnapping? Got an awful lot of money here and we both know you can't play poker." Jacob snorted.

When Danny came into the area of the westbound tracks, he saw a hat on the ground and picked it up. Could it be Katie's? He turned back the way of the fleeting train again, wondering. Did she throw her hat off the train to help him find her? Then she must have seen me. And here I am the great rescuer. He shook his head in disgust. Perhaps I should get a horse and ride for the next stop. He turned back to hurry to the station when he was stopped dead by something in the bushes.

A woman's skirt and petticoats stuck in the bushes. He drew closer.

"Hello. Are you alright, Ma'am?"

"Danny?"

"Katie! Oh, Katie." Danny hurried over and knelt down, gathering her up in his arms. He held her gently as he picked the brush out of her hair. "Katie, you're here. Are you hurt? Did he hurt you?"

She shook her head. "Oh, Danny," she clung to him nearly choking him. "I jumped off the train. I saw you through the window when Markum pushed me onto the train. He was afraid someone was after him so he told me to run and hide. I went to the end of the caboose and jumped off the steps. God told me to. I hurt my ankle, but made it to hide here. I wouldn't have hurt myself if I had jumped when God told me to do it. But Danny, never mind me. It's the children—he has the children. I don't know what he has done with them. We must do something." She turned her head into his chest and wept.

The joy of seeing her took flight. His heart sank. What would Markum do with the children? Little Sarah and Jeremy gone?

Father this is a nightmare. Help us, please.

Tom ran over to them. "She okay?

"Tom, Katie says he has the children somewhere." Katie nodded.

"Your two children, Ma'am?"

"Yes." She could barely speak, sobbing heavily while gripping Danny's coat.

"Why, I saw them with Grandma Gwen at her place, just before I got here. They are fine."

She looked up, her eyes bright with hope. "Are you sure?"

"Yes, I'm sure. Say, what is this all about?"

"He told me the children would be hurt if I did not come quietly with him. I wanted to scream or run but I was so afraid for them. But when I saw Danny..."

Danny tightened his arms, drawing her closer to him.

"She thought he had already taken the kids, I guess," he said.

Katie nodded, her head burrowed back into his chest.

"I wondered why she didn't yell out or try to run. Poor lass, she's all done in. Take her home, Danny. She's had quite a time. I will be by in a little while to find out more." Tom tipped his hat and walked away.

Danny carried her to the depot and called for a wagon. He sat her in it, retrieved his bag, and took a deep breath.

Thank you, Father. You did keep her safe. I guess you had to let her go through this in order to put that evil man behind bars which should come by way of Jacob. Hopefully the mastermind behind it all will be caught soon.

As Danny carried Katie through the door, Gwen came hurrying toward them. It felt so good to have her in his arms. He hated to have to put her down.

"The children are in the side yard. They don't know what happened."

"How is it that you do?" Danny asked Gwen.

"Tom was by, checking on the children. You can fill me in on the rest later."

When Katie heard the children's voices, her body shook. Danny carried her to the couch. She clung to him tightly. Poor girl.

"Is she hurt?"

"Just bumped up a bit. Ankle's hurting. Maybe I better go get the doctor."

"No, don't leave. Please." Katie's frightened eyes held him in check. He couldn't possibly ignore her plea.

"I will get her some arnica and a cup of soup. What shall we tell the children?"

"Later," Katie interrupted. "We'll tell them later. For now, I just want to see them, please." Danny went right out to retrieve them.

"All right child, now you rest. I am so glad you are home." Gwen gently kissed her forehead.

"Where were you, Mama? What's wrong? Are you sick?" Sarah came running in with Jeremy right behind.

"She is fine. We just need to let her rest a bit, she had a fall." Danny assured them.

The children nestled up to their mother and she held them tenaciously. When she finally released them, Jeremy went over and climbed into Danny's lap.

"Dandy, I am so glad you camed home."

"Me too, little chap. Home to be together and never far away again." He looked over at Katie and she smiled in agreement.

Katie ate her soup, resting on the couch while Gwen fed the rest of them at the table.

The children were the only ones who didn't jump at the sound of the knock at the door. Danny answered the door and found Tom ready to talk.

Danny whispered, "We haven't told the children yet, so give us a chance to get them in the back before you mention what happened."

Grandma, always savvy, told the children she would read them a new story in the back bedroom. She knew Katie wouldn't abide the children going outside right now.

"How are you feeling, Ma'am?" Tom asked her.

"Much better now that I am home. Thank you so much for coming to help me. How did you know?"

"Millie. She saw the scared look on your face."

"You'll be glad to know Jacob wired and they telephoned to Millie's and she ran right over and told me they would be coming in by stage. Now, I need to know all about this."

After Katie's story was told, Danny insisted she go to bed.

"But we must tell the children," she protested.

"Tomorrow—let them sleep peacefully and you won't be going to work either." He wanted her to understand that she really was home and he would take care of everything. She nodded.

"Be right back, don't go away, Tom," Danny said as he carried Katie to her room.

"I'm fine really, I think." She protested but he wasn't giving in to it. It felt good to coddle her a bit.

He put his lips to her ear and whispered, "We're home now. I am not leaving, my sweet Katie."

Tom squinted, clearly taken aback. "Gretch?"

Danny explained the sordid tale that lay beneath the surface of the crime.

"She was jealous of Katie. She arranged the whole thing," Danny said as he finished.

"I see. Well, I can't say she didn't have it in her. The shoe fits. But if the old man is dead, what evidence do we have?"

Danny put a few more pieces of the puzzle together for Tom, from Bitter Springs.

"Sounds like the hotel clerk would never forget her, just like the rest of us. Imagine Gretch in the Arizona Territory." He shook his head in disbelief. "She must have stuck out like crazy. The White Rock nightmare—that is what she is and always has been." He shook his head in disgust. "She's gone too far this time. Nothing would please me more to see justice done to her. To tell you the truth, I think she was more than capable of murder." His jaw tightened.

"To think I nearly married that nightmare." He ran his fingers through his hair.

"She *is* a beauty. You just happened to be her target, from the first."

"I guess I still am. Her beauty is only flesh deep. I have seen hell in those black eyes."

"So have I, for too many years. I always thought she was the reason little Laurel nearly drowned. The day before, Laurel had called her a name. And there were so many other stories but anyway, I will be working on this and will get back to you. Maybe a few more things will fall into place." He grabbed his hat and started to leave. "We'll see what we can get out of that Markum fella. Jacob's bringing him in on the stage. He's not the type to be honorable, even among thieves."

Gwen came back in after getting everyone to bed. "May I get a quick rendition, so I can at least sleep tonight?"

"Of course, but do you think I could get something to eat. I haven't felt much like eating in the last couple of days."

"My poor boy. How about you, Thomas?"

"No thanks, Ma'am. Gotta tend to the prisoner coming in soon. But I won't say no next time."

Danny explained enough to satisfy his grandma's curiosity with the promise of the whole story tomorrow, as he happily ate a second portion. Then she handed him a plate with coconut cake.

"You had coconutted cake without me? Now, I am really feeling left out."

"Don't be silly. I can always make another one."

"It is so good to be home and I do have really good news to share tomorrow with everyone, but when I am done with this cake, I am going straight to sleep."

"I will make up the couch."

"No, you have done enough. I can do it," he protested, with cake stuffed happily in his mouth.

"Pishposh, I will have it done in a jiffy."

Katie was exhausted and fell asleep quickly but every little noise woke her. She constantly checked on the children, leaving the adjoining door open. She tried to go back to sleep but kept seeing Markum's angry red face coming toward her. She hoped he wouldn't escape from

Jacob. She hated having him in the same town but she would have to accept it. She wanted the fear scriptures Gwen had written out for her in her Bible, but her Bible was in the living room.

Late into the night, she hobbled out to get her Bible. Moonlight streamed through the windows. When she saw Danny asleep on the couch, she thought back on how wonderful he was and what a miracle that he came at the same time she was being taken away and then to miss jumping onto the train and be right there for her. His Bible lay open. A strand of hair was placed like a bookmark in the book of Ruth. It looked like hers and made her wonder. She tiptoed back toward her room, her Bible in hand. She felt better with him being here in the house. Yet, she knew it was God who brought all these answers to prayer. She would have her Bible when dawn lit her room. She heard him turn on the couch and quickened her pace.

Thank you, Father, for everything. Take these awful memories from me.

Had he put a strand of her hair in his Bible? And, of all places, in the book of Ruth.

CHAPTER TWENTY-NINE

The Whole Story

Katie limped into the kitchen half dazed after pondering all that had happened the day before and feeling a little sore and stiff.

"Good morning, Katie." Danny didn't wear his usual grin. She saw only concern in his countenance as he got up quickly to help her to her chair.

Gwen came from the kitchen. "Good morning, child. How are you feeling? Would you like a glass of juice? First let me give you another dose of arnica. I was going to bring breakfast to you."

" I will be fine. The arnica is helping. Thank you, you are a dear. Juice sounds wonderful. I just can't seem to get myself together this morning."

Danny gently took her hand across the table. And it felt so good.

"I think that is to be expected. Well, don't worry about your job. I went to see Mrs. Perkins and explained what was needed to keep you home and rested today."

"You did? Oh dear, I guess the whole town will know

sooner or later."

"More like sooner," Gwen said matter-of-factly, as she finished setting the table.

"This is awful. I wonder if I will lose my job? And what will people think?" She put her hand to her forehead.

"Katie your job is quite secure. Mrs. Perkins said she could never get along without you. You are 'absolute perfection' she said." Danny animated with his chin high and hand twirling into the air, making her smile.

"So when do we worry about what people think, child?" Gwen said. "These people will think exactly what they thought the day they met you, that you are the prettiest and sweetest young woman in town."

"Oh, thank you both. You are so kind."

"The doctor will be by later just to make sure you are all right."

"Maybe it is a good time to share what happened in Bitter Springs, before the children wake. We'll want to give them a shorter version, I am sure."

"Bitter Springs? What about Bitter Springs?" Katie looked from Danny to Gwen.

"Let me put all the pieces together as we go. I do have a wonderful piece of news that has been hard to hold in since then but I need to start from the beginning."

Danny explained about the letter he received to go to Uncle Tyler's deathbed. "I didn't know if it was a trick or not and I wanted to find out before I told you. Tyler contacted my lawyer friend, John. He was hoping to settle some business before he died. John thought it would be better if I handled it considering the situation."

"Shouldn't you have told Katie?" Gwen asked, as she

settled into a chair next to Katie.

"Not necessarily, because he didn't ask for Katie to come. He asked for a lawyer. I did not want to subject her to any more pain, if it wasn't necessary. I was the one who arranged the papers to keep him away. I was the contact he was looking for. And like I said, I wasn't sure if it was some sort of trick. I didn't want to put Katie in any danger but it seems she was in danger despite my efforts."

Katie waited impatiently for Danny to continue.

"Anyway, he was truly on his deathbed. It was his heart and he looked like a corpse, ashen and thin—a far cry from the big tough man I had seen on my previous trip. He had lost weight. He said it was consumption and dropsy. It was good he got the dropsy, as he didn't suffer long. His heart wore out with the coughing. He kept pushing me to go save you. He didn't mean for this to happen. Originally he thought if he could get you to come back, he would say he was sorry, especially for hurting Jeremy. I told him later he didn't hurt Jeremy. He could hardly talk about it. He went through a great deal of torment. He mentioned his mother and the cruelty of his father and trying to sort out what was truth and lies in the things that were told him as a child. His father must have been a horrible man but his mother a Christian woman. Anyway, the whole situation gave rise to me giving him the gospel."

Katie sat in awe of the whole story.

Danny continued. "I have to tell you, though, I went through torment to stay there. I didn't know what was going to happen to you. I was so torn, but I knew if I was obedient to the Holy Spirit that God would take care of you. And you were not harmed, although frightened. I told your uncle that

God loved him and sent his Son to die for those sins he had done. He said his mother told him that but his father told him it was all lies and that he was just no good and beat him for things he hadn't done."

"What a horrible childhood he must have had," Gwen said, her hand at her throat.

"Yes, I heard a little of that from Aunt Nora. It was part of the reason I stayed as long as I did but please go on," Katie urged.

"Well, after awhile he broke down more and I told him the full gospel and the story of the thief on the cross. He seemed to relate well to that. He knew he could not fix his broken life except to call on God at the last and I am happy to tell you that he did."

"Oh, Danny, you did what we could not do. I am so glad. It is such a miracle." Katie put her hand to her mouth and tried to hold back the tears.

"Ah, but he attributed much to the love of his mother, Nora, and you. And he was ashamed of his drinking and his behavior. He really was a changed man. He called to the woman of the house who takes patients in for the doctor and told her God loves her and that he found Christ as his Savior and she needed to find him, too. I guess his transformation was too much for her because she shrieked and ran out of the house and down the street." Danny was in his usual animated state waving his arms as he told the story. "After overhearing some women talking as I left, I presumed she might have run all the way to the local preacher."

The women laughed, though teary-eyed.

"He kept telling me to go and save you from Markum,

but I assured him you were safe. I wanted to be there with him at the last, although it was a hard time for me. I learned a strong lesson in trusting God. The change in his countenance was remarkable and when I preached to him, his labored breathing softened. He was glad to hear that he would see his mother and Nora and that you and I and the children would be there someday to see him. I was able to see that peaceful face at the point of death."

Katie dabbed at her eyes as she realized her tormenting uncle was now with God. It was overwhelming for her.

"Danny, how can I thank you. At the time I left, I had little faith in his coming to the Lord. Thank you for being so faithful."

"My years at the mission prepared me for that encounter, but the real preparation was done by those who came before me." He smiled lovingly at her and melted her heart.

After a long pause, Danny sighed heavily.

"However, I must tell you this whole incident with Markum comes back on me."

Katie looked up, startled.

"What on earth do you mean, Daniel?" Gwen asked.

"Well, Tyler did not hire Markum this time."

"Who did?" Katie barely choked the words.

"Maybe not now, Daniel. Katie has been through so much," Gwen said.

"No, I must know what this is all about." Katie was insistent. Maybe the things Markum said to her would make sense.

"It was Gretchen."

The two women gasped in unison.

"She went to Tyler and he wouldn't do it himself. But he did tell Markum at the saloon and he met with Gretch."

Katie was remembering. "He said that. I remember now. He said I made an enemy and he was paid a lot of money just to dump me...off the train...even in the desert."

Gwen gasped, her hand grasping Katie's arm.

"Well, Tom needs to know this." Danny was livid.

"Oh my...something else, Daniel," Gwen said. "Awhile back, Gretchen went to visit Ruby. She set an entire bakery full of sweets before her and asked her all sorts of questions about Katie. I thought it was strange. Gretchen would never go near Ruby before."

"Really, to see Ruby? Yes, Grandma, she hated her. Called her names. It used to make me angry. So, Gretchen was bribing her. I need to tell Tom all of this."

"Why would she do such a thing?" Katie shook her head in disbelief, still trying to take it all in.

His eyes met hers. "She knew how much I cared for you. She wanted you out of the way. I guess it was obvious that I was—in love with you."

Katie was stunned. Tyler had come to the Savior and gone to heaven, Gretchen had paid Markum to do away with her, and Danny just said he was in love with her. She sat with her mouth ajar. Out of the corner of her eye she saw Gwen smiling.

Danny's face was ablaze with color. He abruptly excused himself saying he had to discuss the new details with Sheriff Tom and left.

"She left for the East," Tom told Danny. "They said she

went to her aunt in New York. We let the authorities know. She could bolt to Europe, perhaps to her mother in France, and we'd never be able to do a thing. I am going to do everything possible to see to it she does not get away with this. I call it attempted murder. Got a few tidbits out of Markum that may help, too. He'll spill more, I'm sure."

"I am sure Gretch's daddy has been fixing things up for her, as always," Danny said, his jaw clenched. "I hope we never have to see her face again. Please keep me posted." He stood and shook his head. "I sure pity Europe. Someday she will meet her match and he will get the better of her."

"Have Katie write down everything Markum said. Go home and rest. It's over. I'll make a call on Miss Ruby soon." His friend slapped him on the back and scooted him out the door.

"I will, thank you."

"You know, you're the talk of the town, you two." Tom smirked. "She's sure a pretty lass. Makes me think of Audrey."

"Yes, and with a heart of gold, like her hair." Danny turned. "Audrey?"

"Well, let's hope we can get the one with the heart as black as her hair behind bars," Tom said.

"You still like Audrey?"

"I guess I really do miss your lovely, free-spirited cousin."

"Hmmm."

"Okay, friend, no matchmaking. Audrey doesn't know I am alive."

"Of course she does." Danny grinned and Tom tossed his hat at him just as he slipped out the door.

Danny meandered toward home thinking about Audrey, his lovable but somewhat scatterbrained artist cousin and Tom the conventional sheriff. He laughed to himself until he got closer to home and remembered he had confessed his love to Katie It slowed his steps and his breathing.

Talk of the town? But how do I face her now?

CHAPTER THIRTY

The Lost Box

"I nearly forgot." Danny bolted from the chair after the evening meal, making everyone jump.

"Forgot what?" Gwen chided. "As if we haven't had enough excitement around here?"

"I'm sorry, I didn't mean to startle you. I forgot about the box." He dug around in his satchel. "Here it is. This belongs to you, Katie."

Her breath caught as she reached for it. "My box. I thought it was gone." She touched it gently, looking half afraid to open it.

"Tyler gave it to me. He said it was yours."

"I can't believe it." She shook her head.

"Open it," he urged.

She looked at the box in her lap and slowly opened it. She pulled out papers and pictures and her eyes filled with tears. "This is my mother and here is another of my father." She handed the pictures to Gwen and Danny.

"She is beautiful... like you," Danny said.

"Yes, you do look like your mother." Gwen compared

the picture to Katie, holding it up.

Involuntary tears started streaming down Katie's cheeks. Danny reached for his handkerchief and dabbed her face gently.

"My mother's locket." She lovingly touched the locket in her hand. "I thought I would never see it again." She opened the little gold locket revealing the little pictures inside. "This is Charlotte, my sister, and this is me. I was five and she was seven."

A big wad of money peeked from underneath the papers. Katie pulled it out.

"He said he never knew the box was there. It had been hidden in the tack from when he brought you home. When he found it after you left, he put all the money your sister had sent in it. I think he held back your sister's offerings because he was afraid you would just run off somewhere with it and deep down I think it scared him."

Katie sat blinking at him. She didn't seem to know what to say. She mumbled, "There were some things I had misjudged about my uncle."

"What is in the envelope there?" Danny pointed inside.

Katie opened it and scanned the papers. "I am sure I don't know what these are. I have never seen them before. Looks like something a lawyer could interpret." She handed them to Danny, her eyes still too watery to read through them.

"They are legal papers of some sort. They were signed over to Tyler from someone, a William A. Donnelly."

"That's my father. How odd."

Danny turned them over and searched for more information. "It appears to be a will, but there are some things that would need to be researched. You would have to have these looked into. I suppose John could help."

"Oh–no-you-don't." Gwen shook her finger. "You are not going to leave us again. If you go, then we all go."

Danny laughed. "Don't you worry, I wouldn't leave you for anything right now. You know, that might be just what we all need—a little vacation."

"But I am working," Katie said.

"Isn't Elvira Perkins planning a trip sometime soon? I thought I heard someone mention it in town," Gwen asked.

"Why, yes she is. She is going back East to her niece's wedding." Katie perked at the opportunity.

"I have some money, I have been setting aside," Gwen added.

"Good. It is settled. I will make the plans. We'll take the papers to John and have him look them over and we'll go to the mission. Finally, it will be a truly happy train ride. I will take you all to meet the fellows."

"Wonderful," Katie said. "That would be best of all."

"They are going to love you. When they heard about you, they were anxious to meet you. And Grandma, well, they think she is a peach without ever having met her and just wait until they meet Jeremy and Sarah. There will be laughter in the mission house on that day."

"I would so love to put faces to those men I pray for every day." Gwen's eyes were misty now.

"I will be in all my glory with my beautiful family."

Katie caught Gwen chastising him a bit with her eyes and he changed the course of the conversation. She pretended not to notice, biting her lip to quell a smile.

Later, when Katie left the room, his grandma whispered, to him, "Daniel, this precious young woman and her children do not belong to you, you know."

"I know. I guess I got carried away. I have always had a problem with sticking my foot in my mouth." Gwen rolled her eyes. "I was eager to have you all see the mission and take you to some wonderful places I know. I am so frustrated. I know what I want but what am I to do about it, Grandma? Do you think she cares about me the way I do her?"

"I think it might be best to ask her and until you decide what you plan to do about it, remember you have no ties on her." He saw a smile that was ever so slight as she said it.

The thought had never occurred to him. She could never belong to someone else. The thought of it made him miserable. She was so precious. It had been settled in his heart but what if it wasn't in hers? After all, he had no job or prospect of one. She had lived in poverty long enough. But how could he write and support them, too. His head was spinning and he knew it was time to go back up the hill and pray. But the women begged him to stay. Go out in the yard and pray, but not far away, they would tell him. He happily complied, not wanting to leave them.

The happy group had made their plans when one thing after another seemed to be against it.

"I am so disappointed." Danny sat rocking in the old rocking chair consoling himself.

"Yes, I think we were all looking forward to it. But God knows best. I suppose it was just not God's timing. We didn't ask him first." Gwen sat quietly with her needlework in her lap. "Katie couldn't help it if Mrs. Perkins' niece postponed her wedding until summer, and I am sorry I forgot about my commitment to Clara, to help her with her daughter's trousseau. We were getting too excited, I suppose. We make our plans but he orders our steps. Maybe it will all come together in the near future."

"I suppose. I will go do your errands now, Grandma." He had to do something besides rock in the rocking chair like a fidgety child.

"All right. Don't forget the mail."

Danny walked out the door and down the street, so deep in thought that he was at the store and hadn't remembered anything about the entire walk there. He tried to refocus on getting the needed items and headed for the post office.

"Hey, Danny."

He turned at the greeting. "Hello, Tom."

"I wanted to let you know, I will be going out of town. I didn't want anyone spreading it too much. Don't want to encourage any varmints."

"Good idea. Mum's the word. Where you going?"

"To Los Angeles. I have to testify in a trial. Want to come with me? You aren't doing anything are you?"

"Oh, no, I couldn't leave them right now. Besides I think they might all hogtie me if I tried."

The two men laughed and conversed as they walked down the street.

"But say, Tom, I could use a big favor."

They made their plans and Danny hurried back to the cottage.

"Grandma, here are your groceries. Do you remember where we put Katie's legal papers?"

"Up on the mantle, under the lace cloth, no, by the clock," she directed. "What are you doing? Was there any mail?"

"Tom is leaving for Los Angeles but don't tell it around town, and he is going to take these to John. He can do it and I won't have to leave you all."

He grabbed the envelope and started out the door.

"Shouldn't Katie know?" she demanded.

"Of course, I am going to stop and see her now at work. Oh, and I will get the mail." He winked and she rolled her eyes and waved him off.

CHAPTER THIRTY-ONE

Gwen's Surprise

Danny finally went back nights to the Overlook House. On Saturday morning he came early to the happy cottage and yet late for breakfast.

"I have a surprise for everyone today," Danny announced to the family as he ate his breakfast.

"Oh, boy." Jeremy scrambled to his feet from his marble game with Sarah.

"What is it?" Sarah's eyes lit up.

"I guess it wouldn't be a surprise if he told you, would it?" Katie tugged at her braid.

"When do we get to haved it?" Jeremy asked.

"Everybody pitch in and clean up and put on your shoes. Grandma, can you and Katie get some kind of lunch together for us to take? It isn't a regular picnic, just so you know." Danny winked at Katie but she hadn't a clue why. He helped the children get their shoes on, then stood guard at the door.

"I wonder what he is up to?" Gwen asked Katie.

"I don't know but he sure looks excited about it." The

ladies happily put together a fine basket of food, almost as anxious as the children to see what surprise he had planned.

"Okay, let's see if our coach has arrived." Danny, grinning from ear to ear, opened wide the front door to reveal a carriage. "Let's go everyone."

Peals of delight rang from one happy soul to the next.

"Now, I think the ladies should ride and the gentlemen should drive."

Sarah's countenance fell and Danny saw it.

"Except little princesses, they may choose where they would like to sit." Danny gave pretense of wiping his brow at the women, who smiled approvingly.

Jeremy giggled. "Giddyuped horsey."

"Not yet, Jer'my, we are not all in yet." Sarah admonished.

All set to travel, the happy company traveled up the road in style, waving to friends as they went. When Danny took a sharp right after going through town, the two women knew they were headed for the Overlook House. Gwen was almost giddy and Katie was delighted just to watch her and Danny, too, who was having great fun with the children as usual.

"He is such a big kid," Gwen said.

"Yes, isn't he."

"He will make a wonderful father."

"Yes." Katie nodded.

The Overlook House came into view and Gwen sighed heavily.

"How long has it been?"

"A year I suppose. Much too long."

Katie watched Gwen's eyes fill with tears as they rode

into the front drive. She reached over to hold the older woman's hand. Gwen turned to her and smiled. Then the carriage jolted.

"Pull the reins, little chap, tighter, and tell him whoa," Danny instructed.

"Whoad, horsey, whoad!" Jeremy shouted, squealing with delight when they actually stopped.

Sarah giggled. "Mama, look we are back at the big house."

"Yes, dear, isn't it lovely."

The house was even more wonderful than she remembered. The wrapping veranda, the cupola, dormers on the outside. Katie knew this was going to be a wonderful walk back into Gwen's life. She would soak in all the stories and enjoy it all. And it was so glorious to be back.

Danny reached for the little ones and helped them down. Their fascination with the horses and the carriage swung to the irresistible tree swing. They scattered like mice for the massive oak tree.

"My considerate boy," Gwen stroked his cheek affectionately, as he helped her down.

He grinned and kissed her cheek and set her gently. Then he reached for Katie.

"A wonderful surprise, Danny, like we talked about. I had almost forgotten." His eyes answered with a warm look. He put his hands to her waist to help her down and it made her long to fall into his embrace. His hands lingered as he set her down.

Danny opened the door into the beloved home.

"It is good to be home, Grandma, isn't it?"

"It surely is. But remember, Daniel, home is where we

are."

"Well, we are here now, aren't we?"

"We are indeed."

Katie sat the basket in the kitchen and followed them all around to the library—the favored spot.

Gwen went right over and sat in her chair. "A fire in the fireplace? Oh, Danny, you are too much and on a day like today." She fanned herself and chuckled.

"Well, it was a wee bit cooler day today." He grinned sheepishly. "At least I left the windows open."

Sarah and Jeremy came running into the library.

"Play the piano, please. Grandma Gwen hasn't heard you play it." Sarah pulled at her mother's hand.

Jeremy nodded his curly little mop head.

"Excuse me, Madam, but the little prince and princess have requested you to play for them," Danny addressed like a courtier.

Katie nodded. "Gladly, sire, but the queen of the castle must give her consent."

"Queen Gwendolyn, would you care for this lovely musician to bless your gentle heart?"

"Oh, please do. I have been looking so forward to it." Gwen leaned back in her chair and smiled.

Katie curtsied and went to the piano. Immediately her fingers spread their wings of flight into the heavenlies. As the music permeated the room, Gwen sighed. Danny sat in his grandfather's chair and leaned back appearing to savor the sonata. Sarah stood next to Katie, fascinated, watching her mother's hands float across the keys. Over the piano, she could see Jeremy watching the fire, happily tapping his heels against the hearth keeping time. Then Katie coerced them all to sing hymns with her and it was a heavenly time of praise. Danny's voice was so wonderful and to hear Gwen sing made it perfect. This was more than she dreamt —a family filled with love and joy.

Gwen and Danny shared more memories than Katie could retain in one afternoon.

"I wanted to show you the beautiful things you missed when you were staying here." Gwen pulled lace and quilts and all manner of exquisite treasures from her trunk.

"Such lovely things." Katie wanted so much for Gwen to be surrounded by all the things she loved.

She pulled out a lace shawl that Katie thought was the most beautiful one she had ever seen. The edging was delicate and so perfect.

"And this, I made myself for my trousseau when Samuel and I were engaged. I want to give this to you." She laid it into Katie's lap.

"I cannot take this from you. It is much too precious," she protested.

"Think of it as a gift of hope. I made it for my trousseau and you can have it for yours."

Katie thought about the words Gwen spoke as she gently traced her fingers around the patterns of the shawl. "Oh, dear one, I will treasure this always and I will save it for Sarah someday, too."

"Child, there will be a man who will be deserving of your affection someday and you will wear it for him."

Katie wondered at her words. Did she consider Danny might be that man? Did she think Katie worthy of him?

The little company fully enjoyed the outing. They picnicked out in the back lawn and Katie heard even more joyous stories from the past.

Later, when the sun waned over the western horizon, Danny knew their day was spent. "Ladies and gent, I hate to spoil this jolly time, as my great grandpa used to say, but we must go now."

Gwen chuckled. "Yes, my father did love to say jolly this and jolly that."

They slowly made their way to the carriage and one by one were gingerly set inside.

As they turned the carriage out of the drive they saw the lowing sun reflected in the window on the west. Like a goodbye glow from a home they all wished were theirs to enjoy every day.

Danny let everyone off at the little cottage and drove the carriage back downtown.

When he returned, they were ready for him with hot tea and buttery shortbread cookies.

"Someday we shall ride in a horseless carriage." Eager young faces surrounded him as he popped the buttery shortbread in his mouth. "I think this is an awfully nice reward for a carriage driver."

"An awfully kind carriage driver, I'd say, wouldn't you, Katie?"

"Yes, so kind and thoughtful. It was a perfect day." She would remember every perfect moment.

"Me and Sarrie drived, too," Jeremy said, looking longingly at the shortbread cookies.

"Then I must share my cookies with you both." Danny pulled the children each one on a knee, cookie in hand and trotted them off on a new kind of carriage ride.

It was dark and Danny seemed happy to be stuck at the cottage. It always made Katie glad to have him near. Gwen and the children had gone to bed and she and Danny did the last minute cleanup together in the kitchen.

"I think your grandma had a wonderful surprise, Danny. I am so glad you did it."

"It was your idea, too, you know. We talked about it."

"I know." She handed him the cookie plate to dry.

"I could have sat there for hours listening to you play and sing." He sat the plate down and pulled her by her apron close to him. "Katie," he whispered.

She melted. They stood just soaking in the moment and their cheeks touched. She felt his breath. His lips moved gently brushing her cheek and she felt herself wanting to fall into his arms again. He drew back a little and they lingered unable to move. He backed away holding her only with his eyes.

"You have my heart, you know," Danny said.

"I do?"

"Couldn't you see it all these months?"

She was speechless.

"Tell me, Katie, is there a chance in this world that you could love me?" His big brown eyes were begging.

"Oh, Danny, I have always loved you. First as a brother and friend but now…" Katie looked down, embarrassed to have spoken it. One of her curls fell and he lovingly reached to touch it across her face.

"You have? Really?"

She nodded, shyly smiling, and he held her at the waist and whirled her around. "She loves me!"

"Shh—you'll wake everyone," she pleaded, suppressing

a laugh.

"I won't be able to sleep all night." He kept his hands at her waist and it sent chills up her spine.

"Nor I."

He drew her closer. "I don't ever want to be away from you again."

Their eyes locked. "Oh, Danny, am I dreaming? Do you really want me—a widow with children?"

"Of course. Why would that matter? You aren't dreaming, Katie—you *are* the dream. You are too wonderful to be true. And you love me, too." He reached for her hand and brought it to his lips.

"But we're a package, you know."

"And don't you know how much I adore Sarah and Jeremy?"

She nodded. She guessed she really did know but fear had kept her from believing.

"Well, I do. I can't imagine my life without you and Sarah and Jeremy."

She absorbed every word into her heart and their hands lingered in a soft goodnight. Katie went to bed, overwhelmed with joy at the blessing God had given her and made sure to thank him. Then she tried to close her eyes and saw only big brown eyes and a dimpled grin and his words played over and over as a song: "She loves me...she loves me...she loves me...."

CHAPTER THIRTY-TWO

Coming to Terms

Sunday's late snack was eaten and the kitchen was in process of being cleaned up, when they heard a loud knock at the door. Danny went to answer.

"Tom, come in," he greeted.

"I just got off the train. Thought I'd stop by on the way home to deliver your package."

"Would you like some supper, Tom? It's handy," Gwen said.

"I hate to impose, Gwen, but I can't think of anything better, that and maybe a night's sleep in my own bed. I'd be a fool to refuse another one of your meals. Living alone is getting a little old."

"That can be remedied with the right woman. Perhaps a charming little artist?" Danny teased and Tom's eyes penetrated him like a double-barreled shotgun. Danny slapped his hand to his heart pretending to be shot.

"It was just a thought. Okay, okay, I'll be good." Danny grinned and the slightest smile snuck out of Tom's bushy mustache.

The women gathered the food they had just put away and made up a plate for Tom.

Danny sat across from Tom and listened as he told him about the trial, while Katie got the children ready for bed. Gwen sat in her living room chair doing her needlework, in the light of the longer summer days.

After discussing the trial and eating heartily, Tom got up to leave. He pushed the envelope that sat on the table toward Danny. "I almost forgot, your lawyer friend gave his best to you and said there's great news inside. Said he'd never get you back now. Whatever that means." Tom shrugged.

"That is strange." Danny picked up the envelope wondering at the peculiar thing John had said to Tom. "I don't know how to thank you, Tom."

"Seems to me I just got paid in full." He winked at Gwen and patted his belly, laughing. "Nothing to it. The courthouse was right there near his office. I best be getting on home now. It's sure good to be back in White Rock. Thank you again, Ma'am. The food was delicious, as always." He gave Gwen a kiss on the cheek and left just as Katie walked back into the room.

Danny turned and handed the envelope to Katie. She opened it and read the letter. "The railroad stocks my father had given my uncle are good. Uncle Tyler never knew." She handed the letter to Gwen, standing next to her. "Look how much they are worth."

"Oh, my—" Gwen's hand flew to her heart.

Danny walked toward them and Gwen slowly handed the letter to him. He read it in disbelief. His joy was quenched. He excused himself and walked out into the yard, but he could hear the women's reactions.

"What's wrong, Gwen? Why did he leave like that?"

"I have my suspicions but I think it best you ask him."

Katie ran out after him. "Danny, Danny, what is it? What's wrong?"

He felt like he was being choked. This was not the way he planned it. It was all wrong. He pointed toward the hills. "I imagined you there on the hill...in the Overlook House as my wife from the first day I saw you there. I would find out what God wanted me to do and then we would all be happy. I wanted to provide for all of you."

"Why does this change anything?"

"Don't you see, Katie? You're rich. You don't need me and I can't live off your wealth. What self-respecting man does that?"

"Can't you see God has provided this so you can do his work and not have to divide your time trying to provide for us?"

"No—it isn't right. I can't do it." He knew his words were curt and cutting and Katie looked like he'd slapped her but he wasn't going to give in.

"I guess your pride is stronger than your love." She snapped back with her ire up. He had never seen her like this. Clearly she was hurt but he couldn't agree to live on her money. He just couldn't. She turned from him and ran away toward the backfields.

Grandma came up behind him. He knew that look. The one that said he had crossed over the line. Her face was flushed and lips pursed. She was livid.

"Don't be a fool, Daniel. God brought you a precious young woman like Katie and two adorable children and then gives you all the money you need to do his work and you would let your pride throw it all away?"

He had been rebuked twice now. They were both angry with him. But he was frustrated. "I don't see it that way," he muttered with his teeth clenched. "Isn't a man is supposed to provide for his family?" He looked out back, wondering where Katie ran to but was too upset to run after her. He ran his fingers through his hair, bewildered, as his grandma continued.

"It is only your pride that is hurt. She is the prize you have been waiting for. Look at me, Daniel." She tilted her head and crossed her arms across her chest. "Would you let her go and marry some other man? She turns heads all over town." Grandma threw up her hands and went into the house.

That hit him—hard. The vision of her with another man made him recoil. She could never belong to someone else— NEVER! She was his and he knew it. To be without her and the children would be unthinkable. He sighed, knowing they both spoke the truth. It was surely his pride.

But it still isn't right, Lord. Your Word says a man is supposed to take care of his family. Why haven't you shown me how to provide for all of us? I just can't see me saying, "Katie, I need money for this," or "Katie, I need money for that." Oh, it is hopeless.

It was an agonizing walk toward the backfields to find Katie, kicking the clumps of grass along the way, trying to wrestle it all out. But he couldn't just leave her out there. He had to try to explain.

When he found her she was in the grasses, on her knees,

sobbing her heart out. He felt like the fool his grandma had called him. What had he done? Hadn't she been through enough?

"Katie."

She looked up at him and it broke every last ounce of pride that remained. Her normally sweet happy face was marred by his insensitivity and callous behavior. He dropped down next to her and wiped her tears away.

"I'm so sorry. I *was* prideful but I didn't mean to be. I wanted to be the one to provide everything beautiful for you. I wanted you to be proud of me."

Her wet curly lashes and red cheeks even now were breathtaking to him.

"I am already proud of you. I know I will see your words in print and be proud then, too. You have the Overlook House and the wonderful blessings of a piano and books and beautiful things your mother has left like the china. I had nothing to offer you. But God has given us this blessing to use to further his kingdom. This is exactly what I prayed for, Danny. I wanted to bless you and Gwen. I wanted you to be able to write and not worry and your grandma to go home to the Overlook house." Tears started cascading her cheeks again.

"Oh, Katie, forgive me. I don't ever want to make you cry. Grandma said you are my prize but you are my treasure. I couldn't bear to lose you."

He cradled her in his arms and she snuggled into his chest and rested there a long while, as he looked across the golden grass meadow and the far south edge of the Overlook House in the distance. It wasn't the way he wanted it to be. He wanted to give it all to her and support her, too.

"I just want to support you always."

She smiled at him, blinking her tears away. "Then you will have to be diligent in the pursuit of your writing. You know, it would only be to get you started until you were published. But please let me have the chance to give for a change." Her dewy green eyes pleaded and he knew the battle was over. He had lost and won all at the same time.

"We could buy a fine carriage for Gwen."

He smiled, no longer struggling. "And a thousand green dresses for you."

"Oh no, I love my green dress. I don't want another. Someone dear to my heart bought it for me."

Danny tenderly lifted her chin. I've been such a fool. She is my gift—a true gift from God's loving hand. "How can you ever forgive me?"

"All I have to do is look into those big brown eyes. Don't think you won't have to forgive me one day for something I have said or done."

"Never. You are perfect."

She laughed. "Yes, that is funny isn't it, after all the muddle I have made of my life."

"I can't imagine anyone on earth like you, Katie."

"You know, Danny, we can help the mission, and give the men a good new start."

He sighed, shaking his head. "See—you are the most unselfish person I have ever known. I don't deserve you."

"Oh, but I *am* selfish, Danny." Her eyes sparkled playfully. "I want you all to myself always."

He cupped her face with his hand and drew it up to his and kissed the lips he had longed to kiss for so many months and she melted back into his arms. He knew she was worth so much more than his foolish pride.

CHAPTER THIRTY-THREE

Danny's Rose

The next day, Danny and Katie went out for a long walk and Grandma Gwen took the children to get the mail. They were back by the time Jeremy bounded into the house ahead of Sarah and Gwen. "Where did you goed?"

Danny picked him up and answered, smiling. "Well, little chap, we have been deciding that I should be your and Sarah's new daddy."

"Really?" Sarah ran over to him and he picked her up. She hugged him tightly.

Jeremy was silent. Katie, Danny, and Gwen looked at each other, perplexed.

"Is there anything wrong with that idea? Isn't that what you wanted?" Danny asked him. They were sure he would be bouncing all over the house with the news, singing some amusing little song.

"Well, I just wondered if you beed our daddy, if our mama can comed, too?"

"Yes, I think that can be arranged," Danny said trying desperately not to keel over laughing, especially when he saw Jeremy's beloved mother bent over on the couch with her hand over her mouth suppressing a laugh.

Gwen threw her hands up in surrender. "You should have named him Isaac for all the laughter he brings."

Sarah giggled. "Jer'my, you are so silly."

"What a wonderful day, and now we have a letter from the east on top of it." Gwen waved a letter in the air.

"Let's hear it," Danny said. "We'll be sending one right back with all our good news." He took Katie's hand in his and sat next to her.

They all listened happily as Grandma read the missive. Danny parents and sister and her husband were planning a trip in late summer. Danny clasped his hands together. "Perfect. We could have the wedding while they are here."

"How perfect," Katie said.

"I can show them my glorious new family. Children, you will meet you new grandparents," Danny said.

A look of apprehension went from Sarah to Jeremy.

"There is nothing to be afraid of. My parents will adore you and you aunt and uncle will think you are amazing."

The children smiled in relief and the little family chattered all through dinner about all the glory of the day. When the sun was setting, they went outside to look at the crimson sunset and make more happy plans together.

"Can we have a big flower garden?" Sarah asked.

"Of course. Grandma Gwen will teach us how and she will truly be our own dear grandma," Katie said.

"Will you play the piano for me every night?" Danny asked.

Katie answered him with a warm but sly smile.

"Can we have fired in the fired place? And can we

bringed the cuckoo clocked? And can we taked the coconutted cake with us?" asked Jeremy breathlessly.

"Sure little chap, we are taking our two special coconutted cake bakers with us."

Sarah looked at Danny, smiling. "Jer'my calls you Dandy, Grandma Gwen calls you Daniel and Mama calls you Danny, but I am going to call you Daddy."

He picked her up." And I will call you daughter; my sweet daughter, Sarah, my little princess." He looked up to heaven. "You are so good to us, Lord. You have made us a whole happy family."

They walked leisurely back toward the cottage door and as Katie turned, the last of the sunset's glow shone on the golden curls that had fallen on her shoulders. She stood—a radiant sight taking Danny's breath away.

Gwen brought out the delicate heirloom shawl she had given to Katie and placed it over Katie's shoulders. "Worn for a man worthy of you." And then she handed Danny one of the pink roses from his rosebush she had cut and he gave it to Katie to complete the vision.

Gwen sighed in perfect contentment, "I always knew you would be…Danny's Bride."

"Jer'my, God gave us a grandma and a new daddy and a new home and look at Mama, she is so happy."

"Sarrie, I tolded you—God will provide." And he rolled his eyes back and sighed.

CHAPTER THIRTY-FOUR

EPILOGUE: A Joyous Occasion

"They're here!"

The shout from downstairs startled them both. Katie stood like one of the model forms they had in the dress shop, waiting to be dressed. Greeting her new family in nothing but her undergarments seemed highly inappropriate. Gwen left her to go directly downstairs.

But what could be done? She stood gaping in front of the mirror, accessing the changes from the once scrawny woman who had come to White Rock from the depths of misery to the woman she was now—full of life and color and health. Even her hair, which hung softly coiling to her waist, was softer and shinier.

Danny's words from after dinner last night kept ringing through her head. "You are everything I ever wanted. You will make me the happiest man in the world to have you for my bride." She placed her hand to her heart as she thought about the sweet things he had spoken. He said he had been captivated with her right from the first. His words took her back to that amazing day. Strange, how the Overlook House was the place they first met and here she stood upstairs waiting to become his bride.

She could hear the happy commotion downstairs. Family. The only one left on her side was Charlotte, but she could not come. Her plans for Europe were all in place. Well, perhaps her brother-in-law, Granville, would not have liked their lovely home or their charming friends. But no matter, she would be part of a new family, now. She had a new life and it was wonderful. She wouldn't want anyone spoiling it. She would visit Charlotte someday.

A rap at her door brought her back to the moment.

"Katie, may we come in?" It was Gwen with Ginny, her new mother-in-law and her new sister Vicky. She recognized them from the picture. She felt so embarrassed to meet them in her such a way.

Ginny rushed over and enveloped her in her embrace. When she pulled back, Danny's wonderful smile smiled back at her in the face of his beautiful mother. His sister, Vicky came from behind and hugged her, too. Vicky was charming and looked impressive in her fashionable light peach traveling suit and large shiny silk collar. She pulled off her huge hat with peach feathers and flowers and set it on the bed. Ginny, her new mother was equally exquisite in beiges and browns with beautiful buttons down her skirt. It was a new world of fashion dazzling her eyes.

Katie stood still as three lovely generations of women chattered and scurried like mice to put her together.

"Now, Katie, don't you worry. Everything will be fine." Her new mother-in-law stood with her sweet appraising head tilted. She meant it—Katie could feel the warmth reaching from her eyes. It made her heart sing, and her fears flew off to unknown places. She wanted them all to merely accept her but they welcomed her into their arms like she'd been in the family forever. Vicky stood with her long slender arm around her beloved grandmother and shook her head. "Grandma, your letter said she was lovely, but Katie, you could go down the aisle in an old housedress and no one would even notice it. How fun it will be to do your gorgeous hair. Oh, I always wanted a sister. I wish we weren't so far away."

Katie was overwhelmed by their admiration. What a charming family. She should have known. It was one more fear that should have never held her captive. Would she ever learn?

The women covered Katie with a quilt and had the trunk brought up. They unwrapped the most beautiful dress Katie had ever seen. It was creamy, buttery satin and the lace formed small rose patterns. Her life seemed to be blessed with roses.

"Well, let's see if it fits. The delay on the train sure didn't help any."

"Yes, Mother, we have a lot of work to do if it doesn't."

"Everything will be just fine," Gwen said as she handpressed the skirt.

They were acting like schoolgirls and Katie was caught up in their fun. They draped it over her petticoats and helped her pull it on.

"Now will it button?" Ginny held her breath.

A light rap at the door, produced a peeking Sarah. "Mama, can I come in?"

"Of course, dear." Katie turned to face Sarah and smiled at her frozen gaping mouth.

"Mama, you are so beautiful."

Gwen retrieved her. "Sarah, you come right over here by your new grandma and Auntie Vicky and watch. Did you see Audrey downstairs?"

"Yes, she is having fun making everything pretty. I like Cousin Audrey, she's funny."

Ginny laughed. "Our darling Audrey, isn't she a character. I am sure everything will be picture perfect with her artistic touch."

"Yes, we have had her here for a week and she put flowers on every piece of furniture in the house." Gwen winked at Katie.

"Wait till you see our wedding gift from Audrey," Katie said.

"Oh my, yes. She finally painted the house with Danny and Katie on the porch and me behind the children who were sitting on the swing," Gwen said.

"And the best part is that she painted herself into the canvas in the yard at her easel painting us." Katie laughed just thinking about it. "She surprised us all. Jeremy still thinks God painted it."

The ladies laughed in chorus.

"How wonderful. I can't wait to see it. Audrey is such a dear, we had a lot of fun together as girls," Vicky said.

Audrey was charming. Katie wanted to keep her. She was like the family butterfly flitting around everywhere. She had set up her easel and insisted Katie sit for her so she could get the feel for painting her later. Danny insisted she paint Katie in her green dress with the children at her feet to hang on the wall in the library. Audrey would be staying for the next couple of months and Katie was going to love it.

"Mama, I met Uncle James and Grandpapa. They are so nice. They brought Jer'my and me rock candy. I tried a piece and it doesn't taste like a rock. It's really good."

The women had another good laugh when Katie explained about the rock candy Sarah had seen and wondered why anyone would make candy out of rocks.

"Smart girl," her new grandmother said as she drew Sarah close.

The uproarious laughter downstairs made the women look at each other with their brows raised.

"It's Jer'my. He was telling them about coconutted cake and when I came up, Danny..er Daddy, I mean, started to tell them about us being properly attired."

Gwen chuckled. "Of course. Well, there will be a lot of laughter in this house."

"Katie, I am absolutely charmed by my new grandchildren. I told Vicky she must learn your child rearing secrets when the baby comes," Ginny said with a crooked smile and a mischievous twinkle in her eyes. Everyone stopped chattering and stared at Vicky, who had stopped buttoning and grinned as she tenderly rubbed her belly.

They celebrated the news of Vicky's expectancy and then went back to work. With the last of the many pearl buttons buttoned, they surveyed the bride.

No one could speak. It was a miracle, the pure grace of God. To bring it all across the country and have no idea whether it would fit her or not. A perfect fit—as if made for her. Finally, Vicky let out a sigh and the whole room came alive again with excitement.

"Well, I am so glad it fit you. I didn't get to wear it. I was much too tall. The sleeves came up to my elbows." Vicky giggled, patting Katie's sleeves down at the wrist.

"I was so hoping it would fit. It was such a wonderful dress to be used only once." Her lovely, new mother-in-law had tears glazing her eyes.

"I am so honored that you brought it to me."

Ginny grabbed Katie's hand and squeezed.

Katie looked in the mirror. She felt like a princess but then she *was* marrying a prince. The lace bodice came up to her chin and trailed down her back and there were many intricate tiny pearl beads sewn into the lace itself.

"It is so beautiful," she said.

"Hmm. Yes, but it is you that make it so, dear." Ginny stood back looking at her.

"And you don't need an awful corset," Vicky said, making an ugly face that made Katie laugh.

"I dreaded to wear a corset but I figured if I had to wear it, it would be only for today."

"Well, thank heaven you don't. They are such evil contrivances. I spent a lot of time getting that tiny waist fattened up some." Gwen looked at her, her head lilted back and forth. Was she remembering her own wedding or perhaps Ginny's in this dress?

"Well, it's not all the style, you know but it's more wonderful and the color is perfect for your rosy cheeks," Vicky said.

Ginny rolled her eyes. "I think being concerned about style in regards to a wedding dress is ridiculous. No one would wear her mother's or grandmother's lovely gowns if that were so. Okay, Vicky, work on her hair and don't do a Gibson style on her. At least not today. Her hair is lovely all itself."

"Yes, Mother, I agree."

"We need to change our clothes, and get Sarah and Jeremy dressed, so come when you are through."

"I would love to steal your hair, Katie," Vicky said, fingering her curls, as the others went downstairs.

"Now they are gone, you can tell me all about the romance. I absolutely love romance."

Katie laughed and proceeded to tell her new sister all about falling in love with her brother and his falling in love with her. By the time the story was told, Vicky had put Katie's hair up in a perfect arrangement of her lovely wispy curls, some of which draped down her back.

"Vicky, it's wonderful. I cannot think what my hair would have looked like without your help."

"Well, I don't know when I have ever seen such beautiful soft curls as yours. It was quite fun. I think God ironed out all mine when I was born." The sisters laughed together as if they had been comrades all their lives.

"I am so excited about your baby. Perhaps we can come after it's born."

"I do hope so. You will be its only aunt, you know."

"James has no sisters?"

"Nor brothers. I call him my spoiled child and he is, but he is so wonderful. So much like Father."

Katie allowed a few seconds of sorrow that her own father was not here to escort her. She had already thought about her mother and let go, so now she would have to do the same with her father. Perhaps they were looking down from heaven.

Gwen stepped into the room in her silvery-blue silk

gown that Danny insisted she get for the wedding. It matched her glistening silver hair perfectly. She carried a box in her hand. Vicky smiled, seeming to know all about it.

Audrey peeked around the doorpost and gasped, "Oh, I must paint you. You look like a fairy princess. Cousin Katie, you look like the glory of the sun...no, maybe the sparkles on the sea...no, I have it—the dew on Danny's roses." And she laughed at her own silliness.

Cousin Audrey was all about paintings and colors and funny repartee. Her childlike heart was like Jeremy's—so trusting and sweet. With every painted word she was like a painting herself. No wonder Tom was taken with her.

Gwen stood still in front of her. "You beautiful child, I fear Daniel will swoon when he sees you." The younger women giggled at such a thought.

Katie waited as Gwen pulled out an intricate veil of delicate lace and cameo combs to set it.

"We have all worn it, Katie, even me," Vicky said.

"It was my own when Samuel and I wed." Gwen gingerly held it out to Katie.

"Oh, it is so lovely." She wiped a tear that trickled down her cheek. How cherished she felt.

"Oh no, no. A bride cannot cry at her own wedding." Audrey hurried and dabbed Katie's cheek as the tears dropped. It made Katie smile and it stopped the tears.

They situated the exquisite veil on her perfectly coiffed curls and pinned it with the beautiful combs.

"Well, you're one of us now, sister Katie."

"To think all you dear ones wore it as well. I am so honored."

"Not me yet. Don't know if anyone will be able to put up

with me long enough to ask for my hand." Audrey smiled and gave a little giggle but Katie sensed hurt in her eyes.

"Oh, Audrey, now you know that isn't so. You are a painting all in yourself," Vicky said.

"Vicky is right. Whoever finally gets the courage will be blessed." Katie thought about a certain big sheriff that turned to mush around Audrey.

"You'll be wearing the veil soon enough, our lovely butterfly." Gwen brushed Audrey's cheek gently.

"I am just glad my dear cousin has found his perfect match." Audrey held her hand to her heart and sighed, in her posed theatrical way.

Sarah and her new grandma, Ginny, came back in arm-in-arm, dressed for the wedding.

"Oh, Mama."

"Oh, Mama, indeed," Ginny said.

Katie stepped once again in front of the elegant cheval mirror as they all gathered around her.

"Let's pray." Gwen and the entourage bowed their heads and asked a blessing on their beautiful new bride and groom. Katie was so overwhelmed. How was she going to keep from crying for joy.

"I think it is time now for you to meet your escort and new father-in-law. Let's go down now, ladies." Ginny let them file out, then she turned and winked at Katie. "I'd say you are a mother's answer to prayer for her son and then some."

What a wonderful family. She was elated that they were all coming to Los Angeles a couple of days into their honeymoon. They would stay at the house getting to know the children and then they would bring them and enjoy the sights and go to the beach. Then they would all go together to see the Men's Street Mission. It was all so perfect

Father, you brought it all so beautifully together. What joy you have brought into my once dismal life: a wonderful new family, this beautiful home, and my beloved Danny, who is truly a man after your own heart.

A light rap stopped her prayer and she said, "Come in."

She turned to see a kind-faced man. There were tiny touches of grey in his moustache and he was built like her own father, tall but not thin. Something about him reminded her of Danny. What was it?

"My dear Katie." He reached out his hand and she laid her little gloved hand into it.

"It is so wonderful to meet you, sir."

"The pleasure is all mine. What a beautiful young woman my son has asked to spend his life with. Except for stories of your delightful Jeremy and Sarah, Danny has talked about nothing but his precious Katie since we came. I feel as if I know you already. I had hoped to be here sooner so you would feel more comfortable walking with me. I am highly honored that you asked."

"I am the one who is honored, sir." She looked up at him in all earnestness and he answered with a smile in his eyes that crinkled at the corners, showing the slightest of age and made her realize what she was seeing was her Danny in those big warm eyes.

"I hope I will be the kind of daughter-in-law you hope me to be."

"From what my mother has told us in all her letters, we might have to live up to your standards, my dear."

He offered his arm and she felt the tender strength of a

father again. How comforting it was. Now she must go to meet her charming bridegroom.

They walked the length of the elegant winding stairway of the Overlook House. Her house. She had not even thought of it before. It was an overwhelming thought that she would be mistress of the house. But everything else about this day had been rather overwhelming. It was as if they were father and daughter and he led her out onto the veranda where their friends and family waited. Gwen waited with her wedding bouquet of Danny's roses and tears were already flowing down her sweet round cheeks.

"You are a sight to behold. I knew you would capture Danny's heart and carry his roses on your wedding day. I have waited for this day."

Dear Grandma Gwen would be her own grandmother. Gwen kissed her cheek and she kissed hers. As she started toward the guests, she saw Mrs. Perkins smiling and the beloved pastor's wife and Miss Ruby who had cropped her garden short to produce the array of color for her wedding. Then she looked toward the arbor. The pink-rosed arbor had been lovingly coaxed back to its former state as had the lush green lawn. Her Sarah stood under it angelically dimpled in her pink dress with flowers in her hair and her little Jeremy was fancied up so cute. She felt everyone's eyes upon her, making her truly a blushing bride. She overheard the lovely shushed comments as she and her new father walked toward her groom. She saw her handsome groom in his frock coat but he almost made her laugh. He was grinning his full-dimpled grin until he saw her, then his jaw dropped.

Lord, this time I know I am not dreaming and I am so glad!

The only thing that made Danny nervous was that someone might come and kidnap his bride but he smiled to himself. No, that won't happen. Then an enchanting creature came toward him, escorted by his father. Ah, she was so beautiful, his Katie. Yes, now he could say it—*his* Katie. The family told him she was wearing his mother's dress and Grandma's veil, and Grandma told him not to swoon and he laughed at her. But if anything could do it, it would be the sight of his bride. She was getting closer. Grandma was right but certainly he wouldn't swoon, would he? His heart pounded faster and faster the closer she came.

He reached for his lovely bride. Around her neck, he saw her mother's locket he had brought back to her. They had delicately set in pictures of her parents in its little ovals just for the wedding. It was her way of having them there.

God had given him so much. She had come to him out of loss and misery. God had directed her steps and brought her straight to little White Rock and to his own grandma's cottage. The words he thought the first day he met her came joyfully back to him...how wonderful to come home to this charming woman and her two children.

You heard me, Father!

Was the sun shining exceedingly bright or was it the blinding glory of his bride? They lingered over their vows looking at each other earnestly, lovingly. Pastor Adkins shared his heart and united the beloved couple in marriage.

"You may kiss the bride," he said with a wink.

Danny wanted to remember this moment forever—to savor it. He had kissed Katie only once and that was to heal her sorrow for hurting her sweet spirit but now he would kiss her in joy. As the newlyweds looked at each other and drew close, the guests hushed and an impatient tug came from the bottom of Danny's coattail.

"Dandy—Daddy...kiss Mama and let's go climbed the tree."

Poof, went the photographer's camera and captured the moment for posterity.

The bride and groom kissed, half-laughing, but their friends and family didn't notice the kiss for their eyes were on the little mop-headed chap who brought down the house.

Author Notes and Acknowledgements

I hope you enjoyed More Than She Dreamt and I want to share some special things with you about the book.

First, I have to tell you about the cloud scene. You might think it was contrived but I actually lived it. Yes, it really happened to me! I was reading the 15th chapter of John at the time, outside, working hard in the Arizona heat, waiting for monsoons many years ago. Two of my children also saw it. I wanted to run and call my neighbor and I realized I couldn't as it was dissipating. It was something just for me and I will never forget it.

I wrote this book in an RV. I don't recommend it. It was where we were and a hard journey but I managed, so no excuses. If God has called you to do something, don't hold back. Better get moving.

Thank you to my beloved prayer brigade: Susan Gahr, Jan Holman, Mary Winzenburg and Kathi Clough. I was so blessed to have their prayer cover and encouragement. And thank you to my budding writer daughters, Cheyenne Wilson and Sierra Helton who gave their input, prayers and help along with my daughter-in-law, Kelly de Lance who prayed and encouraged along the way. I would also like to thank lovely calligrapher, Mindy Sato, for her beautiful work on the scripture page and for her encouragement on the home stretch. And a thank you to Carol Fielding at www.allaboutrosegardening.com for her rose history help. And a very special thanks to our beautiful cover model, Erin Franklin.

MORE THAN SHE
Dreamt

Rose Arbor Brides continues with winsome Cousin Audrey on a painting tour when big surprises turn up in 1906 San Francisco in **More Than She Imagined**. Watch for it!

Join me on my website page for bio and blog and be sure to sign up for my newsletter to find out when the next book publishes.

Website: www.sandyfayemauck.com
Facebook: www.facebook.com/sandyfayemauck.author
On Twitter @sandyfayemauck
Pinterest: www.pinterest.com/sandyfayemauck

Did my book minister to you? If so, I would love to hear from you. Contact me through my website above and click on the contact page.